Whose
Side
Are You
On?

BOOKS BY KERRY FISHER

After the Lie
The Island Escape
The Silent Wife
The Secret Child
The Not So Perfect Mother
The Woman I Was Before
The Mother I Could Have Been
Another Woman's Child
Other People's Marriages
The Woman in My Home

THE ITALIAN ESCAPE SERIES
The Rome Apartment
Secrets at the Rome Apartment
Escape to the Rome Apartment

Kerry Fisher and Pat Sowa
Take My Hand

Whose
Side
Are You
On?

Kerry Fisher

bookouture

Published by Bookouture in 2025

An imprint of Storyfire Ltd.
Carmelite House
50 Victoria Embankment
London EC4Y 0DZ

www.bookouture.com

The authorised representative in the EEA is Hachette Ireland
8 Castlecourt Centre
Dublin 15 D15 XTP3
Ireland
(email: info@hbgi.ie)

ISBN: 978-1-83618-782-0
eBook ISBN: 978-1-83618-781-3

To Giselle with love and thanks for our fifty-nine years of friendship

1

JACKIE

We'd been coming to Philippa and Andrew's holiday home for over two decades. For the first ten years, I'd leapt out of the car, done that arms wide open, 'Oooh careful, careful, about six inches, STOP!!' thing, as Ian did five hundred manoeuvres to squeeze into a tight spot on the seafront in Deal. But I'd come to the conclusion that marriage, family, all of it, started off with a fat well of patience and by about year fifteen, most people were peering at the unmistakable view of a silty bottom. As I saw it, there were three choices: shuffle off the mortal coil obscenely early, pack your bags and get out now or be a lot more sparing about how often you were going to engage with other people's ineptitude or moaning.

I'd ticked option three in my head, which had allowed me to navigate marriage somewhere on the spectrum between benign neglect and intense periods of emergency focus. Today was at the benign neglect end of the range, so I was full-on ignoring Ian and his complaints about the tight parking, leaving it to my daughter Scarlett to do the honours. The festive season was my second most hated period of the year. Scarlett had already exhausted my Christmas Eve patience by getting into the car and immediately whingeing about how early we'd all have to get up on the twenty-seventh so she could get back to London for her job dogsitting a Pomeranian – 'God forbid they could leave their precious Miss Moneypenny on her own for five minutes while they head off to "a little luncheon".' Followed by a moan about why Philippa had invited us in the first place. 'I mean, I'm fine with it – it'll be great to see them all – but she's always made such a big deal about Christmas being "special family time".'

I knew why. So did Ian. A few weeks shy of her thirtieth birthday, I was pretty sure that Scarlett could handle the truth, but still I'd muttered, 'I think they just fancied a change.' Partly out of loyalty to Philippa and Andrew, but mainly because we were struggling to believe it was real ourselves.

I could see a Christmas tree in the sitting-room window on the top floor of their Georgian townhouse. Philippa would have decorated it with care. Maybe even extra care this year. We'd always joked about how we went to all the effort of choosing a colour scheme, white and gold, or purple and silver, then messed it up with all those sequinned stars and salt dough Santas that we'd saved for twenty-plus years since the kids were in primary school. The coloured lights wrapped around the tree in the little courtyard garden, sparkling their welcome, made my throat tighten. That glittering glow should have heralded good times ahead, many more springtimes braving the sea earlier and earlier each year, many more summers sitting under the stars with the sound of the waves drifting over to us.

I had no idea how Philippa was putting on her jolly face when mine threatened to crumble at any minute. But there she was, her blonde highlighted hair straightened within an inch of its life, which reassured me. The trials of the last few months hadn't impacted her lengthy beauty routine.

She threw open the garden gate and flung her arms around me. She whispered in my ear, 'Thank God you're here. Thank you, thank you, thank you. All distractions welcome.' And in that moment, a spark lit inside my sadness. One day, I could see that we might turn this into a story to laugh about. How my best friend for fifty years – bonding over our roles as sheep in the school Nativity play in primary school – had needed me to put on a performance that wouldn't have disgraced a celestial band of trumpeting angels.

She'd begged me to carry her through one last family Christmas before she and Andrew told their only child, Abigail, that they were getting divorced. 'I know she's an adult with a life of her own, but she loves Christmas. I just want a chance to revisit all our traditions for a final time, so she doesn't feel so cheated.' Personally, I thought the chances of her feeling totally pissed off that the happy family Christmas had been a complete sham, an announcement-in-waiting, would be far worse, but I was the last person to lecture Philippa about stellar parenting decisions.

When I'd told Ian, I'd sobbed. Deep sorrow for the fact that out of everyone we'd known during our married life, we'd spent more time with Andrew, Philippa and Abigail than anyone else. Our daughters had gathered sea glass together on the beach, squealed into the freezing water on sunny Easters, hiked with us from Deal to Dover along the clifftops, spurred on by the promise of ice cream and scones. I'd tried to persuade Philippa to talk to Andrew, to investigate ways to put the spark back into her marriage – 'Christ, you're not suggesting we join some weird swingers club, are you?'

They'd got married in 1995 after a six-month whirlwind romance, three and a half years after us. Since then, we'd done our fair share of offloading about our husbands' misdemeanours, but I'd always thought we were both one hundred per cent in it for the long haul. I had to bite my tongue when Philippa complained about Andrew because a lot of what she said sounded like the inevitable familiarity of a long marriage. 'If he's not talking about some database system he's project managing or how he's going to take much more adventurous holidays when he retires – sorry, but there's absolutely no chance of me wild-camping in Botswana – he's wanging on about his running. How his feet are holding up, how his new shoes have shaved half a nanosecond off his personal best, which challenge he's going to train for next. And none of it bears any relation to what I want. I'm sick of pretending not to mind that he spends most of every holiday twitching to respond to an email about why some piece of code isn't performing properly rather than engage with Abigail and me. Suddenly, I don't feel like being that woman any more. I want better than that. I want to feel seen. Thought about. Desired.'

My own view was that one of the greatest perks of married life was having a stable home to glitter away from in brief bursts without having to put on a weirdly fanfare-ish performance behind closed doors. Much to Philippa's horror, I'd embraced my grey hair, stylishly bobbed still, but no longer a slave to my roots. Ian had just looked puzzled when I'd asked him if he minded that I'd stopped colouring my hair. 'Why would I mind? It's your hair.' I was pretty sure he also wasn't losing sleep over the fact that my days of strappy sandals – or anything that aggravated my bunion – were over.

But despite my best efforts at trying to convince Philippa that a marriage of nearly thirty years shouldn't be thrown under a bus for a dazzling disco ball of a new suitor, she still pulled the plug. I'd fought Andrew's corner, listing his qualities. At times, I felt as though I was scraping the bottom of the barrel. However, in my opinion razzle-dazzle often ceded to the superior quality of solid reliability over the decades. 'He can barbecue a chicken breast without giving everyone food poisoning.' 'He always leaps up to investigate things that go bump in the night.' And I didn't hold back on the obvious either: 'He's got a bloody good pension!'

However, she'd been determined that she was destined for more and I admired her. The sheer guts to turn her back on everything she'd known and take a plunge into alien territory. I wondered if my resistance to her leaving Andrew was partly to do with how parochial her bravery made me feel, how unadventurous, how suburbanly content with life. Undeniably, a part of it was that we loved them both and wanted to cling onto our 'Fabulous Four'.

But she was my original friend – Andrew came later. So here I was, championing her in the prelude to the unknown and dragging my family along as secondary cheerleaders.

I struggled to keep my composure as we trundled into the kitchen, as we had hundreds of times before – the same, but now different, with Andrew clapping his hands and saying, 'Who's for a drink? Sun's over the yardarm somewhere in the world!' Even Ian reached with uncharacteristic enthusiasm for a glass of champagne.

Scarlett and Abigail were busy hugging each other, slipping back into that pattern of people who've known each other since they were babies – laughing with the sheer delight of being together, diving into a random topic. Today that was Abigail demanding to know whether the piercing in Scarlett's nose hurt and if she was conscious of the stud in her nostril.

Guy, Abigail's boyfriend, appeared in the doorway and came over to shake Ian's hand and give me a hug. 'How are you? How was the drive? Great to see you again.' There was something so wholesome about him – he never looked as though he'd dragged a T-shirt off the floor or hadn't shaved. He was one of those classically handsome young men the gods had smiled on, arranging his features in a way that made you want to stare, even if only to see whether his eyelashes were actually that long.

It was embarrassing how much I envied Philippa for the fact that Abigail had found a decent, solvent, charming and ambitious boyfriend. Scarlett had had a parade of unsuitable oiks, although the older she got – as I was keeping my eye on the window for grandchildren – I found myself parking their unsavoury quirks in the category of 'no one's perfect' and 'as long as she's happy'. Insanely loud apple-crunching, nail-biting, unwillingness to eat anything that wasn't a variation on lasagne or sausages – I was forcing myself to overlook more and more. Sadly, Guy only had a younger sister, otherwise I'd have been manoeuvring for an introduction to his brother.

Philippa beckoned to me. 'Right, let me show you where you're sleeping,' she said meaningfully as though I hadn't slept in the same room with the view over the sea for years.

Ian moved to bring the cases in, but a little shake of the head and an eyebrow raise from me had him sinking back onto his stool.

I followed Philippa up the stairs. 'How's it going?'

She turned round. 'Do you know the hardest thing? Now I know that we're splitting up, it's like I've got one foot out of the door already and can't stomach the slightly annoying things I've been putting up with for years.'

My heart broke a little for Andrew, who, as far as I could make out, hadn't really wanted the split but had graciously accepted that Philippa's mind was made up and was trying to make the unravelling of the marriage as painless as possible. Normally, I would have sympathised with husbandly irritation, but I didn't want to hear it today. Didn't want to witness the petty pebbles of contempt that had gathered so much moss as to become insupportable.

Philippa, however, was like a beast who'd spotted the keeper arriving with the key to her cage. 'I can't stand how he swills his tea round in the mug to mix the milk. Get a bloody teaspoon out of the drawer! And you watch, when we go to bed tonight, he'll say, "Will you bring the water glasses up?" as though I need reminding after literally doing it every single night for years.'

I mustered up a smile. 'I suppose now you know there's an end date, you allow yourself to be properly irritated by everything you simply put up with before.'

I didn't want to join in. I wanted these people I loved to stay together, but if they couldn't stay together, I wanted them to love each other apart so that Ian and I wouldn't have to take sides.

Philippa opened the door to 'my' bedroom and flumped down on the bed. 'Sorry. I don't want to be horrible about Andrew. I know he's a decent man. But I feel as though I know every single word that is going to come out of his mouth before he even thinks it. And the only time I see him truly animated is when he's training for a bloody running race or measuring how much protein he needs to put on some piddling amount of muscle. I don't care! *I don't care!'*

I could have listed five hundred things that irked me about Ian. Ordinarily, when neither Philippa nor I was intending to leave our marriage, I'd probably have taken the opportunity to lift the valve on the marital pressure cooker and reduce the frustrations back to a simmer. Contrarily, now I wanted to list all of Ian's glorious qualities, and Andrew's as well. The way neither of them flirted with waitresses or made lewd comments about actresses on TV. How they'd organised races on the beach when the kids were young, while Philippa and I took ourselves off round the shops. How now the children were adults – though secretly we still thought of them as children – our men were genuinely interested in helping out with advice on house buying, career progression, the necessity of starting a pension sooner rather than later...

Yes, maybe they were small things, but they added up to a big whole. And as much as Philippa moaned about Andrew being a workaholic, that particular fault had also provided the upside of a cleaner, gardener and many sunsets and cocktails in foreign lands.

I turned to head back downstairs.

'Listen, we've decided to tell Abigail once she's back at work so she's got a routine to focus on. Probably the first weekend in January. I feel such a terrible mother.'

I tried to make a joke to banish the heavy feeling in my chest. 'Well, it's about your turn.'

Philippa smiled. 'Thank you for keeping it all a secret for now, though.'

'Only a few more decades and we'll be even.'

Philippa's face turned serious. 'That was another lifetime ago.'

Yes, it was. But I hadn't forgiven myself yet.

2

Pigeons. So many of them. Squatting high up in the porthole windows. On the arches. Flitting in and out with twigs and straw and scraps of paper to make nests on top of the ornate pillars, seemingly undisturbed by the trains screeching to a halt beneath them. Even a stupid pigeon managed to stay with the same partner for life.

I huddled on a bench at the far end of the platform, listening for the announcement of my connecting train to Middlesbor-ough. I angled my face away from the group of teenagers taking it in turns to swig out of a cider bottle. They wouldn't be interested in me; they had all of their lives ahead of them, hadn't yet made any decisions that would dominate their futures. The girls were far more interested in pretending to hate the boys, sarcastic comments and put-downs their inexperienced tools for flirting. The boys retaliated with fake-fighting, grabbing the girls by their coats, swearing, as though somehow that made them cool. Their youth, their laughter both called my attention and repelled me with the envy it engendered.

We'd been like them once. Sixteen, the last time I was here. On the cusp of the rest of our lives. Would I have wanted to have *known what lay ahead? Would it have been possible to choose a different path? I didn't know. Lucky them that they still had the freedom to make mistakes that it was possible to recover from. The best I could hope for now was that everyone would forget I ever existed.*

3

JACKIE

Ian and I loved to luxuriate in bed on a Christmas morning. Twenty-odd years after Scarlett had stopped bouncing in at 5 a.m., we still relished the fact that we hadn't been woken up to see if Rudolph had eaten his carrot. But in karmic payback for being a parent who preferred a solid night's sleep to early-morning child excitement, I was wide awake before any hint of dawn spread its tendrils across the sea.

I left Ian snoring and crept downstairs, savouring the idea of sitting in the kitchen by the warmth of the Aga and allowing myself a moment to reflect on all the fun we'd had at this house over the years. To pay proper homage to our memories so that I could consolidate all that we'd had together and keep it safe from being tainted with whatever came next in our friendship chapter.

Guy was already downstairs.

'You're up early,' I said, trying not to mind that he was in my space. 'Happy Christmas to you.'

'And to you. I had some gifts to wrap.' He laughed, acknowledging the last-minute preparation. 'The café has been insane for the last few weeks – people have been going mad for our cinnamon-spiced chai – so I haven't had much time. Plus, Abigail is terrible – she loves to prod and poke her presents, so I like to put them under the tree at the last possible moment. She's such a child.'

His voice was laced with so much affection that I pondered on how the years transformed those idiosyncrasies we loved to annoyances that grated. Mind you, Guy was so blinking perfect, he'd probably be the type of husband to up the ante even further in forty years' time. He'd no doubt be presenting gifts wrapped in wild flower seed-impregnated paper made out of grass fibres, alongside recordings of him reading his own love sonnets.

I was already preparing myself for a 'meals in under thirty minutes'-style cookbook and who knew what practical gadget from Ian. Vacuum cleaner you plug into the car cigarette lighter? Rotating bathroom scrubber on a handle? Spot clean steamer for the sofa? It was my own fault. I'd once told Ian I only wanted practical presents rather than any more clutter and now it was far too late to establish myself as a diamonds-or-die kind of woman.

I made myself a cup of tea and slipped outside into the garden. I switched on the fairy lights, pulled my dressing gown tight, letting the freezing sea air settle around me. My mind drifted to Scarlett's single status. Of course finding a man wasn't the be-all and end-all. Or at least that's what I told her – and myself. And the rational part of my brain didn't believe it was. It was just, well, when I imagined her life once I was dead, I wanted to know that there was someone looking out for her who would love her at least as much as I did. Still, I knew better than to allow those thoughts to shape into actual words that left my mouth.

Before I could get any further down this well-worn track, Guy came out with some banana bread drizzled with honey. 'There have to be some perks of owning a café. It's all organic.'

If I was Philippa, I'd be nailing him to the floor and begging Abigail to propose to him.

I was just dotting up the crumbs with my finger when Scarlett appeared, followed by Andrew, both in their running gear. There was a flurry of wishing each other merry Christmas, plus lots of shushing in deference to the people who didn't want to be awake at 7.30 a.m.

'Are you going running now? It's not even properly light,' I asked.

Scarlett laughed. 'Yep, I made a bet with Andrew last night that he wouldn't run before breakfast after all that booze.'

Andrew threw up his hands in defeat. 'Can't let these young ones think they're the only ones with all the stamina.' He gestured to Scarlett. 'Let's see what you can do then. We'd better get going before Philippa wants me on kitchen duty.'

His voice was neutral, giving no indication that this was anything other than a decades-old breakfast tradition, Andrew chopping mushrooms and grilling sausages to keep everyone going until the big turkey feast mid-afternoon. Nothing 'last' about it, nothing significant. I wondered if he was hoping that Philippa might change her mind at the eleventh hour.

With that, they headed off along the promenade, where a few early dog-walkers were putting their hands up to each other in festive greetings. I watched them silhouetted against the dark morning, the easy rhythm of Andrew's tall frame followed by Scarlett's athletic body at a steady pace, her brown curls flying about in the wind. I didn't know how she stood all that hair flapping around her face, but she never seemed to notice so many things that bothered me.

When Ian arrived next, hungover from too many cocktails the night before, I heard him grunt a greeting at Guy before he came outside to find me.

I got up. 'Merry Christmas,' I said. I couldn't say those words to Ian without wondering if he still thought about that dreadful Christmas. If his stomach knotted when the carols started playing in the shops, if he had to work hard not to let that one terrible year taint the many good celebrations that followed.

He hugged me before stepping back and frowning. 'Bloody hell, it's freezing out here.'

I laughed. 'Should clear your head at least. I knew you were in trouble when Andrew started with the Winter Pimm's. You know brandy doesn't agree with you.'

'Do you think Guy will make me a coffee?' he said, closing his eyes against the brightening sky.

'I think that would be a bit cheeky – a busman's holiday for him, but as it's Christmas, your wife will do the honours.'

Ian squeezed my fingers and said, 'I knew there was a reason I'd stayed married to you all this time.'

I hurried off. I never knew how to absorb comments about being a good wife at face value. Even now, after so many years, I wanted to sabotage the moment, to remind him. To *tell* him.

When I returned with Ian's coffee, he was making noises about going inside. I put out my hand, wanting to savour this moment before we got swept into the day with all its underlying and competing currents.

'Do you think Scarlett is happy? I do wonder whether she's lonely in London. And I don't want to say this to her because she'll see it as a criticism of her life choices, but that couple with the Pomeranian, they really take advantage of her.'

'I'm not sure the freedom to disappear off to Bali when the fancy takes you goes hand-in-hand with employee rights and pension contributions,' Ian said, a familiar version of the same comment that he'd been making since Scarlett dropped out of art school over a decade ago.

Before we could discuss it any further, the rest of the party came clattering down to the kitchen, crowding around the central island or squashing up against the Aga. Ian and I drifted inside to a flurry of greetings and shouting at Alexa to play 'Once in Royal David's City'. If I ignored the looming dread of change and separation heading towards Philippa's family, the morning felt joyful and relaxed. I tried not to be that woman who found Guy and Abigail a bit over the top with their matching woolly slipper socks and cards embossed with 'To My Darling Boyfriend'. I couldn't believe anyone of that generation bothered with cards any more. Surely there was some digital equivalent of the padded musical card that was far cooler. Just as I had that thought, Abigail squealed as she opened her card from Guy. Yep, he'd recorded himself singing Ed Sheeran's 'Thinking Out Loud' for her. Of course he had. Unfortunately, Scarlett and Andrew bursting through the door, each fighting to be the first one home to prove which one of them was the fittest – 'Can't keep an old dog down!' 'I could have run to Dover and back twice in the time it took you to run along that promenade' – rather spoilt the impact of Guy's grand gesture. Nevertheless, he was setting the bar high early on.

After breakfast, Philippa and I tidied up in a well-honed ballet of scraping, stacking and clearing, a routine born from combining our households on frequent occasions. We shuffled everyone else off to sort the presents in the sitting room for the grand opening ceremony. When we were all assembled, Andrew began distributing gifts with a theatrical flourish – 'Is it a bird? Is it a plane? Or could it be a book?' But it wasn't enough to distract Abigail from the fact that Philippa and Andrew hadn't bought anything for each other.

'Where's Mum's present?'

Philippa stepped in. 'Honestly, we decided this year that we didn't need any more clutter and that we would buy each other an experience instead.'

'So what are you going to do?' Abigail asked, in a tone that reminded me of Scarlett when things she took for granted as part of the family furniture changed without warning.

'We haven't decided yet; we thought we'd do something in the new year, give us a treat to look forward to.'

I looked down. I wasn't into lying to adult children, or any children really, especially when the big fat lie would be exposed in a matter of days.

Philippa deflected attention from her lack of presents by handing Abigail a beautifully wrapped gift. I envied people who could be bothered to faff about curling ribbons and writing name tags with their italic fountain pen. My family were lucky if I'd managed to take their presents out of the Amazon box.

Abigail opened a gold bracelet, which she slipped onto her slim wrist, alongside a couple of other bangles. She turned her arm this way and that. 'Thank you. I love it.'

My stomach was refusing to take pleasure in Abigail's joy, churning with the impression that Philippa and Andrew had spent more money on Abigail this year to compensate for the hammer blow about to fall. Before I could work my way through the logic of that, Guy was handing Abigail a gift about the size of a shoebox. She did a dramatic rattling and shaking and pressing her ear to it. I was aware of Scarlett doing the face wrinkle of 'Mate, it's probably a pair of AirPods'.

Abigail lifted the lid and pulled out a smaller box that had the unmistakable look of something jewellery-like. I glanced at Scarlett, whose face was unreadable. I could never decide whether she was a super-independent woman who refused to compromise – good for her – or whether the flames of desperation were beginning to flicker as her big birthday loomed in a fortnight. But if she was wishing that she had her own wholesome bloke presenting her with chi-chi presents today, she was doing a fantastic job of keeping her expression in Switzerland.

The box was fiddly to open and Abigail insisted on teasing the bits of ribbon undone rather than scrabbling and ripping at them as my family would have done, so our interest started to wane and conversation turned to which party game was first on the list. I was a fan of Pictionary despite having the artistic skills of a toddler. Scarlett showed a bit of animation for a game of Articulate, which made me immediately want to play that, unable to shake off the mantra that had guided me through every family holiday – 'As long as Scarlett is happy, I don't care what we do.'

Ian was just putting his bid in for Monopoly when there was a gasp from the other side of the room. Guy was down on one knee, all big eyes and hope, with Abigail clutching a ring between her thumb and forefinger and the words, 'Will you marry me?' reverberating around the room.

Abigail clapped her hand over her mouth, then delivered a very confident 'Yes!' Everything dissolved into a flurry of congratulations and 'Did you know this was going to happen?' and 'When do you think the big day might be?'

There was immediate posing in front of the Christmas tree with the diamond in the engagement ring sparkling in the lights and the whole tableau looking Instagram perfect. Philippa kept saying, 'I can't believe my baby is going to get married.' The timing of the announcement seemed a bit ironic, given that Abigail's parents were just about to blow apart the notion of 'till death do us part' in favour of 'till one of us can't face another thirty years of same old, same old'. But there again, marriage was always a bit of a spin of the roulette wheel. A solid partnership at twenty-seven could either calcify into an immovable monolith over the next forty or fifty years or be eroded by so many storms that it was just a matter of time until it crumbled into the sea.

And as with all big announcements in tight family or friendship circles, underneath all the surface congratulations came the inevitable assessment of 'what this means for me'.

Scarlett wasted no time with her incisive investigation: 'Didn't you do well to get a ring exactly the right size?' with its subtext to Abigail of 'Did you choose this ring, and if you did, why was I left out of the loop and didn't know this was imminent?'

Abigail took the comment at face value, responding with 'I did have a little input a month or so ago.' She flickered her fingers at Scarlett. 'Got my nails done just in case,' she said with a wink.

Scarlett's surprised jerk of the head showed me that Abigail's answer had landed painfully, demonstrating to Scarlett that even a lifelong friendship was no match for the allegiance to a serious boyfriend. That secrets were going to be – and should be – kept. But still, because she was my daughter, I wanted to hug her and say, 'It's hard when your life is at a different stage from your best friend's. But be generous-hearted – you can be part of the new chapter too.'

Abigail and Guy seemed far more concerned about capturing their best sides for Instagram than focusing on the enormity of agreeing to get married. Abigail was ruffling her long blonde hair to give herself a 'surprised on Christmas morning, you'll have to excuse the bedhead' look. Maybe I was just picking holes because, secretly, despite the doctrine I had never deviated from in years – 'You don't need to get married. You create the life you want and if you find someone to share it with, then that's a bonus' – I found myself to be rather jealous that Philippa and Andrew had someone else to take care of Abigail, who would love her as much as they did.

I glanced round at Ian. He looked terrified by the overt display of romance, the puckering of lips and eye gazing. I had to beg Ian to feature in any photo, let alone one where we were supposed to be demonstrating the longevity of romance. But I'd still rather have someone who would drive out into the woods in the middle of the night with me to free a mouse from the humane trap in our attic than someone who looked adoringly into my eyes over lobster on Valentine's Day.

However, we were nothing if not good guests, lining up

obediently for supporting cast photos. If they managed to snap one of Ian without his eyes rolling into the back of his head, I'd be amazed.

There was a definite upside to this announcement, though – Andrew uncorked the Christmas champagne earlier and by the time we sat down to eat, we were all giggly and full of suggestions for the 'big day'. Thankfully, all the outrageous ideas served to make us look invested and excited about the engagement. 'You could ride in on llamas!' 'Why don't you get married on top of the O2?' 'You could have the ceremony in a nuclear bunker!'

Abigail and Guy tolerated all of this with good humour before saying, 'We've got a tight budget, so it will probably be a simple church service – the registry office in town is just too soulless – and a pub.'

Andrew frowned as he forked in another Brussels sprout – 'Only eat them to stop Philippa moaning that she doesn't know why she bothers' – which, in the circumstances, I thought was loyalty continuing above and beyond. In fairness, he did seem to be washing them down with great glugs of Rioja. He tipped his head on one side and, with a noticeable slurring of his words, said, 'We'll obviously chip in for the wedding, so it doesn't have to be totally bargain basement.'

Guy reached for Abigail's hand and Abigail delivered an answer that they had obviously rehearsed. 'That's really kind, Dad, but the important thing to us is that we make the day about our relationship, rather than about how much we spend.'

'No, no, I'm not having my daughter, my only child, having chicken in a basket in a pub on her wedding day.' There was something subtly aggressive about his insistence.

Philippa bristled immediately. 'It's not up to you. If they're old enough to get married, they're old enough to decide how to do it.'

'You've probably got a little while yet to make your minds

up, unless you're intending to get married next week,' I said, aiming to lighten the atmosphere.

Guy nodded gratefully, relieved to be able to smudge over the detail of the day. 'We're not going to leave it too long, but nothing is set in stone yet.' He squeezed Abigail's hand and, with an air of deferential son-in-law-to-be, he turned to Andrew and said, 'Whatever we do, if we're as happy as you and Philippa have been, we'll consider ourselves very lucky.'

Philippa gave a watery smile, but appeared to see the humour as well as the irony in that statement, widening her eyes at me with a discreet 'if only he knew' expression.

Andrew guffawed out loud, making a noise that bore no resemblance to anything that could be considered funny. 'Well, that's a huge joke,' he said in a tone that sounded menacing rather than comedic.

Ian got there before I did. 'Andrew,' he said, 'do you know where the matches are to light the Christmas pudding?'

In that moment, I loved my husband with an intensity that made my heart constrict. Unfortunately, wine had made Andrew brave and belligerent; the feelings that he'd either not been admitting to, or had resolved to keep in a tidy box until a convenient moment, suddenly spewed forth. I watched his mouth forming the words, reminded of the powerful jet of the fountain on Lake Geneva that we'd posed in front of when we'd gone on a weekend break together, two couples, a long friendship and marriages we all took for granted.

Abigail caught something in the air, like a deer sensing human footsteps. 'Why is that such a joke?' she asked. She didn't yet understand the magnitude of her question and how she very much wouldn't want to hear the answer, right now, on this exciting day.

None of us was quick enough to deflect. Andrew's reply strangled out into the room against the background crooning of

Bing Crosby's 'White Christmas' that I hadn't even noticed but immediately sounded loud and mocking.

'Because your mother has decided that all these years working as a software analyst – which, I might add, I do not enjoy – to provide a good home – actually two homes, including this one – has made me over-focused on my career. Apparently I'm "horribly selfish" about the time I spend running to keep me sane when I'm not at work. So, in short, she's not going to put up with me any more and wants to divorce me.'

Philippa was first to recover, flying out of her chair, her face twisted with fury, shouting about the absolute bastardness of him and if he wondered why she was divorcing him, well, frankly, his behaviour today was enough to justify it. Abigail was curled into Guy, crying. I didn't blame him for looking as though he'd been short-changed. He'd obviously thought he was joining a stable family with many jolly Sunday lunches and shared weekend breaks away but instead had inserted himself into a bag of trouble. Scarlett was semaphoring at me, mouthing all sorts of things I couldn't quite decipher but was pretty sure they amounted to 'Bloody hell/did you know about this?'

Ian was trying to lever Andrew up into a standing position to take him outside. 'Come on, chap, a bit of fresh air will do you good.'

I didn't fancy the look of the next few months when despite us all making an effort to keep the show on the road today, it had still shot off the rails so spectacularly.

4

SCARLETT

Whether or not I felt a sense of cosiness or a temptation to ignore the ringing when Mum's name flashed up on my mobile depended entirely on whether I was in child or adult mode. No one could reassure me like Mum – she always made me laugh about my tendency to let my thoughts out into the atmosphere before I got my filter in place. 'One of my dog-walking clients handed me this bag, saying, "I don't need this any more so I thought you might like it". I genuinely thought she was giving me some rucksack thing to keep her dog's bits and pieces in, so I pointed to my bumbag and said, "Oh, that's kind of you, but I don't need it, thank you, I keep the poo bags in here." Of course, it was only a flipping Prada.'

'You're a breath of fresh air. Your lack of airs and graces will be one of the things employers love about you,' was her generous spin on my many social gaffes. And I'd wallow in that snug feeling of there being one human being in the world who insisted on seeing my slip-ups as charming rather than stupid.

On the other hand, Mum was infuriating in her perpetual quest to 'adjust' me – 'I hope you won't mind me saying this, darling, as you know, I have no agenda except for you to be happy...' – before launching into the countless ways my life would be better if I were more like her. Given that I'd left home eleven years ago and was a perfectly adequate adult, her unasked-for advice made me hold the phone away from my ear with one hand and give it the middle finger with the other. 'Remind me to bring you this serum I've been using on my hair. It stops the ends getting so dry.' 'Now, I find that if you get your washing done on a Sunday, you're not starting the week on the back foot.'

I was always on the back foot. And, frankly, quite comfortable there, one foot off the ground but one eye on the next bit of fun, never really making decisions, more reacting to an endless turn of events. Flexible thinking I liked to call it. I couldn't imagine ever acquiring the required skills for Mum to accept that I'd nailed life. With Mum working in HR and Dad as a purchasing manager for an international hotel chain, they'd kind of assumed I'd end up in the corporate world or some fancy-arse design job. Definitely a 'role' – as they liked to call it – that would signal to the world that I was 'on my way'. Disappointingly for them, 'on my way' often meant a flight ticket to a far-flung destination to live in a shack at the beach in the winter, preferably somewhere with hammocks and spices and sarongs, smug at avoiding the grey skies. But despite Mum's lip-pursing when I told her that I was off to Thailand or when she caught sight of a new tattoo – 'Oh Scarlett, what will that look like when you're my age?' – I could take her for granted. She was predictably there. Although she was quite keen to point out the millions of ways I could improve, her comments rolled off me. It was almost like a game we played to pass the time, with no one particularly invested in winning, one of those warped family ways of connecting and caring.

But when Mum called in early January to ask a favour on Philippa's behalf, I was undoubtedly in child irritation mode. 'You know Andrew moved into that flat they own in Clapham on New Year's Day? She's worried he will just work and drink, so I told her you'd invite him out for a run now and again?'

'Why did she throw him out if she intended to be responsible for his welfare?' I asked, still annoyed about them involving us in their drama over Christmas. I'd rather have been sitting on my own in my flat watching telly on Boxing Day. Instead, we'd all been pretending not to hear Philippa rowing with Andrew upstairs while Guy comforted Abigail in the kitchen.

My mother did her theatrical sigh, the breathiness of it containing the very essence of 'When you're older and have managed a relationship longer than a few months, you'll understand.' The desire to recycle our perennial argument about how women of my generation didn't need a man to complete them versus the 'it's not now, it's when you're older' hummed across the surface of my paper-thin patience.

'She still loves him, he's still Abigail's father, but they want different things from life. Andrew is so restless – always wanting to book the next holiday, the next adventure. Philippa just wants to enjoy the lovely home she's worked so hard to create. She doesn't want to keep packing a suitcase and climbing on and off planes.'

'Won't he think it's weird, a thirty-year-old offering to show a fifty-seven-year-old the London ropes?'

Mum snorted in that way she had when I offered an opinion that didn't match hers, as though, when it suited, I could be bossed about like a five-year-old.

'You've known him all your life, for goodness' sake. He's probably quite lonely. I think he'll be rather touched that you want to spend time with him.'

'I don't want to spend time with him. *You* want me to spend time with him...'

And so the conversation went on, with Mum doing an array

of noises designed to represent the fact that she knew best and I knew nothing. However, while presenting her request as an optional favour that I could do whenever I was minded to, history had shown that Mum would eventually adopt a water torture approach: 'Did you manage to introduce Andrew to your running club?', 'I was just wondering if you'd spoken to Andrew yet?', 'Philippa was asking me whether you'd seen Andrew?'

I knew she'd break me eventually. So I resigned myself to an awkward reaching out to my best friend's dad, feeling oddly embarrassed about contacting a man I'd seen several times a year for three decades. I'd spent Sundays, holidays, weekends away with him. Nevertheless, I'd always been insulated by my parents and that odd sense when I was with them that I was still a child and therefore could abdicate all responsibility for making any social occasion a success.

By the third week in January, it was either contact Andrew or live with pre-emptive fury of the predictable conversation whenever Mum called. I texted him.

Mum tells me you've come up to the Big Smoke from the burbs! I run three times a week with Great Strides Running Club (just round the corner from me in Clapham), so let me know if you want to join me any time. Hope all well.

I added a x, then deleted it as weird. I prayed that he'd be way too busy and I wouldn't have to jog around Clapham Common with yet another corporate type forcing me to defend my decision to work as a dogwalker and guinea pig feeder for the type of people who employed not just cleaners but chefs. Dad was always encouraging me to aim higher, increasingly disguised as 'I was just thinking about how creative you are, how good with images and words – I think advertising or marketing would be a great career for you'. I didn't need someone else sprinkling their disappointed dust over my life choices.

Surprisingly, Andrew jumped at the chance to join me. And without Abigail, without Philippa, he seemed far less like my dad. Far less 'What are you going to do about a pension?' and 'Have you shopped around for contents insurance?' Far more 'With your experience looking after animals, you could spend your life housesitting around the world. If I was your age, I'd be taking off to New Zealand for the winter – sure you could find some fantastic properties to look after there.'

Probably the first time anyone among my parents' friends hadn't done that 'Yes, yes, lovely that you spend your days with a Bernese mountain dog and Labradoodle but renting a room at your age? When are you going to get a proper job?'

Soon what had seemed like a chore became something I looked forward to. We challenged each other to find new running routes outside the club. He'd tease me about my laid-back lifestyle – 'Dawn run around Hampstead Heath? Do you actually get up before ten on a Saturday...?'

I'd make jokes about him being a stuffed shirt – 'Assume Shoreditch is far too trendy for a man of a certain age, but there's a route through Victoria Park and along the canal calling to me.'

We ran, miles and miles, sometimes in an easy silence, sometimes exchanging superficial chat when we weren't running uphill – the best spots for coffee, whether we thought we'd survive any of the reality TV shows. 'I'd back myself for *I'm A Celebrity*,' Andrew said.

'I definitely couldn't eat a kangaroo's penis,' I responded and then blushed. I was suddenly embarrassed to have said 'penis' out loud, as though I was still in primary school and knew that it was a naughty word but wanted to see how the grown-ups would react.

Occasionally, we'd have deeper conversations about how

marriage was a lottery. 'I mean, really, you're incredibly lucky if you grow together with someone in the same direction. Philippa was brave to address the fact that we might be happier going our separate ways.' I felt both privileged and uncomfortable that Andrew was sharing a window on his private life. He offered up intimate stories about a woman who'd so often been a fixture in our kitchen, helping me with my handwriting (she'd failed), showing me how to do my eye make-up, allowing me the pick of her wardrobe for Abigail's seventies fancy dress party.

As the weeks went by, though, I found myself making excuses to text him features about training shoes, about muscle groups, about nutrition, in the hope that he might want to 'grab a drink' to talk further. I upgraded my running kit to something a bit more stylish. I forgot the deference to his seniority, to his status as the ex-husband of my mum's best friend, father of my best friend.

The year seemed to gallop towards spring. I had none of that sense of endless grey skies that usually had me trawling the internet for bargain flights to Asia, the weeks dragging with exaggerated slowness towards lighter evenings and longer days. As February gave way to March, the occasional tendril of puzzlement that had curled around my thinking was shifting into something more solid. Disbelief and belief were starting to compete. I asked myself whether I was reading Andrew's invitations all wrong: to have 'a spot of lunch' after our runs, a drink at a rooftop bar one of his colleagues had mentioned. In eight short weeks, I'd gone from reluctantly complying with my mum's request for a favour to wondering about whether he was sitting in his flat, wondering about me. I lay in bed every morning allowing myself a fifteen-minute daydream about when I'd next see him again.

While I walked the dogs, my mind whirred with how I might drop hints about meeting up at the weekend. As I filled water bowls or groomed the dogs, I replayed our conversations, sieving for a meaning beyond middle-aged man with an empty life who was eager to have company – any company, not necessarily mine. I didn't dare assume he also sensed our conversations running on two different planes. Sentences that should have been superficial, innocuous, but appeared – to me, at least – to carry weight because of the magnetic charge push-pulling our words. Was I alone in feeling that every exchange glittered with subtleties, unspoken questions, boundaries that we didn't yet dare breach? I had to be.

Maybe Mum was right, that 'all this playing the field' would eventually pall. Perhaps I was now fixating on the one bloke I'd spent time with in the last few months who didn't pull the duvet back over his head when I got up to go for a run but instead wanted to join me. Or maybe I was mistaking his ability to stick to plans rather than blowing me out because 'he just wasn't feeling it' for something other than old-fashioned good manners. I forced myself to believe that his separation from Philippa had decimated his friendship group. That while Abigail was so caught up in organising her wedding, he'd rather have dinner with me than sit alone with a tikka masala and Netflix.

Then, that Saturday evening. So British. Dinner overlooking Covent Garden at the top of the Opera House. He ordered a bottle of Albariño: 'Organic – should mean we don't get a hangover if we order a second bottle,' he said.

'I'll tell my mum that you're a bad influence.' I cringed as my joke reiterated not only the age gap, but the family history standing between us like a disapproving sentry.

But that was the moment something shifted. Despite everything I'd told myself, that this crush I had on Andrew was akin to a teenage infatuation with a member of a boy band, a reaction crossed his face as though he was tussling with many competing thoughts. He didn't laugh or make a joke or let the comment fade, another bit of banter of no import. The words sat heavily between us, and we locked eyes. His lips twitched. My stomach tightened as I braced myself for a conversation that must surely end with him letting me down gently. A humiliating exchange when he would tell me that he was flattered, that he liked spending time with me but his feelings were fatherly – 'I'm hoping I didn't give you the impression of anything else?'

I couldn't even contemplate the other option: that he might admit to finding me attractive. That would be a tripwire of trouble on so many levels. But my stupid heart didn't want to listen to reason. My head could send all the warning signals it wanted, but I could feel my breath catching in my chest, urging him to say something out loud that would confirm that I wasn't a lovesick idiot, deceiving myself into seeing a depth of emotion that didn't exist.

Before either of us could say anything, a waiter arrived to take our order. I chose wood pigeon and venison and was rewarded with Andrew saying, 'You're such a pleasure to take out because you try all sorts of things. You've got a great attitude to life, always up for an adventure.'

I had a flashback to last summer when our two families were at a pub celebrating Andrew's birthday together. Philippa had sent back her steak – 'I have to have it well done, can't bear any blood.' I felt a little surge of triumph that I compared favourably with Philippa in one area at least, then immediately frowned at my childish pettiness.

As the food arrived, Andrew seemed to relax. The initial tension engulfing us dissipated as we discussed films we'd like to see, the people on the other tables, whether Banksy would one day decide to reveal his identity. Somewhere between starting the next bottle of Albariño and discussing the various merits of lean venison over beef, Andrew raised a glass to me and said, 'To you. Well done for staying true to yourself. Don't ever change.'

We clinked glasses and I said, 'That's all very flattering, but

I'm not sure anyone would agree with you. I think it's been less about being true to myself and more about never committing to anything.' I dabbed my mouth with my napkin, suddenly conscious of Andrew looking at me intently and terrified I was sporting a rogue blob of beetroot.

'Have you ever been in a serious relationship?' he asked.

The question took me by surprise. 'Surely you remember Dan the Dickhead? I brought him to Mum and Dad's twenty-fifth wedding anniversary party. He drank too much Châteauneuf, tried to move one of the tables to the edge of the room so we could dance and it collapsed, smashing all their Waterford crystal.'

Andrew laughed. 'Oh yes. I guess that wasn't a relationship cementer.'

'I'm not very good at relationships. I go for total losers who can't tell you whether they're free that evening more than two hours before we're due to meet. Or the other type who seem to like me because I'm not particularly conventional. They always end up wanting to "fix" me, encouraging me to get a different job, save up for a house. I like knowing that I can up sticks whenever the mood takes me, that I'm free to come and go as I please.'

Andrew leaned back in his chair, sipping his wine. 'I admire that about you. Your willingness to embrace uncertainty, to go with the flow. I wish I'd met someone like you years ago.'

I was astonished how keen I was to hear him imply his entire marriage to Philippa had been a mistake, that she'd been so cautious and staid and had bored him silly with her endless collecting of handbags. And as swiftly as I had that thought came a rush of shame that I was eager to hear negative things about a woman I'd loved all my life, who'd treated me like another daughter. I did not want to be that person. Surely I was better than that?

I waited, leaning into the table, anticipating, longing for but also dreading words that would mean we had to stop pretending. Sentences that would move us from people who had dinner and ran together to people having to make decisions about how the hell this might play out. I thought about Abigail's messages: *Dad says you've taken pity on him and you go running with him. Thank you! I hope he's not cramping your style. Come and see Guy and me soon... bridesmaid dresses to choose xx*

'Do you want to get married?' Andrew was asking.

Was he testing the waters about whether I was up for a romantic relationship? Or – like the rest of my family – eyeing up the fact that my thirtieth birthday had come and gone and subtly pointing out that the egg-timer was looking short of sand? No one was going to 'desperate old spinster' me. 'Not really. Can't imagine ever meeting anyone who'd put up with me forever, to be honest.' Now I was becoming the sort of woman I despised, fishing for compliments.

A grin spread across Andrew's face. 'I'm sure you'll find someone up to the challenge.'

That sensation again of dancing around the topic, of neither of us being brave enough to address what was happening. Though perhaps nothing was happening except a drama in my head. I needed to step back, stop this nonsense, if only to free up more space for other thoughts. I didn't need all those couples' activities that Abigail posted on her Instagram – Guy helping her choose a new dress #MyPersonalShopper, the two glasses of champagne on a sunlit terrace #JustTheTwoOfUs, Guy carrying her bags #HelpAtHand. Yet, without any evidence that Andrew saw me as anything other than an alternative to joining a gym, I was obsessing about when he might suggest seeing me next. Walking the long route past his block of flats in the hope of bumping into him. Signing up to Facebook – the social media graveyard of old people – so I could see if he was posting anything. Which he wasn't.

To save my sanity, this was the last time I was going to have dinner with him. I wasn't that sort of woman, the type to moon about, hoping that a man would make a move. If I wanted to hook up with someone, I either asked them directly or made it so obvious that they'd be able to read my intentions from Mars. But this was too difficult, humiliation at family gatherings a possibility forever more. What if he told my mother I'd tried to get with him? 'That daughter of yours is pretty forward. I didn't see that one coming. Bit awkward.' No. 'Madness this way' was signposted in neon lights.

We finished our wine. I said no to coffee and we wound our way through the crowds. A steady drizzle was falling and the hubbub of Saturday night revellers rushing to take shelter was a welcome diversion from the quiet that had descended between us.

'Cab or train?' Andrew asked.

'I'm still stuck in my student mentality. Cabs are only for emergencies.'

He laughed. 'Even when it's raining? You're a cheap date.'

I hated the idea that he thought I was a tightwad, given that he'd already insisted on paying for dinner, so I said, 'If you're in a hurry to get home or afraid of shrinking, I can make an exception.'

He took a deep breath. 'I'm never in a hurry to leave you.' He swallowed and pressed his fingers into his eyes. 'Let's get a cab. But I'm paying.'

I followed him without speaking, still processing his words and fumbling about for possible meanings. Was he just being polite? A declaration of something more?

When a cab pulled up, we clambered in, Andrew on the fold-out seat opposite me.

He ran his fingers through his hair, so much less corporate-looking than at Christmas, with dark grey waves curling over his collar. Younger. Definitely not the epitome of a broken-hearted husk of a man that Mum kept conjuring up every time she asked about him. He glanced over his shoulder to see if the cabbie was listening. Then he turned back to me and, in a loud whisper, said, 'I've been wanting to say this for weeks. I love spending time with you. You are just fun to be around.'

'Thank you,' I said and we sat, staring into each other's eyes, as Trafalgar Square came into view. 'You too.'

He shook his head. 'There are other things I want to say.' He glanced out of the window, his face silhouetted against the lights as Nelson's Column loomed, then faded in my peripheral vision.

'What other things?' I tried to sound ballsy, as though I was laying down a challenge, but my voice came out gentle and pleading.

He ran a finger across his eyebrow. 'I'm scared to say them in case I am so wide of the mark.'

Someone was going to have to be brave. My turn to see if the cab driver was showing any interest in us – I really couldn't face an 'Is this man bothering you?' scenario.

I stretched out my arm and reached for Andrew's hand. He didn't respond, just let his hand rest in mine. All the voices of doubt swirled into my head, the horror that he might be sitting there wondering how to free himself without embarrassing me. Finally, gloriously, his thumb caressed my palm and he leaned forwards.

'What's the worst idea you've had in your whole life?' he asked.

Anticipation rose in my chest, a fluttering of excitement tinged with a desire to show off, to shock him with how outrageous I could be.

Showing off won the day.

'How long have you got?' I said.

'As long as you need.' That half-smile, that teasing. But also that sense that he was all in for every misdemeanour. The time I filled up my employer's car with diesel instead of petrol and the engine conked out down a deserted lane in the backwaters of Sussex. The day I'd decided to let the guinea pigs have a little run around inside and I'd had to beg the handyman to dismantle half the kitchen to retrieve them from behind the fitted cabinets. Never mind the champagne and roses, a man who listened without talking over me, without assuming his experience was superior to mine was the biggest aphrodisiac I could dream up.

I rested my forehead against his, our lips just centimetres apart, breathing in the scent of him. That spicy cinnamon after-shave that made me think of Marrakech and markets and searing sunshine. Realising then that a scruffy black cab on a rainy evening with Andrew won hands down in terms of panorama. 'Frankly, there have been so many. Where shall I start?' I murmured. If he didn't hear those words as the ultimate come-on, I'd better start downloading applications for a convent.

He didn't disappoint. 'With me?'

'You're as bad a mistake as any, so I guess you'll do.'

And we sat, our heads touching, our eyes both smiling and challenging each other to the next move. Longing coursed through me as though I'd smeared the menthol cream I used when I pulled a muscle in my calf over my whole body, a tingling heat colonising every skin cell.

When the cab came to a halt outside his flat, Andrew drew back and raised a questioning eyebrow.

'I think we should explore my very worst idea,' I said, scrambling out of the cab.

'Are you sure?' he asked, once we were on the pavement. 'I can soon flag down another cab.'

In reply, I took his face in my hands and kissed him, bold with the relief of knowing, giddy with the realisation that this – whatever 'this' was – was the maddest thing I would ever do. A tiny part of my brain scrambled into the pulpit of reason, preaching for restraint, for reflection. But my heart was championing the art of freefalling, tumbling through the air, shrieking with joy.

I stepped back, but he pulled me to him again. Caution and consequences skittered away like an empty beer can across a deserted park.

What a wonderful mistake this was going to be.

5

JACKIE

A few days before my birthday in May, Philippa bustled in with a rose in a pot. 'You're currently the love of my life, given there are no other takers at the moment, so I bought you this – just a little something for your birthday on Saturday.' I hated birthday presents, but social etiquette meant I didn't want to sound ungrateful and at least it wasn't another thing to clutter up the house. I did love my garden, so if I had to suffer a present, a plant was probably the way to go. Philippa carried on, oblivious. 'Fifty-seven! Where did those years even go?'

I loved her for skating over the fact that my birthday was also the anniversary of the thing I attempted to forget. But, try as I might, I could never view it as a day of celebration.

I ushered her into the kitchen, where Ian was pulling a chicken curry out of the microwave. 'Sorry for gatecrashing your romantic dinner à deux. Didn't realise it was date night,' she said.

Ian laughed. 'The more, the merrier as far as I'm concerned. I'm not sure Jackie would take me seriously if I suggested a date night. You'll know by now that she's not really one for candlelit dinners. She just about lets me give her a birthday card. Even

WHOSE SIDE ARE YOU ON?

then, she's always telling me to recycle the one from the year before.'

'That's obviously the key to a successful marriage, refusing to get sucked into doing what society dictates couples "in love" should do. We always did the whole presents and cards rigmarole on Valentine's Day, birthdays, anniversaries, "just because you're so damn marvellous" days and look where that got us.'

There was a silence while we all pondered what the correct response could be. I had a distinct sense that Philippa's initial euphoria at her freedom was waning now the reality of being single was kicking in.

I defaulted to 'Have you heard from Andrew?'

'We've had a few exchanges about finances and that sort of thing. I think he's doing okay. To be fair, it must be a bit weird moving back into the flat he had when we first met, almost back to square one.'

'It's only temporary though, isn't it? When Ian spoke to him, he sounded glad that he'd rented it out all these years and had somewhere to stay without a great big palaver. He's taking the opportunity to do a bit of decorating while he's there.' I admired how accommodating Andrew had been, offering to move out when he hadn't even wanted the split.

Philippa rolled her eyes, but not in an unkind way. 'He never could sit still. That man is never happier than when he has a project. Anyway, what's the plan for your birthday?'

I wondered if there was a wistful tone to Philippa's voice. The recognition that by leaving her marriage, all the high days and holidays would require a bit more thought, a bit more effort, rather than taking it as a given that she and Andrew were the fulcrum around which everyone else would pivot.

I was relieved that I could make my birthday sound less than ideal. 'Scarlett had planned to come over and help Ian cook lunch because the thing I love most is when we're all at home together.' I cringed at my clumsiness, my tactless brag about my happy family. I didn't know how to address it without sounding patronising, so I carried on. 'With excellent timing, the bloody oven has decided to give up the ghost this evening, hence the unsatisfactory curry in the microwave scenario. Good job I had that in the freezer. Apparently, there's a three-week waiting list for repairs.'

'So what are you going to do?' Philippa asked as Ian started serving the curry into bowls.

'We're now having to trek up to London with everything so we can do it at Scarlett's. On the upside, her housemate is away for the weekend. On the downside, she's not a great fan of housework, so she's already telling me not to give her a hard time about how messy her house is.' I laughed. 'As long as I don't find unidentified objects in my food, I'll survive. I'd be quite content to knock it on the head, but you know what my lot are like about birthdays.'

'Why didn't you ask me to host, you twit? I wouldn't have minded,' Philippa said.

I could feel Ian's eyes boring into me. I'd wanted to ask Philippa if she could help me out, but Scarlett in particular was still banging on about 'that shitshow of Christmas' and had made a big deal out of wanting some time with 'just our family'. I had a hunch that Abigail getting married had unsettled Scarlett more than she was willing to admit. True to form, she sidestepped any discussion about feelings and shut me down whenever I enquired about how much Abigail was involving her in the wedding. 'I've got the bridesmaid's dress. I don't know what else I need to do except organise a hen party.'

If I was honest – which I wasn't because I didn't want to admit that I was a bit jealous that Abigail's life was all plotted out while Scarlett was still aimless and untethered – I'd found Philippa's obsession with wedding detail a bit tedious. Cream or white invitations? Wildflowers or single stem roses? Scallops or smoked salmon? So the last thing I wanted to do on my birthday was play piggy-in-the-middle, engaging in Philippa's wedding talk while pretending to Scarlett that I had every confidence she'd find her own path when she was ready. I could already imagine my little laugh as I said, 'There's no rush at all. What's meant for you won't pass you by.' All the usual guff I told her so she didn't worry while I lay awake fretting myself.

I opted for a half-truth. 'I know you would have had us all over, thank you, but Scarlett was adamant. She's been a bit tricky lately so I just went along with it.' I added, 'Don't sit at home imagining that it'll be all jolly family time. Ian and I will be tiptoeing through the minefield of topics we cannot bring up in case she snaps our heads off. Such as the temptation to do a forensic investigation into why Scarlett has never had a long-term partner.'

'She's a great girl. She'll find the right person when she's ready. Abigail was just lucky to meet Guy when she did. I hope she doesn't leave it to thirty like I did to have a baby, though. I want to be a grandma as soon as possible,' Philippa said.

I'd been married at twenty-five, and Scarlett was born within eighteen months. But I didn't say those words out loud because we all knew how well that had turned out.

6

JACKIE

Ian acted as though he never thought about what I'd done. He never mentioned it. Perhaps he hoped that focusing on the 'Happy Birthday' of this year would smother the memory of the very unhappy birthday of yesteryear. And despite his best efforts and my best efforts, that year stood out, a big black crow in our history, and weighed on me, harvesting carpaccio-thin slices of joy each time I clocked up another year. My favourite moment of every birthday was getting into bed, knowing that it was three hundred and sixty-five days until I had to face it again.

But this year I was particularly tetchy. Scarlett had texted to tell me that she was intending to get lunch on the table for two-thirty. She wanted to do some deep-cleaning before we arrived and wouldn't have time to do it on Friday night as she was going out. I rang her. 'Listen, if it's too much trouble, let's postpone until the oven is fixed here. I don't want to put you out when you're so busy.' Although I didn't mean a word of that. What I really meant was 'Either stay in on Friday night or get up at the crack of dawn on Saturday. Or, brilliant idea, don't live in such a pigsty that people coming for lunch means you have to spend a whole day cleaning.'

The desire to tell her to forget it, that I hated my birthday anyway and I didn't care if I spent it huddled under a blanket eating peanut butter straight out of a jar, was almost irresistible. But Ian wouldn't let me get away with that. Scarlett knew he wouldn't let her off the hook either, so reluctantly she agreed to get cracking early doors on Saturday morning.

I was wide awake at six-thirty and got up as soon as I opened my eyes. It wasn't always effective, but I knew from previous years that it was better than allowing any space for my mind to drift down dark alleys.

Ian groaned as he sensed me leave the bedroom. 'You don't have to get up, love,' I said.

But Ian took his role of making tea in the morning for me very seriously. He might not be all flowers and chocolates and 'your hair looks nice', but the right colour tea – properly strong – in the right mug was his love language and he never deviated from it. And every time my fingers closed around that purple mug with its caramel-coloured liquid, I felt safe.

So, within ten minutes, we were sitting in the kitchen, with Ian reading the Saturday papers, and me gathering up the food from the fridge and putting bottles of wine in a box. He handed me a card – my one concession to birthdays. He never properly understood why I didn't want a present, but he'd long since given up buying me anything as it inevitably led to a row about how it was my right not to want gifts.

As he reached for another section of the Saturday supplement, he looked up. 'You're fidgety, aren't you?'

'I know Scarlett is plenty old enough to clean her house herself, but I wouldn't mind going over a bit earlier to help. Otherwise she'll be all stressed and then that will spill over into the day. And I just want to have a nice time.'

'Why don't you text her and tell her we'll be there about eleven?'

'She'll tell me not to come. Let's just get ready and go. If by some miracle she's already finished the cleaning, we can get a head start on lunch.'

'Well, getting your rubber gloves on doesn't sound like much of a birthday treat to me,' Ian said.

'As long as I'm with my family, I don't care what I'm doing. Really.'

All the things we never talked about glittered above our heads for a moment before vanishing into Ian's reluctant but tolerant scrape of his chair. 'I'll go and get showered then.'

We drove up to Clapham and managed, miraculously, to find a parking space not too far away from Scarlett's flat. 'She might not even be here if she stayed out last night,' Ian said, attempting to disguise his annoyance at the interruption to his Saturday morning routine as a legitimate concern.

I peered into the downstairs windows but couldn't see anyone moving about. 'We'll just have to go for birthday coffee if she's not.'

I rang the bell and waited for quite a while, unwilling to accept that Ian might have been right about sticking to the appointed time.

Scarlett finally appeared at the front door, bleary-eyed in her T-shirt and pants with something that looked like utter horror on her face. She threw her arms up in the air. 'Why are you here so early?'

Ian muttered, '*Happy birthday, Mum, thank you so much for everything you do for me.*'

Scarlett ignored him. 'I thought we said twelve-thirty to start getting lunch ready?' She rubbed at the corners of her mouth. 'It's not even nine-thirty yet.'

I employed the humorous approach, doing a little dance and miming hoovering and cleaning windows. But she carried on frowning, leaning on the door jamb like a no-entry sign. Her welcome bore absolutely no resemblance to the 'You're here early! Wonderful! I get to spend more of your birthday with you!' delusion that I'd been labouring under.

I explained how I thought she'd appreciate the help – 'I know how busy you are with work. I love having a good old spring clean. I've even brought my limescale remover for the taps and toilet rim – so satisfying!' I said, grinning to show I was up for any disgusting job she cared to throw at me. It didn't have the desired effect though as her mouth was hanging open in exasperation. While we were having a stand-off on the steps, Ian was unloading the wine and food.

'Hello, darling,' he said, acting as though Scarlett was delighted to see us. 'This meat needs to get in the fridge as soon as possible.' Which was one of the most inflammatory things Ian could have said. Both Scarlett and I became infuriated with Ian's obsession over not leaving anything out of the fridge for more than five seconds. We both operated on a 'hang on tight to anything you haven't finished with' basis when we were having breakfast as Ian whisked the milk away before it could ever make contact with a tardy Weetabix.

Scarlett still stood blocking the entrance, but did reach out to take the cool bag from Ian. 'You can't come in at the moment, because I'm, er, cleaning. Why don't you go and have coffee at the café round the corner and I'll text you when I've finished.'

This was the woman who had had no qualms when she lived at home in letting me pick my way across a room of yesterday's underwear, food wrappers, discarded T-shirts. I waved dismissively. 'I've seen it all before. I'll give you a hand.'

'Mum.' She was trying to indicate something to me, glancing at Ian and widening her eyes as though we were having a secret conversation.

I struggled to follow. Then suddenly the penny dropped. 'Have you got company?'

'Yes. I have.'

Ian wasn't quick enough not to pull the face of distaste that he always made when confronted with the fact that his daughter was now old enough to be having sex, possibly with someone she would only see once.

'Okay, why don't you hide him in the bedroom while we bring all the food and drink in? Then I'll get Dad a flat white so you can say your goodbyes. Or we're very happy to be introduced?'

Ian shook his head as though he didn't have all day to be standing debating the finer points of Scarlett's love life and squeezed past her, chuntering about how he needed to get the Sauvignon in the fridge. 'Nothing worse than tepid white wine.'

'Dad! Don't—' Scarlett spun round and shot in after him and I followed.

Before I crossed the tiny hallway into the large kitchen diner, I heard Ian's voice, full of surprise. 'Hello. What are you doing here?' followed by 'Oh shit. No. Oh my God.'

I ran in to see what the calamity was. I looked down the corridor that led to Scarlett's bedroom to see Andrew scooting across to the bathroom, bare-chested in a pair of bright blue boxers with dancing bananas on them. His dark hair bore the distinct mussiness of sleep. My brain was slow. So astonishingly slow that my first thought was 'Wow. That's a jolly pair of boxers' as I compared them to Ian's sober black and grey selection. Then I realised.

I felt my mouth drop open, which I'd always thought was a dramatic gesture to denote surprise that authors used in books but that never happened in real life. But no, the May breeze that was blowing in from the front door I hadn't yet closed whistled round my teeth.

Ian was glaring at Scarlett with a fury that I'd only seen on rare occasions in our married life and never directed at his daughter. 'What's going on? Please, please tell me this isn't what it looks like, though I can't see how it could be anything else.'

Scarlett's face was mottled with both defiance and a desire to burst into tears that reminded me of when she was a young teenager and I wouldn't let her go to Manchester for a pop concert unless I went with her.

Unusually, Ian and I reversed roles. I patted the air, appealing for calm from Ian. To Scarlett, I said, 'Do you want to go and put a dressing gown on?' thinking that a T-shirt with 'I don't kiss ass, I kick it', which was short enough to allow glimpses of a zebra print thong, wasn't really the attire we needed for a serious talk. 'Then it's probably a good idea if we all have a bit of a chat...' That last sentence crept out with all the energy of a hairdresser saying, 'Do you like it?' while the client was already wailing into a tissue and poking regretfully at great chunks of hair on the floor with her toe.

Scarlett's face darkened. 'No one under the age of forty owns a dressing gown.'

I didn't think arguing the toss on that point was going to fix today.

As soon as Scarlett left the room, Ian was shaking his head in disbelief. 'Is she sleeping with Andrew? Was she having an affair with him while he was still married to Philippa? At Christmas?'

'I don't know,' I hissed, narrowing my eyes as I replayed the days we'd all spent together at Christmas, sieving through the mealtimes, the various combinations of people distracting and comforting each other for something I'd missed. But there was no 'a-ha!' moment. 'They did go running one morning, but I don't recall any funny stuff.' I tutted to myself, hearing the ghost of my mother's instructions during my own teenage years about 'not getting up to any funny stuff'. This was so far from funny.

'He's old enough to be her dad,' Ian said. 'He's older than me.' Which were valid enough objections, but he was overlooking the one taking centre stage dancing and whooping at top volume in my head, which was 'What the hell am I going to say to Philippa?'

Before we could exchange any more of our shocked thoughts, Scarlett and Andrew reappeared in clothes that didn't force us to imagine what they'd been up to the night before.

Scarlett had her chin up and her shoulders back, practically a parody of any Instagram meme about how to walk into a room looking like you mean business. Andrew was far more concilia-tory in his stance. At least he had the grace to look embarrassed. He turned to Scarlett and said, 'Would you like to speak? Or shall I?'

Scarlett did that twitch of her lips that took me back to the many stand-offs we'd had right up until she left home for good. It was code for: 'You can say what you like, but I'm doing it anyway.'

Eventually, she said, 'You can.'

Andrew sat down on the sofa and Scarlett plonked herself down next to him, but thankfully didn't hold his hand. After decades of watching Philippa swing her feet up onto Andrew's lap, I was battling to accept what was in front of me.

Andrew put his hands out in a gesture of submission. 'I'm really sorry about this.'

Scarlett stiffened.

He turned to her quickly. 'Not sorry for being with you,' he said, gently.

I didn't know whether to be glad he was so obviously on Scarlett's side or repulsed that he was using such a loving tone with my daughter, whom he'd watched grow up.

Unbidden, a memory rushed in, a swimming pool in Spain, set high in the mountainside against a backdrop of cacti. Philippa was heavily pregnant with Abigail and we were lying under the umbrella in the shade discussing baby names. Meanwhile Scarlett, who was about two and a half, played with Andrew in the pool, squealing with delight as he launched her into the air.

He took a breath. 'I'm sorry you found out like this. It's not what we wanted. And I'm well aware of what you will think, all the reservations you'll have. I would have them too if it was the other way round, if Ian was with Abigail.'

Ian made a grunt of disgust. 'Is this why you and Philippa split up?'

Scarlett wrinkled up her face. 'Dad! I'm not a homewrecker. We've only been seeing each other...' She paused, grappling for the right words. 'Andy joined my running club, so we've been exercising together a lot.' She coloured up as she realised that 'exercising together a lot' might be misconstrued. The unfamiliar 'Andy' rather than 'Andrew' registered. The intimacy, the shift from our closest family friend, whom we knew far better than Scarlett, to a separate relationship, on a different level, governed by the sort of knowledge that was only possible if you were lovers.

Andrew 'Andy' stepped in. 'There was nothing going on while I was still living with Philippa. I didn't plan this, neither of us did, it's been totally left of field.'

'You can say that again,' Ian said, pacing about in a parody of *Meet the Parents*.

Scarlett's voice took on a belligerent tone. 'Dad, I'm a grown woman. Plenty of women my age go out with older men. It's no biggie.'

Ian looked as though he'd seen a unicorn run through the kitchen. His voice took on a menace that I didn't recognise. 'No biggie? *No biggie?* I would say this is quite a sizeable biggie. It's verging on incest!' That horrible word made my heart leap.

Andrew was shaking his head, his hands placating. 'I know what it looks like. But all I'm asking from you is to give us a bit of time and space. It's all happened very quickly and taken us both by complete surprise. I do recognise it's not ideal for you guys. I'm not surprised you feel protective.'

Ian shook his head. 'Not ideal? One of our best friends leaving his wife and hooking up with my daughter? No. Not *fucking* ideal at all.'

'Does Philippa know?' I asked, but I already had my answer. There was no way that she wouldn't have been straight on the phone to grill me.

Andrew looked at his feet, then met my eye. 'We're waiting for the right moment to tell her. We hadn't planned to say anything to you – or anybody – yet. Just wanted to find our feet first without dealing with everyone else's opinions. I'd appreciate it if you'd let me speak to Philippa when we're ready. We were hoping to get Abigail's wedding out of the way first. Neither of us wanted to overshadow that.' He glanced at Scarlett, who gave a nod of encouragement.

I gasped. 'But that's four months away. I can't be expected to keep this a secret from Philippa until September. She's my best friend.'

For one moment, I thought Ian, this man who released trapped moths outside, who massaged my shoulders when I spent too long at the computer, was going to go all 1950s father and take a swing at Andrew for bringing his daughter's virtue into disrepute. His voice came out strangled, as though he had something obstructing his airways. 'I can't listen to this. You're not who I thought you were. Not at all.'

Ian stood with his hand on the food bag he'd carried in from the car, back when this day was supposed to be a celebration, a run-of-the-mill, all-the-family-together kind of day. The sort of day where Scarlett would boss Ian about and he might make a joke about it being no wonder that all the men her age were running for the hills. Depending on her mood, she'd either give as good as she got, which could be quite entertaining, or throw a strop. I'd tell them off for bickering but, ultimately, we'd muddle along in that predictable tutting-but-loving kind of way. He beckoned to me. 'Let's go. I'm sorry. I know it's your birthday, but I just need some time to get my head around this.'

His distress was contagious, upset ricocheting off every surface like a child's rubber bouncy ball. It obliterated any notion that this situation was resolvable, that there was in fact a solution that could satisfy, if not delight, all parties involved. But the fact that Ian, who'd never wavered, not once in our whole married life – not even *then* – couldn't find the strength to summon up a brave face, couldn't keep it together for the next four or five hours until we figured out a long-term plan, frightened me more than anything else had ever frightened me.

Somewhere I found room for a sliver of anger, a rage that he simply wanted to walk away from it. And that was despite knowing that Ian's behaviour would be less damaging than my modus operandi of getting into a vicious slanging match and backing everyone into extreme corners of self-justification.

I tried to keep the tears out of my voice, just missing the mark of sounding agreeable rather than snappily acquiescent. 'You're right. Let's cancel. I hate my birthday anyway.'

Andrew stood up, walking towards me. 'Jackie, I'm sorry this came out the way it did. I shouldn't have stayed here last night and allowed this to happen.'

'No, you shouldn't. You really shouldn't. This is so unfair on everyone.' I walked over to Ian, who was already half in the hallway.

Andrew turned to Scarlett. 'What would you like me to do? Do you want me to leave you to talk to your parents? I'm not sure what would be best. I'll do whatever you want.'

Just hearing him speaking to her like that turned my stomach. This friend of nearly thirty years, a man I often stayed up late talking to, even when everyone else had gone to bed. I had never felt the slightest flicker of flirtation or vulnerability, and now he was suddenly the biggest threat to everyone I knew and loved.

Scarlett leapt to her feet. 'This is not Andy's fault. He's not some creepy old man taking advantage of me. I want to be with him and he has every right to stay here whenever it suits us. I chose this. Of course, I know it's complicated, but it's what I want. What we want.' Although she sounded marginally less certain about the 'we' than the 'I'.

If it had been any other situation, I would have rushed in to say, 'He'd be lucky to have you.' Instead I was afraid. Afraid that he would recognise how funny and kind and generous-hearted she was under her spiky exterior. Terrified that against all the odds, the age difference, the friendship and family history – the thought appalled me – he would properly love her. That after all these years of quietly crossing my fingers that Scarlett would find a good man to have a serious relationship with, this was where the chips had landed.

I screwed up my eyes. I could not conceive of Andrew – the man who chaired board meetings, understood databases and could offer a brief CV of every Cabinet minister – with Scarlett. The woman who turned her house upside down to find her passport every time she went on holiday and was so chaotic, she still sometimes resorted to using washing-up liquid instead of shampoo.

'Okay, okay. Let's talk later in the week,' I said, giving in to Ian's impatient tapping on the door jamb. Rage was emanating off him in waves in a way that made me scared that if we didn't leave immediately, words would be said that couldn't easily be undone. Despite everything, I wanted Scarlett to know I was her mum, that she could talk to me, that I might not agree – definitely didn't agree – with what she was doing, but that I still loved her.

She jutted out her chin. 'I'm going to do what's right for me. And I'm sorry if that doesn't meet with universal approval.'

And with those words – those simple, yet astonishingly complicated words – I realised that this was about to become my second most disastrous birthday ever.

7

SCARLETT

I'd fought hard never to think about the day when my parents would find out. And I'd been largely successful, kicking all my worries into the long grass, as something to deal with when absolutely necessary. But now that moment was here and it was so much worse than I could have ever imagined.

Dad looked so disgusted, as though he was struggling not to throw up. Mum reminded me of our old Labrador who hated it when family members didn't stay in a tidy group and ran between us in a frantic effort to gather her tribe. I didn't know how I'd kept my nerve, how I hadn't folded under the burden of their horror, how I'd managed to deliver a calm and solid response.

But when Dad slammed the front door and, through the window, I saw him sling his arm round my mum's shaking shoulders, I had to work hard not to cry.

Andrew stepped towards me, his hands in half-surrender: 'Are you okay?'

'Give them something to talk about on the way home, anyway.'

He held his arms out. 'You don't have to be brave with me.

For two pins, I'd sit down and cry myself. I've made life very difficult for you.'

I leaned against his chest, briefly wallowing in the theatrics of the moment, the enormity of 'this' becoming real, something that other people, people who loved me, knew about. That they'd take seriously and, by default, we'd have to as well. Or get out now in the tiny window before we rolled a Molotov cocktail into the lives of everyone else we loved. Overnight we'd moved from two people gently mapping out each other's contours to a couple who were going to have to survive the avalanche of other people's opinions.

Andy and I had discussed this outcome on a regular basis since that night back in March when I must have said, 'Yes, I absolutely want to do this' a hundred times. I'd known that at some point in the not too distant future I would have to face the harsh reality that Mum and Dad would never approve and I would need to suss out a way to be comfortable with that. Of course, I understood why they would find it hard to stomach. Frankly, if one of my friends had told me they were embarking on a similar relationship, I would have pulled every vomit-making face available in my muscle range. However, it felt right, in a way that logical examination wouldn't allow for. Over the two months that had elapsed since what we referred to as 'our glorious first mistake', I'd ceased to think of Andy as Mum and Dad's friend or Abigail's dad or Philippa's ex.

As a result, my parents' shock and disapproval felt under-standable from their point of view and incomprehensible from mine. As far as I was concerned, the age gap and family history had paled into such insignificance that I barely thought about them. To me, Andy was, quite simply, a man whose enthusiasm for life made me feel as though the world was glittering with opportunities. Not bound by the sorts of reservations my own dad had – 'I'm too old to go setting up my own business now'/ 'I'd love to live in a sunny climate but I've left it a bit late to start again'/'I did think about joining the tennis club but they're all youngsters down there now'.

The more I got to know Andy – it was astonishing how little I'd taken on board about a man I'd known all my life – the more I became convinced that age was an attitude of mind. He pored over the Sunday supplements, reading about golden visas in Malta, Cyprus and Portugal. 'I quite fancy buying an old farmhouse by the sea and seeing if all this cold water swimming will help me live to a hundred.' He talked about becoming a business angel, investing in start-ups. 'The young ones, who've got a bit of fire, a bit off the wall, you need that quirkiness sometimes, to have the imagination to look forward, to see what the future might need.'

It wasn't even that I thought he'd do it, it was that wonderful sense that he was open to the world. That he would embrace any experience that might present itself, make new friends, and never talk himself out of something that might be, could be, fun or interesting. The opposite of everyone who surrounded me, with their grey and heavy refrains about the trappings of adult life, as though there was a mutually exclusive choice to be made between pleasure and stability. I'd been fed the gospel right up until I left home that if you hadn't got life sussed by the time you were thirty, you were somehow failing. In Mum and Dad speak, that required me to be on the housing ladder with a clear career trajectory, partner and an agreement about when I might start a family.

But despite Abigail gliding into all those things, ticking off the milestones with aplomb, Andy laughed in the face of these 'rules'. 'Who gets to decide how you live your life? If I'd listened to my mum and dad, I'd have trained to be a vicar. Never even went to church after the age of eighteen. You're supporting yourself, you don't ask them for anything. You're a decent and kind and funny person... you're an adult in your own right...' he'd said. 'Though some of your decisions are a bit suspect.'

He'd bent to kiss me and his words ran around my head – 'Who gets to decide how you live your life?' His confidence in me, his certainty that I was where I needed to be until I found another path to skip down – with absolutely no need to apologise for it – was so unbelievably attractive. I loved his conviction that you didn't have to know all the answers before you started, otherwise you'd never do anything. 'I'm a big fan of doing some basic research so you're not a total idiot, but the most important thing is trusting yourself and believing that you have the capability of dealing with whatever life throws at you.'

He'd looked at me then. 'We're going to get a lot of shit for this if people find out. I don't want to drag you into anything that you're going to regret.' His expression was serious. 'I think we both know what this looks like to the outside world. Your parents will hate me and I don't think Abigail or Philippa are going to take kindly to it.'

Now, as we stared at each other, both processing the sudden leap from secret love affair to publicly contentious relationship, I understood exactly why Andy had been at pains to reiterate what was at stake. I hadn't wanted to listen, hadn't wanted to dwell on the consequences. Whether it was dopamine, pheromones, oxytocin or a simple penchant for pushing boundaries, I couldn't imagine regretting for a moment the fact that a favour I'd been doing for Mum – 'Philippa's worried he'll just work and drink – so if you could get him out for a run now and again?' – had spiralled into this sparkling thing that consumed me. That caused me to smile suddenly. That made me like the world so much more. That slowly, quietly, stopped me wondering what was wrong with me, that I was at such a different stage from all my peers, from Abigail. But, in the end, I didn't care about understanding. I cared that Andy believed in me, that I could glance over at his head bent over his laptop and have a secret smile just because we were in the same room.

After the hundredth time that he'd outlined all the possible consequences of what we were doing, I'd lost my temper. 'Are you looking for the easy get-out, a way to let me down gently? Because I'm not sitting here waiting to be rescued. I've been surviving quite well on my own for years, so if this is all too much for you, just say the word and we'll go back to clinking glasses at Christmas and forget that we've seen each other naked.'

For the first time ever, though, I'd known that I was all in. If we split up now, I would be broken-hearted. Not broken-hearted in the way I'd imagined myself to be before when I'd spend a few weeks sending drunken texts and waxing lyrical about how we should try again. Coupled with hanging around pubs the object of my affection frequented before getting a grip and reminding myself that Scarlett Dalton wasn't put on this earth to beg anyone to go out with her. But Andy, Andy was different. I hadn't bothered to cultivate an edge of insouciance so I could tell myself afterwards that I didn't care anyway. Much, much too late. I wanted this to work more than anything I'd ever wanted.

Eventually, once I'd stopped shouting, I'd articulated those thoughts out loud.

His eyes had crinkled at the corners as a huge grin spread across his face. 'I do too, Scarlett. I do too. But it doesn't stop me worrying about the fallout. We are going to have to exist in a world beyond this,' he'd said, gesturing to us sitting naked in bed. 'There's so much at stake. I don't know how Abigail will react.'

I had put my head on his chest. 'She's very generous-spirited and, also, she's settled in her own life, so with any luck, she'll come round to it in time. As you say, if you wait to have all the answers before getting started, you'd never do anything.'

Andy had sighed and I had felt young and childish. How could I possibly understand his fear of falling out with Abigail? Parents were supposed to act well, protect their children and forgive them when necessary, not the other way round.

And now, here we were, revisiting those same questions again. The ones that had such simple answers in my imagination when no one knew about us. But the here and now had slammed its way into the party and it was cards-on-the-reality-table time.

He took my hand, caressing my skin with a gentleness that somehow made me want to cry. 'If this is just a bit of fun for you and you think in six months' time, you'll be sick of my snoring and everything else that comes as part of my old man package – ex-wife, daughter, universal disapproval – then we should call it quits now. We are going to hurt people and their reactions will probably hurt us, there's no getting away from that.'

Again, my immediate response was to double down on fighting for us against all the odds, wanting to hear him say that nothing else mattered as long as we were together. But this wasn't a time to buy into all that Hollywood 'you and me against the world' fairy-tale nonsense, even though those sentiments felt far removed from a cinematic invention now. I played devil's advocate instead. 'But you could easily get fed up with everyone saying, "Oh is this your daughter, the one that got married?" every time we go anywhere. And I'm never going to be a woman with matching handbags and shoes and an Ottolenghi recipe for every occasion.' I left out the 'like Philippa', but I might as well have spray-painted it across the wall of the flat, so pointed was the reference. 'You might get fed up with my repertoire of lentil pie, aubergine casserole – and salmon when it's pay day.'

'I won't,' he said. 'I won't.'

'What's in it for you?' I asked, aware that I was fishing for compliments that I'd use to reassure myself whenever we were apart.

He looked so serious, I wondered if he was trawling every

last brain cell to offer me something, anything, rather than admitting that the question defeated him and he just fancied sleeping with someone twenty-seven years younger.

Eventually, he looked at me, almost shamefaced. 'I'd forgotten to take joy in the small things. You, you appreciate everything, always pointing out the flowers when we're out on our runs and saying, "Wow, look how clever nature is." You spent several minutes marvelling at that purple snake's head fritillary. You were glowing that day when you were looking at the young beech trees against the blue sky, fascinated by the vibrant green. You talk to anyone, and have this way of getting them to trust you with their life stories. I don't feel that you're waiting for the next big thing, that you need a new car or a new coat or a fancy restaurant to be happy. When I'm not with you, I have this idea of you in my head...'

I sent up a wish to the universe that it wouldn't be some horribly unflattering image at odds with how I'd like him to be thinking about me. Me in my winter dog-walking gear, bundled up like a set of Russian Matryoshka dolls; me with a face full of spots just before my period; me in just about any picture when I invariably failed to be photogenic. Mum generously said I had an expressive face, but there was no denying that most photos of me had something of the Scooby-Doo fleeing a flock of ghosts about them.

Andy cupped my chin in his hand. 'When I think about you, which is embarrassingly often, I have this picture in my mind's eye of you spinning around in the middle of a spring meadow, your arms flung out, rejoicing in a sunny morning. You don't need a lot to be joyful and I find that so so refreshing.'

My default setting was to make a joke, to say, 'You're just thrilled I'm a cheap date.' With difficulty, I accepted the compliment because he'd turned everything that everyone else thought was weird about me into a quality. What other people took for slovenliness – my lack of interest in clothes, or at least a preference for the student fare of flares, dungarees and Doc Martens – he found appealing. It would be interesting to see if he could embrace my propensity for wild camping and staying in hostels. Might have to consider some compromise there. Even I had been scarred by my experience of being on a bottom bunk in a New Zealand hostel while a couple had sex on the top.

He ploughed on. 'After so many years of planning, of making provisions for the future, which is now not even the future I thought I'd have, I'm totally bewitched by your ability to live in the moment. You don't weigh yourself down with what ifs and the desire to control everything.'

Now I really did think he was getting carried away. 'That's easy for me though because I only have to look after myself. It's a whole different ball game if other people depend on you. If I lose my job, get evicted, run out of money, I can go back to my parents, precisely because they have made provisions. Whereas you *are* the parent.'

He shrugged in agreement. 'I suppose so. But I can't help feeling that the more you have, the more you become trapped in a mentality that you should have the latest phone, a better car, a new watch. With that comes the need for more insurance, more stuff to worry about damaging or losing, just more flaming admin. Whereas you seem to breeze through satisfied with your lot, with a lightness of spirit that quite frankly I envy.'

I believed him. Or at least I really wanted to, more than I'd ever wanted to trust anyone about anything. I felt simultaneously immature – like a child desperate to believe in Father Christmas – and adult, as though I'd finally clocked what a good relationship might look like.

And for the next few weeks, knowing that our heady idyll was existing on borrowed time, our relationship fast-forwarded into something much more serious. While we waited to see whether the news would break, we delighted in discovering each other's strengths in the hope that we'd be solid enough to withstand what was heading our way.

There were so many things I loved about Andy. How he could explain complicated world events in a way that finally made sense to me. His knowledge of hidden corners of London that I would never have discovered, leafy tucked-away squares, pastel-coloured mews, historical alleyways. And – surprising to me as a millennial, who'd previously considered herself above such fripperies – his lovely manners. I hesitated to admit that his solicitude around making sure I had the right drink, food, temperature translated into me feeling cared for. Prioritised rather than demeaned as though I was too feeble to speak up for myself.

He, in turn, seemed enchanted by the way I could be ready to go out in ten minutes, was up for everything he suggested – Highgate Cemetery tour? Searching for the seven noses in Soho? Looking for antlers in Richmond Park? – and saw the funny side if our days didn't turn out as planned.

Slowly, we shifted even further from the constant 'Should we be doing this?' to an understanding that we *were* doing this. That it was no longer a risky indulgence but a necessity and we would have to buckle up.

Which felt easy and right and logical when we were in that cocoon of stealing kisses in the pergola on Hampstead Hill and feeling affronted that we had to separate to go to work. Unfortunately, much more difficult when I was having stilted and defensive exchanges with my mother, my heart alternating between steely and vulnerable every time a message from her popped up. Dad wasn't even trying to contact me.

I tried not to show Andy that their attitudes upset me. He saw right through my façade of indifference, pulling me close and stroking my hair. 'Scarlett, it's not too late to call a halt to this. I'm pretty sure your mum and dad would keep this to themselves if we finish it now. They'll probably never speak to me again, but they will forgive you.'

I shrugged him off. 'Why do I need forgiving? I didn't split you and Philippa up. I haven't done anything wrong, and neither have you. I've had a consenting relationship with a man I love.'

I gasped as the truth that I'd been holding back shot out into the room like a cannonball.

'That's a big word,' he said.

Something in my chest shrank with trepidation, as though Andy was going to rip a cloth off a masterpiece and expose an empty frame.

Instead, he lifted my chin up. 'Look at you, all ferocious and fearless. I wish I'd been a bit more "to hell with the consequences" at your age. My life would have been very different.' He paused, speaking quietly but clearly, his eyes sweeping over my face with all the intent of someone who is preparing for battle. 'Impossible for my heart not to love you, whatever my head says.'

8

JACKIE

Present-day me laughed at the naivety of past me. Throughout Scarlett's childhood, I'd clung onto the idea that by the time she was eighteen, Ian and I would be stretched out in hammocks strung between palm trees, marvelling at how free we were from worry now that Scarlett was an adult.

Instead, I spent the night of my birthday sleeping fretfully, with myriad disastrous scenarios running around my brain. I rang her the next morning. She didn't pick up. A moment later, she texted *I'm sorry for ruining your birthday x*

After much typing and deleting, I wrote: *I don't care about my birthday. I just want you to be happy and this was a shock x.* Then I waited and waited for a reply that didn't come.

How I wished that the only way to discuss something was to pick up the phone, rather than hide behind texts, emails or even deflect from a proper conversation with memes featuring dancing dogs. In the days that followed, I was desperate to call her, but I had a flashback to when she'd have tantrums when she was younger and I'd send her to her bedroom to calm down. I'd go up five minutes later and she'd turn the tables on me, refusing to come out. She'd keep it up all day until we'd end up begging her to join us for dinner. In the interests of keeping communication channels open, I knew not to back Scarlett into a corner.

I had no choice but to acquiesce to her preferred manner of talking to me without actually speaking to me. My natural bent was to see a problem and fixate on it with relentless intensity until I nuked it into submission. Unfortunately, if I applied that to Scarlett, she would add strobe lights, sequins and church bells to the crisis just to prove her point.

So in a test of how grown up I was, I put all the 'for goodness' sake, you idiot' to one side. I reminded myself that just because she was too proud to listen to what I might have to say, it didn't mean she wasn't feeling overwhelmed by the potential repercussions. In my twenties, I'd made a terrible mistake and I'd still had people on my side. I knew how hard it was to see what the options were. With Scarlett, though, it was impossible to force the issue. I had to let her come to me.

Two weeks after my birthday, she finally got in touch: *I am happy, Mum. Really, really happy. I know you think I don't know what I'm doing, but I have never been more definite about anything. It's not ideal and I'm sorry we've put you in a difficult position. Please don't say anything to Philippa yet x*

When that message popped up, I took myself off for a walk in the woods, desperate for some fresh air to clear my head. I stomped along for miles, swearing to myself, failing to imagine a family Sunday lunch with Andrew as Scarlett's partner. Waves of pure adrenaline flipped my stomach as I thought how Philippa finding out was becoming a certainty. I'd be right at the epicentre of her hurt and horror.

Alongside my fear, a side order of anger flamed towards Andrew for crossing that unmarked but self-evident boundary. And, behind that, a desire, fierce and strong, to shelter Scarlett from Philippa's wrath, as well as the heartbreak when Andrew realised that a thirty-year-old was far too immature for a man of fifty-seven.

I distilled that down into three short sentences that got nowhere near encompassing my thoughts. *I'm not the one she should hear it from. Let's talk soon. Love you x*

Scarlett came back quick as a flash: *Promise me. Please.*

I attempted to convince myself that as Philippa had wanted the split, she might even be glad she no longer had to feel guilty, once she'd recovered from the shock. A couple of stiles, a cow field and a hill later, I had to disabuse myself of that notion. It was far more likely that Philippa would go bat-shit crazy.

Me: *I will really really do my best, but I can't give you a hundred per cent guarantee. If she asks me right out, I will have to be honest. I simply cannot bareface lie.*

Then I spent the rest of the walk watching the dots of Scarlett typing and waiting to see if her response would be mature or a teenage tantrum. In the end, I was none the wiser. Whatever she'd written, she'd deleted and that was the last time I had any communication from her, despite sending her a photo of a cake I'd made as a non-threatening attempt to touch base.

Time and time again, I made an attempt to discuss the best way forward with Ian. We flirted with the idea of insisting Scarlett and Andrew came clean with Philippa. 'In the end, though, it's not really our business. I suppose it's up to them how they manage that particular dynamic,' Ian said, doubt threading through his voice.

I put myself in Philippa's position, imagining Abigail and Ian getting together. Or I tried to. I just couldn't. 'I'd hate to be the last to find out though,' I said.

'For God's sake, Scarlett has no idea how to navigate a relationship with someone our age. She's only just stopped thinking that Custard Creams are a proper breakfast. Once, you know, the novelty has worn off...' He winced as his dad brain was obviously veering into territory that he wasn't keen to acknowledge.

'Let's just cross our fingers they split up very soon and we never need to think about it again.'

'But the first question Philippa is going to ask me when she finds out is "Did you know?"' The mere thought made my stomach twist.

'If we're lying for Andrew and Scarlett, perhaps they'd be so kind as to return the favour and say no one else knew so that we don't end up the bad guys?' Ian picked up his newspaper and started to walk out of the kitchen. Everything about the set of his shoulders signalled that his fury at the situation meant anything I suggested was going to be met with rage, rather than careful consideration.

'That's just more lies on top of lies, though.' I wished I wasn't quite so tempted to put a big tick beside that option.

'What do you want me to say?' he snapped. He gave the impression there was plenty he'd like to say but had decided not to in case it turned into a mudslide that engulfed a whole land-scape of familial resentments, not just the current drama. 'Let her get on with it' was his parting shot, which sounded like he was annoyed with me for not foreseeing this in my parental crystal ball and nipping it in the bud before we got to this stage.

Despite knowing he was blowing off steam from a place of hurt and worry, I still wanted to stand behind him flicking the Vs and launching into a historical excavation of his crappy fatherhood moments. With an additional rant about how he managed to convince himself that all the glowing moments of parenting fell under his stellar influence but the shitty ones were attributable to me.

Even without Ian's comments, my head churned with ques-tions that I would never be able to answer, not yet, anyway. Could this last? Could we ever move our brains from Andrew friend to Andy son-in-law? I didn't even want to consider that. If they did stay together, would that mean Scarlett would never have children? How would Abigail ever come to terms with her best friend taking up with her father? Was Philippa going to blame me? Hate me? And then, with a shock that it had taken so long to think of this, would my best friend tell everyone my secrets, to get her own back? I dismissed that thought as soon as it came. None of this was my fault. I hadn't done anything wrong except take a gamble that this – I didn't even want to give it the title of 'relationship' – stupid infatuation would fizzle out before our friendships and families imploded.

I wanted to protect Philippa. However, now that I'd considered that her 'I will not breathe a word as long as I live' might translate to 'I will not breathe a word as long as you and I remain the best of friends', I wanted to protect myself more. Ian would tell me I was wildly overthinking things, that there was no way that she would do that, not even if she was incandescent, because, ultimately, she was an honourable person. I crossed everything that he was right. And with a sick lurch of fear, I hoped that if she didn't do it for me, she'd do it for him.

And somehow, almost another month had slipped past since we'd had any contact with Scarlett and, with it, a large chunk of my sanity. I missed my daughter. Missed the two-minute chats when she was killing time waiting for a bus or for her employer to come out of a meeting. I longed for one of her slightly hysterical cooking questions: 'Does salmon always smell really strong when it comes out of the freezer?' Those frequent little connections that meant I had a sense of her daily life and my incoming disaster radar could remain on standby. Until now.

Today, on the first Saturday of July, I'd read a piece in the paper about how one in five families was estranged from a family member. Enough was enough. I'd been pussyfooting about for six weeks now. I was going to make Scarlett speak to me – words out loud, discussions with sound attached. I would see if I had any magic ideas that could drum some sense into her and let us all off the hook.

I waited until Ian was outside mowing the lawn then rang

Scarlett's mobile, sad at how hard my heart was hammering at the prospect of speaking to my own daughter.

'Hello, Mum.' Her tone gave me no clue about how this conversation was going to unfold. At least she picked up.

'How are you?'

'Great,' she said.

Tears were building in a knot at the base of my throat. That definitely wouldn't help.

'I'm just checking in to see if you're okay. It's a bit of a funny situation at the moment and I wanted you to know that you can talk to me about anything. I promise I only want the best for you and I'm not judging you. I've made loads of mistakes in my life, love, still am.'

'But you are judging me. You're already assuming this is a mistake.'

This bore no relation to the script I'd prepared in my head. 'Sorry, that came out clumsily. I meant that sometimes you go down alleyways in life, and especially when you feel people disapprove of your choices, it's really easy to get entrenched in a position or be reticent about discussing things.' I'd run this conversation through thousands of times, yet here I was, blundering about as though I'd put a motorcycle helmet on the wrong way round.

'We've decided we can live with other people's disapproval. I know you don't want to hear this, Mum, but I'm in it for the long haul.'

I pushed down the need to rush at her with all the objections, all the obstacles she'd face, how difficult it would be, how he'd be seventy when she was forty-three. How she'd never have children. I blew out my cheeks and tried to get my breathing under control so that I could give the impression of a practical, sensible mother, with whom she could calmly discuss difficult decisions. Rather than who I actually was: a mother who wanted to shout – if only she could force the words out through the hysteria blocking her throat – 'Wake up! You've got the whole of your life ahead of you! Don't tell me that in all of London there isn't a single man you could go out with who is less than twenty-seven years older than you!'

Before I could speak again, she said, 'I need you to support me in this, Mum. Dad will follow your lead.'

I focused on the bit I had a fragment of certainty about. 'Dad knows his own mind, love.' Which had largely resulted in him burying himself in work, and refusing to engage with the debates about catastrophic outcomes that I favoured.

'But he listens to you.'

'We listen to each other. Anyway, the reason I'm ringing is not to debate the rights and wrongs of you and Andrew, but to see how you are.'

Scarlett did a disbelieving snort down the phone. 'To see how I am? Is that code for "if I've come to my senses yet"? We're happy. *We are happy.* That's all there is to it.'

I didn't know whether she was repeating that mantra to convince herself, but if it was true, I was resentful but also envious of her ability to isolate her own needs from the impact on everyone else's.

'That's all I want for you, darling. Really. Anyway, I'd love to see you. Would you like to come for dinner this Friday?'

'Is that a single or double invitation?'

Oh, the absolute irony that I'd been saying to Scarlett for years that she should always feel free to bring any 'friends' to meet us, that everyone was welcome. Except this one man.

Ian would kill me, but I couldn't formulate the words to say, 'Surely you don't expect him to come and sit at our table, drink our wine and for us to fix our faces as though it is perfectly normal that he has swapped my best friend for my daughter?'

'Whatever you think is appropriate, Scarlett. I just want to see you.'

I could almost hear Ian's incredulity as the words burbled

out of my mouth. 'You invited Andrew? That's going to be an interesting chat about how many years he's been lusting after my daughter.'

'I'll talk to Andy and see what he thinks.'

I couldn't keep the need out of my voice. 'But you'll come whatever, won't you?'

Her voice was brittle. 'As long as it doesn't turn into an interrogation or nagging session.'

I tried to make a joke. 'When has that ever happened in your whole life?' I asked, manufacturing a laugh to disguise the sob that was sitting at the bottom of my throat like a cat ready to pounce on a mouse.

There was a tiny note of amusement in her reply. 'I'll let you know about Friday. I've gotta go.'

'Love you,' I said, but I didn't know if I'd been quick enough for her to hear before the phone went dead. I ruminated on how when Scarlett was little, she'd gone through a period of asking how much I loved her in the guise of 'Would you still love me if...?' Her fantasy misdemeanours usually ranged from eating all the biscuits to locking next door's cat in a cupboard for a week and I always answered, 'I'd be very sorry if you acted like that, but there's nothing you can do that will stop me loving you.' That truth still stood. Though in all our imaginary scenarios, I hadn't realised that I might have to choose love for my daughter over love for my best friend. I told myself that Philippa would never push it as far as that, that she would see that I was the unlucky woman trapped in an impossible situation through no fault of my own.

A few days later, I walked up the gravel drive to Philippa's house. We'd always congregated here more because she had so much more space than we did in our home on a modern estate. I loved the large Edwardian rooms with the fireplaces and ornate mantelpieces – Philippa had an eye for interior design and I'd always admired how everywhere was so stylish but still cosy and welcoming. Yet now, I was afraid to ring the doorbell. My stomach was burning with the acid anxiety of disturbed nights and lack of sleep. She'd been bombarding me with WhatsApp messages of *Who knew internet dating would be such a mine-field? Please come for dinner and help me sift through the bald, the bastards and the barking mad!* followed by a row of laughing emojis. Every time I saw her name pop up, I felt a rush of nausea, which, ironically, was reminiscent of the morning sickness I'd had when I was pregnant with Scarlett.

It was the first time ever that I'd wanted to avoid her. This woman who had seen me not just stumble, but plunge catastrophically into an abyss and who had never breathed a word to anyone. If I'd managed to hang onto my own marriage, it was in no small part down to her. I was going to pay her back by lying. Lying by omission, but still looking her in the eye, sharing a bottle of wine and choosing not to tell her something that she deserved to know. That, in fact, in a twist of work diaries and social calendars and life fuckery, my daughter and Philippa's not yet ex-husband were probably coming to dinner the day after tomorrow as a couple.

As she threw open the door, sweeping me into a hug, I had that odd sensation of wanting her wise counsel about my dilemma before remembering that she was the last person I could seek advice from. I'd been in her house hundreds, thousands of times over the years. I'd breezed in, launching straight into any old story – the annoyance of my mother commenting on my weight, me thinking I'd wet the bed when my hot-water bottle had split, my shame at bursting into tears when I had to fire a young lad at work – with no thought for how anything I said would be received. Now, I was finding it difficult to meet her eye in case she immediately homed in on this massive secret sitting at the forefront of my brain. If she challenged me directly about why I was being so weird, I'd probably pull the pin out of the grenade and watch everything I cared about blow up right in front of me. I struggled to remember how to chat freely. All my words felt stilted and manicured as I sifted them through the lens of what I couldn't say.

I chose Abigail's wedding as my opening gambit, which would require lots of listening and not much input from me. Philippa was in her element talking about corsages – 'White, surely? Go with everything. But carnations just seem so old hat...' – before moving on to the merits of tiny jars of Love Heart sweets over sugared almonds – 'I mean at our age we don't want to challenge everyone who's got a mouth crammed full of those old mercury fillings – I guess that's all of us – do we?' I nodded along, my own views on anything designerish easily balanced on a pinhead but grateful to be on terra firma. Then suddenly a shift of the tectonic plates. 'I guess Andrew and I will sit on the top table together. That's not weird, is it? Even if we're not together?'

'Of course it's not. You're still her parents.' I instructed myself to make the comment I would have made before. 'And you're technically still married.'

Philippa's face relaxed. 'I know. I'm just overthinking it. It's a good job the wedding is only a couple of months away and we don't have to navigate the bumpy road of new partners.'

My shoulders shot up around my ears at the panorama I resisted letting my mind examine. If Scarlett and Andrew were still – what? – seeing each other? Dating? – as chief bridesmaid, would Scarlett be sitting next to him at the top table? Or next to Philippa? My knowledge of top table etiquette was underwhelming. If the stakes weren't as high, I might have been tempted to giggle hysterically and intone 'What could possibly go wrong?' on a never-ending loop.

I shifted topic. 'How is the dating scene?'

Philippa drained her wine glass and babbled on about the

men she'd been talking to and how just as she thought she'd found a connection, they ghosted her.

I tried to relax, to make the same jokes I would have done if I wasn't suffocating under the weight of what I knew.

She ladled bean and spinach soup into my bowl. We were united in our love for legumes, despite their flatulent effect on our ageing digestive systems. 'Upside of living on my own, no husband to complain!' she said.

'So have you arranged any dates?' I asked, clinging to the notion that the universe might dovetail into a happy-ever-after for Philippa, with a by-product of making her less livid about Andrew and Scarlett.

She ran her fingers through her hair and sighed. 'I'm only telling you, but don't breathe a word. I'm not sure how Andrew would react if he knew I was sticking a toe in the actual meeting-up-and-dating waters, rather than quietly seeing what's out there online. I do worry about him sitting in that little flat on his own. I mean, I'm still here, with you fifteen minutes away and all my familiar stuff. He's living like we did when we first met. I don't suppose he's eating properly either. He never did learn how to cook much beyond pasta. I know he's responsible for his own happiness and I try not to feel guilty, but I can't help it.'

I was conscious of clenching my jaw in order to keep my face neutral. I interrupted her. 'We'll deal with Andrew later,' I said, hoping that we would never have to return to that subject. 'So. Back to your dates. Sounds like something interesting is happening?'

She bit her lip in a coy way that was at odds with her usual cynicism. 'I've been out for dinner with a guy a few times.'

'Oh my God. Is he nice?' I forgot for a moment about the big unspoken thing hanging between us and reverted to type. 'You should have phoned me, at least let me know you were going. What if he'd turned out to have cable ties in the boot of his car and held you in a cave never to be seen again?'

She did her 'stop catastrophising' look. 'I was going to text you before I went the first time, but I was a bit wobbly and I thought you might talk me out of it, so I just decided to take the plunge without discussing it with anyone.'

I felt a stab of hurt that she felt I might spoil things for her. A first glimpse of how our lives might diverge now she had no constraints on when and where she went. I would still have to negotiate my freedom. Not that Ian minded what I did – or, truth be told, even listened much to what I was up to – but I did have to consider him some of the time.

I shrugged my shoulders. 'Why would I talk you out of it? You're not going back to Andrew...' I couldn't even say his name without my voice going tight.

'No. No, I'm not.' She frowned as though she was still having to process that concept.

I hurried on. 'Go on then, who was he?' I asked, catapulting myself to familiar territory as I slipped into my role of digging dirt and detail.

'He's called Noah.'

'I read in the paper that's now one of the most popular boys' names in the UK, so I'm assuming he's either a toyboy or as old as the Ark?'

Philippa laughed. 'Neither. He's fifty. That's not so bad, is it? Seven years difference.'

'Where's he from?'

'Tooting.'

'Does he look like Wolfie out of *Citizen Smith*?' I said, grabbing onto what passed for our normal banter like a lifebelt. Philippa had a handbag and pair of shoes for every possible colour combination, so I was already conjuring up an Andrew lookalike – corporate, groomed and tidy.

'He doesn't wear a beret,' she said, then pulled a face. 'He's got long, curly hair, quite boho really.'

'Wow. That's a change.'

She threw her hands out. 'If I'd wanted what I'd got, I'd still be living with Andrew.'

A note of defensiveness had crept in, so I hurried to backpedal, allowing myself the relief that she was still in the mode of wanting someone different. 'No doubt about it. God knows what I'd choose now if I wasn't with Ian.' I allowed myself to consider the possibility, but my brain didn't offer up any ideas of what an alternative husband might look like. 'What does he do?'

'I'm not exactly sure. I was terrified of looking like some spoilt housewife who'd lived in a gilded cage, so I didn't dare ask too many questions and expose my total ignorance of how these things work – but he manages a community gardening project. And he's also an artist.'

My lips twitched. In ordinary times, I'd make a joke about Philippa's penchant for rose petals on the pillows in top-end hotels rather than impecunious creatives. I needed her to be all in for this man, so instead, I said, 'What sort of art?'

She flapped her hand. 'He showed me a few photos of his paintings. It's mainly portraits and a few dogs.'

'Is he good?' I asked, praying that he wasn't the cliché of a penniless artist scratching around in a garret and might be a contender for Philippa's heart. If she fell in love, she might be generous about who Andrew had chosen.

'He is. He's had some exhibitions in local galleries and some of his paintings were in an art festival in the south London libraries. I'm not thinking that he's going to be the next Banksy and make millions, but he sells a few.'

'So do you like him?' I tried not to sound too eager for a positive response.

'It's so odd being out with a man who isn't my husband, but yes, I think so.'

'Were you nervous?'

'I was a bit teenagerish on the first date. I think I tried on about every piece of clothing I own, but he was really easy to be with, so once I got to the pub I didn't feel that self-conscious, except in a trying to be witty and entertaining and not a total loser dullard sort of way.'

I raised my glass to her. 'To my lovely friend who could never be a loser dullard.'

She rolled her eyes. 'Anyway, enough of him, what's going on with you?'

My heightened super-sensitive radar took a beat to fret about whether her 'What's going on with you?' instead of 'How are you?' had some hidden meaning, but Philippa seemed relaxed as she got up to open a second bottle of wine. I steered everything towards my work woes. 'It's a bit late in the day to ask myself if I'm in the right job, but HR is so stressful now. I spend half my life trying to stay on top of the legislation and protocols rather than doing the bits I enjoy, like supporting employees back to work. Though I get far more anxious about how our decisions impact on people now. I used to be far more clinical in my approach...'

I gabbled on for a bit, discussing how I felt sorry for the young people working from home. 'I mean, never mind missing out on knowledge and guidance that they'd absorb by osmosis just by being in the office, what about all those little flirtations passing them by? Back in the day, a visit from the guy who used to fix our Amstrads could make my week. I don't know how they go about meeting anyone these days.'

'Welcome to my world,' Philippa said. 'Winking, liking and swiping.' She took another gulp of wine. 'I do sometimes wonder if I've made a mistake. I know Andrew had his faults – as do I – but, essentially, he's a decent man. I just couldn't be what he wanted. I don't want to go sleeping in yurts in the desert or trekking up Machu Picchu. I don't need big adventures. I like being at home fiddling about with my bits of sewing and experimenting with my breadmaking.'

I didn't offer the opinion that Noah sounded far more likely to want to go backpacking than Andrew.

She grimaced, then sighed. 'But I also hadn't anticipated how much I'd miss the little things. You know, someone waiting up for me when I've been out for the evening. That shout up the stairs to see if I want a cup of tea. Stupid stuff, like picking up some bananas when he fills up with petrol. Nothing I can't do myself, but, I don't know, those thoughtful gestures that knit together to provide a safe platform in the world.' She took a long slug of wine. 'If I'm totally honest, I'm a bit lonely and I know this guy isn't right for me. He's interesting and fun and sexy, but I'm not going to join in all the things he's interested in: roaring about on the back of his motorbike, or climbing Snowdonia or even helping him plant carrots on the allotments.'

'Why not? You might discover you love it.' And it would be excellent timing if Noah swept Philippa off her feet right now.

'If I was going to become adventurous, I'd still be with Andrew.' She paused. 'I have done the right thing, haven't I?'

I reached for my good friend hat rather than my defensive mother shield. 'Only you can be the judge of that. You seemed quite clear about why you didn't want to be in the marriage any more: that you were existing rather than thriving and that you didn't feel you and Andrew had the same view of retirement. I thought you were brave to act on that. Plenty of people wouldn't.'

I hoped these were the words I would have said in normal circumstances, even if Scarlett and her 'We love each other' weren't dancing around my brain.

Philippa started to cry. 'I just don't know what I want. When I was with Noah, it was all such an effort: worrying about what I looked like, if I was funny enough, whether I was too square for him.'

'But isn't that just part of the process when you're getting to know someone else? Of course it's bound to feel different from someone who's seen you changing into your pyjamas at seven o'clock on a Sunday night.'

Philippa did a sob-laugh. 'How would I know? I haven't dated anyone new for twenty-nine years!'

By the time I'd phoned Ian to pick me up, Philippa had rambled on about all the things she still loved about Andrew, how it was his fifty-eighth birthday soon – 'Would it be weird to send him a birthday present?' – and how much she wanted to discuss every detail of Abigail's wedding with him. 'Even though he wouldn't be interested, he'd listen because he loves her... and no one else will ever love our daughter in the uncomplicated way we do,' which brought on a fresh wave of tears. As I pulled on my jacket, she said, 'I meant to ask, have you heard anything from Andrew lately? Do you know if he's missing me?'

Panic surged through me. If I admitted he might be coming for dinner in a couple of days, I'd crumble if she asked a single question, singing like a canary with everything I knew – and didn't want to know.

And there it came, out of my cowardly mouth, the first direct lie. 'No, not that recently. I haven't spoken to him for a while. I think he's exchanged a few texts with Ian. He's doing all right as far as I can tell.'

Then I fled, to the sanctuary of my husband, my head thumping with the strain of striving to be the friend I was before the big unspeakable turned me into a liar.

9

JACKIE

The next morning I kept picking up my phone to tell Philippa the truth. One, because she deserved to know. Two, because I was sitting in the narrow window between fat lie and fessing up, counting down to the second when I could no longer get away with, 'Apologies. I'd had too much to drink and panicked. I'm sorry I wasn't honest with you straight away – I didn't know how to say it in that moment – but this is actually what's happening.' When forgiveness might still be possible.

I told myself that I could wait until I'd seen Scarlett and Andrew the following evening. Until I got a clearer picture of what was happening, whether this was just a nauseating and hideously misguided crisis of judgement from Andrew on the back of Philippa's decision. I guess if he was feeling rejected, there was something appealing about having a younger woman with less experience of the world look up to him. In the end, same old, age-old story. But even if his ultimate fantasy was finding a woman nearly half his age, there were many pools he could have fished in that didn't involve my family.

Less surprising was that Scarlett had pushed the boundaries in this way – impulsive undertakings of hare-brained acts had always exercised an intoxicating pull for her. Over the years, we'd learned to expect the unexpected. 'Mum, I'm calling from Ko Samui. I know it was a bit spur of the moment, but the weather was getting me down.' 'I handed in my notice yesterday. My boss was being an idiot. No, she probably won't give me a reference.' I consoled myself that Scarlett had thrown herself into so many things – veganism, Buddhism, 5:2 fasting, am-dram, hiking – becoming furious if we didn't share her enthusiasm for her new-found fad. Maybe Andrew would last about as long as her commitment to the Rock Choir, which she'd jacked in as soon as someone accused her of being flat.

I prayed that this wouldn't be the one time that Scarlett's grasshoppering about from shiny new thing to shiny new thing settled into something far more solid that meant we'd all have to gird our loins for a deeply uncomfortable ride.

With perfect timing, Scarlett messaged mid-morning to accept my invitation the next evening on behalf of them both. I had prayed she'd come alone so that I'd never have to own up to my husband that I'd invited Andrew as well. I took the coward's way out and left Ian a voice note while he was at work.

I received one straight back. 'No. I'm not having him in our home. Not now, not yet and maybe not ever.' The finality with which he'd said it infuriated me, as though he was the master of the house and owner of the last word.

Ian and I rowed about it as soon as he walked through the door, an argument that carried on in stops and starts for hours. The battlelines we'd drawn were deep and divisive. My stance roughly distilled down to 'no point in telling our daughter that she can always come to us with any issue if what we mean is we'll freeze her out if she does something we don't agree with'. Ian's position was that Andrew had betrayed us all. That no, Scarlett wasn't blameless either, but he wasn't going to sit around pouring out his best Pinot Noir while trying to blank out the idea that Andrew was screwing his daughter. We went to bed in a fug of hostility, without agreeing on how to handle dinner the next evening.

As I sat at the breakfast table on Friday morning, my eyes scratchy from tears and lack of sleep, I said, quietly, as calmly as I could, 'I understand why you're so upset. Of course I do. But I'm frightened. Frightened that this whole thing could spiral into so many directions that we can't control. I think we need to stay close to Scarlett so we at least know what's going on, even if we can't influence anything. Please. Trust me on this.'

He ran his hand over his greying stubble, scratching at his chin. 'I can't have them here, Jackie. I just can't. It feels wrong on so many levels. I think we can be forgiven for meeting them on neutral territory in London tonight in an effort to resolve the situation, but if Philippa finds out we've been hosting them without saying a word... that's much dodgier.'

I quickly agreed before he cancelled the whole thing. 'Okay. Let's go up there then. I'll ask Scarlett to suggest somewhere to meet.'

I made up some nonsense about wanting a change of scenery, which she didn't question, even if she didn't believe me. She chose a traditional London pub just round the corner from her flat in Clapham. They were already there when we walked in, sitting next to each other in a booth. I didn't want to see if they were holding hands.

Andrew leapt up to shake Ian's hand and I willed him not to reject the gesture. He put his hand out, stiffly, but he did it. I loved him for not turning up the tension unnecessarily.

I gave Andrew a peck on the cheek and Scarlett a hug. There was something contained and wary about her. I wondered whether we'd ever regain that family ease, talking over each other in my kitchen, teasing and shrieking, launching ourselves into chicken and roast potatoes as though we hadn't been fed in a week. Those insignificant times when Ian and I would ponder about where we fancied going for a weekend and Scarlett would plead poverty and ask if we could get an Airbnb with a pull-out sofa. I had to clear my throat to stop my eyes filling at the simplicity of those interactions. Ian would bicker with Scarlett about how 'at your grand old age, you shouldn't be coat-tailing on your parents' holidays' and she'd fight back with how expensive rent was because of the greedy Boomers hogging the real estate. But underneath all of our exchanges, there was a deep and affectionate undercurrent, the sense that we were all on the same side if push came to shove.

Ian went to get drinks while I plastered on my sunny-side-up face as though we were just gathering here for a swift pint before we all headed off to the theatre, Philippa's absence down to a bout of flu.

'So...' I said, before finding that I didn't know how to finish the sentence, because anything I wanted to say sounded judgemental and nosey.

Andrew, because he was a lovely man, said, 'Thank you for coming tonight. It means a lot.'

Scarlett flicked her eyes towards Ian. 'Is Dad all right?'

'He's struggling with it.' And then because it felt unfair to put the onus of being difficult about this shitty development onto him, I said, 'I guess we all will, to some degree.'

Scarlett's face clouded with defiance. Andrew caught my eye apologetically.

'Have either of you seen Abigail?' I asked.

Andrew's face relaxed at the prospect of a concrete question with a concrete answer. 'Yeah, I've had dinner with her a few times, to talk about the wedding and what she wants me to do, and what she wants Philippa to do.'

I sneaked a glance at Scarlett, whose jaw set at the mention of Philippa's name.

'She's so excited and happy. Guy's a good man. It's nice to see.' He paused. 'Thank you for not saying anything yet. I promise as soon as the wedding's over, I will speak to both of them.'

Ian arrived with my wine and his pint. He'd obviously caught the tail end of the conversation. 'For what it's worth, I think they'll feel more cheated that you let them go ahead with the wedding without telling them. When they look back at the photos, that's what they'll see: two of the people closest to them putting on a charade while betraying them in the most spectacular manner.'

'Dad!' Scarlett said.

Andrew put his hand on her arm. 'Let Ian, er, your dad, have his say.'

My stomach was doing that dropping and clenching thing when confrontation is inevitable and it can only be bloody. I turned my body fully towards Ian, in a gesture that I remembered as the 'Look at me, look at me!' instruction when Scarlett was tiny and teetering on the verge of a tantrum. 'Ian, Ian...' My voice was gathering urgency.

He took a long swig of his beer. 'Sorry, but it's true. They can't avoid feeling deceived. No one wants to listen to me, but if this' – he flapped his palm towards Scarlett and Andrew – 'if this is going to continue, then everyone should be making decisions with all the facts at their disposal.'

'I'm her chief bridesmaid, Dad! We're going for the alterations fitting next Saturday, then for afternoon tea afterwards. I've organised it all. What am I supposed to say? "I've got a little something to tell you over the cucumber sandwiches, nothing to worry about, but I'm going out with your dad."'

Ian shook his head. 'But surely neither of you thought there wouldn't be a whole ton of collateral damage?'

Andrew sighed. 'I am torn about this. I really am.' He looked at me beseechingly.

I had to force myself to remember that this wasn't our usual type of exchange, where Andrew and I would sit on a sofa and he'd ask my opinion about how to deal with a difficult member of his team at work, or how best to help his mother, who was losing her memory.

He looked stressed to the hilt, but the thought of Philippa's hurt made me harden my heart. 'Torn about what?' I asked. 'This?' I said, flicking a forefinger at the two of them. 'Or being honest about it and facing the consequences?'

It was then I saw it. A blaze of emotion between Scarlett and Andrew, a complicity that you couldn't manufacture, which reaffirmed that they were in this together, two misunderstood lovers against a harsh and judgemental world.

Andrew leaned forward with more poise and fewer nerves. 'This was not what we wanted. I know – of course I know – how it looks. Scarlett and I were just running together, it was something to do when I first moved here. There are lots of evenings to fill when you're on your own all of a sudden. Abigail was also keen for Scarlett to invite me, she was worried about me being lonely. She knew Philippa would have you both to rely on. But...' He puffed out his lips, a tiny twitch of a smile catching the corner of his mouth as though what he felt for Scarlett was bigger than any common sense or real-world considerations.

I couldn't watch. I couldn't bear to see this youthful display of infatuation.

'Mum, Dad,' Scarlett said. 'What we're trying to say is we didn't plan this, we're well aware of the complications...' She broke off, turning towards Andrew and her whole face softening. 'I'll speak for myself here. I feel like I have found the right person for me. It's not what I expected or what I would have actively gone looking for. But' – she raised her eyes and bit her lip to stop herself crying – 'I want to be with Andy and I am going to do everything I can to make that work, so you can either support us, or not. But I'm not going to change my mind.'

He took her hand. 'I'm not either.'

Ian stared at me, his face a mixture of stunned and horrified. I jumped in before he could speak, and before my own tears overwhelmed me. 'So, if that is the case, why are you waiting to tell Abigail and Philippa? If you're truly certain that this is the real deal?' I couldn't help putting a slight comedy emphasis on the last two words. 'Don't they have a right to know? They might accept it,' I said, hearing the 'but that's very unlikely' tone.

Scarlett flared up. 'Philippa ended it with Andy. So, in my view, she doesn't get to say who he dates next. She wanted out and now she's out. Abigail's marrying Guy. So why should they dictate how we run our relationship? Who we fall in love with? What about our privacy? Our right to choose when we tell people our business? We're not hurting anyone. We haven't split any other marriages up.'

Scarlett's naivety made me want to shake her. Ian was blowing his cheeks in and out as though he was warming up his lungs for a bumper pack of party balloons. I was marginally more relieved than frustrated by his silence. I was having enough trouble managing my own reactions, but at least I had a bit of warning about what might blunder out of my mouth.

I was half-expecting Andrew to attempt to reassure us that he wasn't trifling with Scarlett with a definitive declaration of love. That could have gone two ways: comforting, but equally gag-inducing. Thankfully, Andrew simply turned to Scarlett and said, 'Your mum is rather caught in the middle here. It's not a straightforward situation.'

Scarlett's face clouded and I waited for her to flare back with a cutting comment, but she nodded. Distractedly, I wondered if this wise father-figure dynamic was what had caused this fatal attraction, a grounding influence in the whirl of chaos that surrounded her.

I was stuck between a rock and a hard place. Part of me hoped that Andrew would soon tire of Scarlett eating peanut butter out of a jar and calling it 'dinner' or ironing her clothes on newspaper on the kitchen table. Yet I persisted with a deep-seated maternal aversion to anything that exposed my daughter to heartache. Before I could think of a suitable response, Andrew said, 'Abigail has been dreaming about this wedding for years. Probably since about two weeks after she met Guy. I'm not fooling myself that this' – he gestured vaguely around the table – 'is going to be easy for her to come to terms with. I know you have torn loyalties and I'm asking a lot of you, but please just let her have the wedding day. Please.'

I sat in front of this man, my only true male friend, and noted the tension in his face, the dark shadows under his eyes. Did he know what I'd done? It was just before he came on the scene. Would Philippa have told him? I'd asked her outright once. Her answer: 'It's no one else's business. No one is ever going to hear it from me.' I wondered if that commitment to protecting me had waned over the years, the truth slipping out after too much wine. Or in a moment of hot philosophical debate as the defining proof that these things did happen and much closer to home than Andrew might have imagined. Was there a slight edge of menace in Andrew's tone? That we both had secrets that it would be 'unfortunate' to reveal?

I breathed out. 'I'll give it some thought,' I said, glancing at Ian for approval, who had the same panicky look as he did when our elderly neighbour sometimes mistook him for her dead husband.

Andrew's shoulders relaxed. 'Thank you, I appreciate that.' Then, like an actor signalling the interval as respite in a particu-larly disturbing play, he suddenly mentioned that he'd seen one of Ian's old colleagues. 'Roger asked after you. Told me he wasn't sure how you'd lost touch after he left the hotel business to work in that gym chain.'

And, briefly, the evening slid into something wonderfully non-descript, with Ian and Andrew plodding about on familiar friend territory, rather than this alien landscape none of us knew how to navigate.

I turned to Scarlett. 'How's work going?' I asked in a bid for a similarly neutral subject, a pretence that this uncomfortable evening could also have some normal aspects to it. A prelude to us being able to meet up as a foursome, my daughter with her unconventional but entirely welcome boyfriend, with ordinary conversations that weren't loaded with baggage.

Except what Scarlett did – dog walking, shifts in a café and some language exchange with Portuguese students – easily tipped into the contentious. Much to Ian's fury, she refused to consider a corporate job that would provide stability and a deposit for a house. Any time she seemed to be gathering some savings and Ian and I started considering whether we should cash in a bit of pension to help her onto the housing ladder, she'd ring up with news that she'd booked a flight to Cambodia and was disappearing for six weeks. 'I just can't do another whole winter here,' which would leave Ian ranting about how he was nearly twice her age and managed to get up at 6.00 a.m., de-ice his car every morning and still make it onto the quarter to seven train to London for work. Where, as he loved to point out, he trod the increasingly difficult tightrope of searching for inventive ways of saving money in the hotel business while not screwing the suppliers so far into the ground that they walked away.

When Ian became really critical, I defended her. 'But at least when she does settle down – if she settles down – she'll really have lived life. She won't feel so hemmed in when she does finally have to face up to responsibility.'

It was a credit to my generous-hearted husband that he let those statements glide into the conversation without comment. He restricted himself to shaking his head with an exasperation I couldn't fully share, torn as I was between admiration for her bravery and spontaneity, while simultaneously worrying about her lack of direction.

I'd long stopped trotting out my line of 'It takes some people much longer to find the right path in life'. Scarlett genuinely didn't seem to care that, despite being thirty, she still had a labelled shelf in the fridge, allocated space in the cupboard and had yet to own a decent frying pan. Whenever Ian moaned about her 'still living like a bloody student', I countered with the only partly true 'As long as she's happy', which now had come home to roost in a resounding manner.

Scarlett ignored my question about work, recognising it for what it was. Everything about Scarlett's demeanour distilled into a 'bring it on' jut of the jaw. She took the opportunity to say in an undertone: 'I don't expect you to understand, Mum. But I'm doing this.'

And all I could think was how I couldn't lose my daughter. Not now. Not after everything I'd done. Whatever it took, I had to make this work.

10

Some days the anger – or was it shame? – within me made me feel as though a wild animal was kicking and heaving under my skin, a furious squirrel trapped in a sack. I punched pillows, I ripped sheets from beds, I beat rugs and scrubbed basins and baths until the muscles in my arms ached and my hair stuck to my forehead. But nothing helped on those days. Not trying to still my mind by walking to the beach and watching the relentless ebb and flow of the waves, attempting to embrace my insignificance in the face of the universe. Not sweating up the steps and sitting in the cool quiet of the church, pleading for forgiveness from a God I had yet to be convinced existed. Not taking refuge in sleep, waking and momentarily forgetting before plunging into a despair deeper than before. Not writing letters I never sent, nor rehearsing conversations I would never have, nor daydreaming about fixing what I had broken. The only way to survive was by accepting that everything that came before was so far in the past that I should just bury it all, even if it meant lying to myself and everyone else about who I was.

11

JACKIE

For the next month or so, Ian and I existed on two planes. One where we would be so exhausted, so bored of discussing the whole thorny issue, that we would shelve the problem of the rights and wrongs, our part in being complicit, in favour of sitting in front of mindless television. And another, much edgier one that consisted of variations on a circular argument. The fundamental baddie was always Andrew, but, depending on Ian's mood, could extend to Scarlett and sweep me into the bin with her. Sometimes we would go to bed so furious with each other that I doubted that I'd ever felt about Ian the way Scarlett said she felt about Andrew.

Philippa rang me the weekend before the final wedding dress and bridesmaid fitting, in mid-August. 'Will you come for moral support? I mean, I love twenty-five discussions about the best possible way to attach a veil without messing up the hairdo and whether the sleeves are a bit too puffy as much as the next woman, but we've already had tears because they've printed the place names on cream rather than white...'

I hesitated, fishing around for the unmissable engagement

that would prevent me sitting in a shop with everyone I loved, who shortly might hate each other.

'There's champagne in it for you... we could go out with the girls afterwards for a posh lunch somewhere...'

My brain froze and I found myself saying, 'I can come to the fitting, but Ian wanted to go shopping for a new bed in the afternoon, so I probably won't be able to do lunch...'

'Stop reminding me that you've got a man in your bed and I haven't,' Philippa said, her voice teasing.

'What happened to your gardener bloke? I thought that was all-guns-blazing down among the courgettes and cucumbers?'

She went quiet for a moment. 'My heart wasn't in it. There were so many little things that annoyed me. On paper he was ideal because we shared an interest in gardening, but I hadn't bargained on fantasising about killing him when he was eating his kefir. I swear he thought twirling his tongue around the spoon was some sort of turn-on, but honestly, he reminded me of the giraffe licking her new-born calf that I saw on safari with Andrew. And don't get me started on bathroom habits – I'll spare you the details – and, I can't explain it, a lack of basic chivalry.'

'Didn't have you down as a woman who needed a man to throw his cloak over a puddle for her,' I said, although I did think she could be a bit of a princess at times. I willed myself to be pleased that Philippa knew her own mind and wasn't compromising to avoid being by herself.

'I'm not like that, you know I'm not, but, honestly, that whole "I've got an early start, so do you mind getting a cab home?" Or falling on the side dishes when we go out for dinner like he's been existing on bread and water and leaving me five grains of rice and half a carrot. And a hundred other silly things that once I'd noticed them really began to grate on me.'

I laughed, just for a moment in the conversation rather than filtering my way through it. 'But wasn't that what you said about

Andrew? That you'd reached the tipping point of a hundred and one irritations?'

'God, I'm beginning to rethink that. I suppose Andrew and I had the advantage of growing up together more or less – it's a bit different when you meet a proper adult bloke that hasn't had decades of my wifely training.'

I had a flashback to Andrew helping me on with my jacket when we'd said goodbye at the pub. The moments over the years when he'd leapt up to go to the bar when he'd noticed my glass was empty. Or when he'd rushed to drape towels around us after Philippa and I had dared each other to take a dip in the freezing sea.

'Andrew does have lovely manners, so you might struggle to find someone to compete on that score. But your problems were more fundamental than that as I recall? Basically, you wanted totally different things from life going forwards? I mean, I don't think you decided to split up because you couldn't stand how he ate his Rice Krispies.'

Philippa sighed. 'I wish I did know what I want. Sometimes I feel as though I threw my marriage away on a whim. Almost like I just needed a break from married life. Andrew has been such a powerful influence on me, that restless energy he's always had. I never stopped to ask myself whether I wanted to go along with all his grand plans – buying the holiday home in Deal, darting off to Nice for a weekend, all the driving tours around Europe. Packing and unpacking every five minutes, fancy car festivals and tennis tournaments and dinner parties and shit.'

In normal times, I would have teased her something rotten about checking her privilege, but the big knowledge I was carrying made me less confident about making fun of her. 'Did you really not enjoy all that travelling?' I asked, allowing myself a petty moment of playing the world's smallest violin as I remembered camping in Cornwall in torrential rain while

Philippa sent me photos of Bellinis in Venice and margaritas in Mauritius.

Philippa gave a little grunt. 'I'm aware of what a spoilt cow I sound. It's not anything to do with the travelling per se. What I'm trying to say is that I never really stopped to consider what I wanted from our life. I let myself get swept along with whatever Andrew wanted, accepting that my job was to entertain a whole load of people who probably wouldn't have thrown a bucket of water on me if I was on fire. I might have felt differently if I'd had a career.'

I ignored the last comment because I'd always felt that Philippa could have done so much more than be at Andrew's beck and call, but I didn't want to annoy her by pointing that out. 'You love socialising. We had to book you six months in advance if we wanted you over for dinner.'

'That's the point I'm making. I've come to realise that I got caught up in the slipstream of Andrew's boundless appetite for change. All those stupid people wanging on about their brilliant kids and the best universities and swanky jobs that, honestly, I couldn't give less of a hoot about.'

I was ashamed of the sharp burst of satisfaction at Philippa finally coming round to my view, that lots of the people they'd spent time with over the years were, in fact, pretty vacuous. It was embarrassing that, at nearly sixty, I still craved the certainty of occupying the best friend slot. I shuddered at how the current situation might impact on my privileged position. For a moment, I forgot to respond to Philippa as I contemplated all the confidences we'd shared over the years, all the snide or disloyal things I'd said, all the times I'd let off steam, sometimes hamming up my familial frustrations to make her laugh.

But Philippa didn't need much of a response. She always processed her feelings by talking about a subject until she exhausted herself. I dragged my attention back to what she was saying, away from the unsettling idea that she might use those snapshots in time against me. I reminded myself this was Philippa, the woman who'd saved me, who'd stood by me and kept my secrets. Both of them.

'We've moved house six times in twenty-eight years. Since Andrew's left, I've realised that the weekends I love the most are when I'm pottering about in my garden and – don't shoot me – cleaning the grouting on my kitchen floor, then sitting in my pyjamas watching Netflix.'

'Cleaning the grouting? If it brings you so much joy, you can do mine.' I gave myself a big tick for coming up with something that normal, non-eggshell me might have said.

'It'll be my birthday present to you next year,' Philippa said with a giggle.

I took a deep breath to ascertain that what I was about to say was only driven by fact not deviousness. 'Andrew's such a busy bee. He loves a project. He's never going to be the sort of man who stays in playing cards. I bet he's loving doing up his old flat. So maybe you were right to separate so you can both spend the rest of your lives doing what works for you?'

I kept checking myself, hoping that I was making the comments that friend Jackie would always have made, rather than manipulative mother of Scarlett. Manipulative mother of Scarlett probably had the slight upper hand, but it wasn't a whitewash.

'So are you – what's the lingo – "talking" to anyone else?'

Philippa let out a snort. 'I'm still doing all the winking and nudging and naff dating-site stuff, but I'm not holding my breath. Half the men are living in a spare room at their mum's and the other half mention their ex-wives in every other sentence before assuring me that they're completely ready to move on.'

She was trying to make me laugh, but I heard the catch in her voice, the hook of loneliness. The certainty she'd had last year when she'd first told me she wanted out of her marriage had faded. Doubt was creeping around her words like a summer clematis, filling me with dread.

'I do miss Andrew much more than I thought I would, though. I'm really beginning to wonder whether it would be worth giving our marriage a second chance.'

12

JACKIE

It was the sight of the roses that did it. That deep burgundy, almost black, unfurling with the promise of good times ahead, of beauty and joy and celebration. Last year, I remembered looking out of the kitchen window and saying out loud, 'What a great day to be alive,' as I took in the pink spires of penstemons showcased against the bright white of the Shasta daisies. Then I'd told Alexa to play Dolly Parton and belted out 'Islands in the Stream' at the top of my voice.

This year, the sight of those roses made me sad, in the face of all that had changed. How much was about to change. How precarious our existence was. They taunted me with the irony of deluding ourselves that now our years were no longer dictated by school terms or the needs of a daughter who would surely be self-sufficient at thirty, Ian and I would have space for us. I'd imagined smiling at each other over the breakfast table, discussing topics of the day, plans for the week. The easy and satisfying exchanges that hovered nebulously in a distant future when we weren't haring around looking for lost homework, phone chargers, gym kit. Or trying to help with art projects – our input invariably scoffed at and eye-rolled out of existence.

With the roses came the realisation that in the space of a year – in the space of a few months, in fact – life now was worse, not better. That an adult child brought problems far greater than a smashed iPad screen or being dropped from the netball team. Problems that we couldn't solve by throwing money at them, or by cooking comfort food, or telling her to 'get a good night's sleep and it will all look different in the morning'. But worse than not being able to fix the problem was the realisation that we could also be swept away in chaos not of our making.

Ian looked up at me over his newspaper as I steeled myself to meet Philippa, Abigail and Scarlett at the bridal boutique to organise the final touches to the wedding and bridesmaid dresses. Philippa had been texting me jokey mother-of-the-bride outfits all week. 'Leopard skin too much? A whole pineapple on my hat?' I had to flick back through our conversation thread to remind me of the sort of frivolous banter I sent before every word I typed felt loaded with betrayal.

Ian grunted a 'Morning' to me and slumped back down behind the doomy headlines. Since the Andrew-Scarlett debacle, our morning greetings had atrophied from a light discussion of things we'd read – 'Did you see the feature about twenty trips by rail through Europe? I quite fancied the one through Switzerland' – to stilted exchanges about domestic logistics on a good day and proper humdingers of rows on a bad day.

Today was not in the good day category. The mere mention of what I was doing this morning engulfed the kitchen in a thick treacle of disapproval. Ian could not accept that I hadn't embraced his uncompromising stance, which amounted to: if Andrew and Scarlett were to pursue their 'stomach-churning' relationship, they needed to put Philippa and Abigail in the picture. 'Now. Not in five weeks' time.'

'I agree, but Andrew and Scarlett need to tell them. Not us.'

Ian's mouth set in a furious line. 'But we're lying to your

best friend. If Scarlett and Andrew didn't want us to say anything, they should have been more careful that we didn't find out until they were ready to be upfront with everyone else. I do not want to be part of their deceit.'

I pushed back in my chair and stomped over to the sink to grab a cloth so I didn't have to sit opposite Ian and see the anger on his face. I started wiping down the fronts of the kitchen cupboards. 'I hate this, too, but if we go behind Scarlett's back and tell Philippa, she'll never speak to us again. You know what she's like, so stubborn. I'm not losing my daughter over this.' As the words came out, I allowed myself to flirt with the idea that we could, in fact, become estranged from her. That this friend of ours, the man we'd laughed with, built campfires with, barbecued with, could take our daughter from us in the blink of an eye and we were powerless to control whether that happened.

Ian lifted his newspaper higher in a gesture that made me want to snatch it out of his hands and shout swear words that I'd never said before in his face. This idea that he could sit high-horsing it, that somehow things would be so much better – wouldn't they just – if we steamed over to Philippa's house, sat her down and told her what was going on. Then watched as her world and ours caught alight, flames licking at the corner of our existence before eventually razing our entire landscape. Christmas without so much as a card from Scarlett. Birthdays without even a text message. A whole life that I might not be party to. My best friend might always be more enraged with Scarlett, the youngest and most inexperienced person in the jigsaw, than with her husband. Her husband whom she'd rejected and who'd opted to ignore all the usual rules of engagement with a child he'd seen grow up.

I wrestled with the tears that were clogging my throat, then surrendered. 'Don't you care that if we don't handle this properly, we might lose contact with Scarlett all together?'

Ian didn't move or respond, just carried on reading.

'Ian? Can you answer the question?'

He let the corner of the newspaper flop inwards and stared at me, his eyes hooded and blank. 'Don't ever ask me to be in the same room as him again. It's disgusting what he's done.'

'That's going to be a bit tricky at the bloody wedding then, isn't it? Perhaps they can book you a private dining room.'

I glanced at my phone. I needed to leave to meet Scarlett at the station. And as I reached for the high heels I was lending her because she only owned flip flops and boots, I thought I might slap him. Fly at him, wrench the glasses off his nose and laugh wildly as I jumped up and down on them. That absolute rigidity, that certainty that whatever else happened in the world, happened in our family, his opinion mattered more than our daughter. That was where he was mistaken. That was where he might find himself eating freezer meals for one and wondering how to make the subtitles work on the TV now his wife had left him.

I walked out without another word, leapt into the car and drove to the station, my usual politesse of waving people out at busy junctions giving way to aggressive tailgating of the car in front.

My phone beeped, no doubt signalling Scarlett's arrival when I was still a few minutes away, which reignited my rage. The need to communicate over every stupid little thing – with the exception of the gigantic life-derailing things – as though if she didn't tell me that she'd arrived, I would somehow forget to pick her up. What happened to waiting patiently for two minutes, trusting the fact that I wouldn't choose today to start being unreliable?

As I turned into the narrow road to the station, instead of allowing me to pass, a van barged its way through, leaving me no alternative but to back up. I threw my hands up in disbelief as he drew level with me and he wound down his window. In normal circumstances, I would have avoided eye contact and quickly sped away. Not today. I couldn't get my window down fast enough.

Before he could say whatever profanities he was gearing up for, I leaned right out and bellowed, 'You must have the tiniest penis in the entire world if that's what you have to do to feel powerful.'

His mate, sitting in the passenger seat with his feet on the dashboard and a joint in his hand, elbowed the driver and said, 'She might well be right about that,' and laughed.

'You stupid bitch,' the driver yelled and I squealed off, waving my pinky finger out of the window.

I flashed my lights at Scarlett, wondering if she was being deliberately provocative with the 'It is what it is' slogan on her T-shirt. I'd long ago trained myself to keep quiet about her clothing choices, but I hoped Philippa wouldn't be tempted to comment on her rainbow Doc Martens and ripped jeans. Scarlett had always had an eccentric bent to her dress – a direct contrast to Abigail's penchant for neat earrings and smart separates. Our daughters really were the evidence that opposites attracted. They'd always yin and yanged – Scarlett injecting excitement and mischief into the friendship and Abigail the only person in the world who could present Scarlett with some harsh truths without getting her head snapped off.

I watched her walk towards me, half of me applauding her resistance to conforming to the expectations of adulthood. However, disappointingly, the people-pleasing part of me that considered appropriate dress an extension of good manners wished she wasn't going to be clodhopping about in Doc Martens among all those fine lacey dresses, no doubt squawking with laughter and commenting loudly on some of the frillier offerings. I consoled myself that bridal boutiques probably witnessed all sorts of extraordinary behaviour, against which bold fashion statements and derogatory hilarity would pale into insignificance.

Scarlett waved, her face brightening. For a single second, I could fool myself that this was an ordinary Saturday.

'Hello, love,' I said, as she slipped into the passenger seat without leaning over to kiss me. I didn't know how to have a normal voice any more, how to say, 'How are you?' in a tone that didn't feel weighed down with meaning or accusation. Instead I hid behind recounting my run-in with the white van man.

She said, 'Mum!' in mock horror and, just for a moment, we giggled together. I tried to hold that feeling to me, that we could connect in a simple way, without a great barrier of intent and defence lodged between us.

We soon fell into a loaded silence though, which I broke by blurting out the first thing that came into my head. 'Have you chatted to Abigail lately? I'm assuming that she has no idea about you and Andrew?'

'We've spoken a bit on text. And no, she doesn't know. Not unless you've said something to Philippa.' Her tone was verging on snappy, belligerent.

I fought, fought hard to be the one who was calm and didn't rock up to a tense situation unable to resist funnelling extra oxygen into the flames at the heart of it. I wanted an apology, an acknowledgement that I was caught in a Catch-22 nightmare that I had not created, but I also knew that wanting was futile. Even as a child, Scarlett's apologies had always carried an air of 'up yours' about them. I stayed focused on getting through today with the least possible drama.

'Of course I haven't spoken about it,' I said, managing to sound as though the thought had never entered my head. In fact, every time I had any interaction with Philippa, I had to concentrate with an intensity I hadn't required since my finals to dissuade myself from honesty.

'Good, because it's none of her business.'

I didn't answer, but my face must have betrayed me.

'Mum, she kicked him out. She doesn't get a say in what he does next.'

And even though I was trying to resist plunging back into this circular argument yet again, the urge to explain Philippa's standpoint, and mine, was too strong.

'This isn't about Philippa having a say; it's more about after such a long marriage, Andrew owes it to her to be straightforward about where he's at, so everyone is clear and can move on accordingly.'

Scarlett's head jerked round. 'Why does she need to know what he's doing to move on? She engineered the split in the first place. Abigail told me she's dating anyway. Why does she care who Andy's seeing?'

I wanted to bang the steering wheel with frustration. 'Because it's not a normal situation. Because Philippa's my best friend. Because Andrew is your best friend's dad. Because I feel as though I'm lying to everyone all the time.'

I was desperate to shout, 'And your dad thinks he's a paedophile and is refusing to be in the same room as him ever again, so goodness knows how I'm going to explain that on Abigail's wedding day.' However, we were only five minutes from the bridal shop and we were going to need that time to dig out our game faces.

Scarlett didn't respond. Just set her jaw and looked out of the window.

'Anyway, today is Abigail's day and we absolutely can't spoil it for her.'

I parked and we walked to the bridal shop where I coerced every muscle in my face into something resembling a cheerful greeting. We all exchanged hellos and hugs and 'how exciting's. I concentrated on Abigail's happiness, her 'I can't believe I'm actually doing this!' rather than my desire to stand in between Philippa and Scarlett as though a physical buffer could somehow defend against an emotional showdown.

Philippa was all smiles as she turned to Scarlett. 'I think I'll have to get myself a T-shirt like yours. "It is what it is".'

Scarlett grinned and I breathed out. 'It's my new philosophy on life. Stops me getting annoyed about the train strikes and the rude gits on the Tube forcing their way on before people get off and other professional dogwalkers who never pick up poo and the bus drivers that see you running and deliberately drive off—'

Philippa interrupted. 'I think I'd keel over if I had to live in London now. Sounds so stressful.' She turned to me. 'When I spoke to Andrew the other day, though, he said he was quite enjoying living there, which surprises me. Though I don't suppose he's sullied himself with the Tube. Probably blowing his half of the settlement on cabs.'

Scarlett broke off her conversation with Abigail and said, 'I always make him get the bus.' My heart sped up. She paused. 'When we go to the running club.'

I breathed again.

I dreaded Abigail or Philippa noticing the possessive tone in Scarlett's voice. I tried to catch her eye to send a warning glare without the others seeing, but she stood, her arms folded, her face settled in a triumphant expression. I recognised that look; I knew it masked a defiance, an unpredictable tendency.

Philippa's eyebrows shot up. 'Well, you're a better woman than I am. And thank you for looking after him a bit. I do still worry about him. Have you seen him lately?' The way Philippa asked it so hopefully, as though an affirmative answer would assuage her guilt, made me want to run out of there, to avoid hearing what was coming next so I could abdicate responsibility for my part in all of this. My blood felt turbo-charged around my body as I braced myself for Scarlett's response.

'We're doing quite a lot of running together. He's considering entering the London Marathon next year.'

I willed her to stop there, to not elaborate with more detail that would raise suspicions that her knowledge of his life emanated from more than a shared love of running.

Thankfully, as Philippa was gearing up for more investigation, the owner of the boutique appeared with a tray of Prosecco and said, 'Right, Abigail, while your friends and family are having a drink, let's get you into that gorgeous dress and check that nothing else needs fine-tuning.'

Abigail beckoned to Scarlett. 'Come with me.'

As Scarlett got up, I glanced at Philippa to see if she minded not being asked, but she was busy filling our glasses.

'Just half a glass for me. I'm driving,' I said.

Philippa kept looking over towards the back of the shop. 'Where did they go, those little girls? One minute they're playing with their Polly Pockets and making perfume out of rose petals, the next minute they're getting married.'

Before I could stop myself, I said, 'Well, one of them is.' I cursed myself for inviting further questioning.

Predictably, Philippa asked, 'Is Scarlett seeing anyone?'

I gave myself a moment to think by sipping my Prosecco. 'I don't enquire.'

'That's not like you. You've always been such a snoop dog.'

Normal, unguarded me would have replied 'Because I'm bloody sick of not liking the answer,' but instead I just said, 'I guess now they're proper adults, they're entitled to a bit more privacy.'

Philippa laughed, but before we could say anything further, Abigail came twirling out in her dress.

I clapped my hands. 'Oh wow, you look absolutely stunning.'

Philippa's eyes filled with tears. 'Perfect. Just perfect. I love what she's done with that neckline.'

Scarlett nodded. 'Gorgeous. You look beautiful.' I took solace from the fact that Scarlett sounded so genuine, immediately followed by an ache of sadness about whether their friendship could survive. Most of Scarlett's other female friends growing up had never seemed to get the measure of her, unable to pigeonhole her. As adults, they'd mostly gravitated towards more conventional women who didn't suddenly disappear to Vietnam because there'd been an irresistible offer on a flight.

Abigail waved her hands about in a show of modesty, but I could see that she was delighted with her choice. She thrust her phone at Scarlett. 'Here, can you take a photo of me to send to Dad?'

Scarlett's face was expressionless. 'Of course.'

'Mum, come on, you get in the photo with me.'

Philippa shook her head. 'He won't want me in it,' she said, in that sort of tone when people want you to insist.

Abigail frowned. 'He'll just be glad we're having a nice day, but whatever...'

Scarlett started taking photos of Abigail on her own. Philippa made a drama of dragging herself over, as though she was an unwilling participant. In reality, I was pretty sure she'd be delighted for these photos of mother-daughter happiness to wing their way over to Andrew. Abigail pulled her into the shot. I tried to imagine what Scarlett might be thinking but failed. Was she jealous of Philippa as 'the ex'? Did she consider Philippa over the hill now, so staid and boring with her tailored jackets and trousers, her delicate gold chain? I wondered if Scarlett recognised the value of her own currency: youthful beauty and energy. All I'd managed to ascertain so far was a slightly aloof and scornful attitude, but I wasn't a hundred per cent certain that was aimed at Philippa. My daughter often looked as though she had a disdainful conversation going on in her head and a day featuring discussions about the right jewellery to suit the neckline would be tapping right into that.

Abigail held her hand out for her phone and scrolled through the photos. 'They're a bit dark. I don't know what's up with the camera on my phone lately. Can you take one on yours? I want Dad to think I'm spending the money he's giving me towards the wedding wisely,' she said to Scarlett.

Philippa said, 'Oh he will, darling. This is such a gorgeous dress. Timeless. When I married Andrew, those great big skirts were all the rage. Hideous. I'd choose something totally different now. He kept treading on the hem when we did our first dance.'

'What was your first dance to?' Abigail asked.

Scarlett's expression darkened as though she didn't want to be reminded that Philippa and Andrew had most definitely been in love once.

'"Love Is All Around" – you know, that Wet Wet Wet song.'

Scarlett snorted and pulled a face. 'The one that Bill Nighy butchers in *Love Actually*?'

Philippa nodded, laughing as though she was oblivious to Scarlett's scathing tone. 'The world and its wife had that as a first dance back in the nineties.'

Scarlett pulled an expression of 'how unoriginal' and I was desperate to move the subject away from Philippa and Andrew's wedding.

'Why don't you take a quick photo of Abigail on your phone so she can change and you can try on your dress?' I asked.

Scarlett scowled at me.

Abigail beckoned to her mother. Scarlett hesitated, then snapped away without waiting for Philippa to get back into the shot. 'Smile! You look lovely. Quite the blushing bride.' Reluctantly, she paused while Philippa and Abigail positioned themselves, took a single photo and said, 'There. That'll give him an idea.'

Abigail moved to look at the pictures, but Scarlett said, 'Hang on a minute, I'll Airdrop them to you.'

'I'll just look on your phone. You can send them over later when you've got Wi-Fi.'

I watched as Scarlett dithered, then suddenly, I understood.

She had photos of Andrew on there.

My brain was scorching with the effort of rescuing the situation, but I couldn't come up with anything other than what I'm pretty sure was an expression that rivalled a Hallowe'en horror mask.

Scarlett didn't hand over her phone but instead stood sentry, gripping it tightly and flicking through the images, her shoulders up around her ears as Abigail leaned in to look.

'That's a nice one of me and Mum. I'll send that to Dad.'

'I'll ping it over to him if you like while you get changed?'

My heart leapt for a moment before I realised that it was okay for Scarlett to have Andrew's number. I could feel my armpits sweating inside my shirt, as though my nervous system was malfunctioning.

Abigail looked puzzled for a moment, then said, 'Great, thanks.'

When Abigail headed off to the changing room, Philippa called to Scarlett. 'Can I see the photo before you send it through? Just checking that you haven't captured all my chins before you remind my ex-husband what a lucky escape he's had.'

Scarlett held the screen up for her.

'Not my best, but I suppose it will do. Can I look at the ones of Abigail?' And without waiting for Scarlett to answer, she started swiping.

It was worse than watching the England football team in a penalty shoot-out. The inevitability of disaster. But just as Scarlett was pulling the phone away, saying, 'That's the last one,' the boutique owner came up and touched her arm to indicate that she was ready for her.

That tiny distraction was long enough for Philippa to flick onto a selfie of Andrew and Scarlett. 'Oh there's Andrew,' Philippa said, peering intently at the screen.

Scarlett snatched the phone away. 'We'd just done a nine-mile race and were comparing who was reddest in the face.'

'He wants to be careful he doesn't overdo it. He's always been so competitive. Is everyone much younger than him at your club?'

'No. There's a mixture of ages. Anyway, he's got more stamina than a lot of people in their fifties,' Scarlett said. I wondered if she'd intended the double entendre and decided that her brusque delivery meant she probably had. She stuffed the mobile into her pocket and marched after the shop assistant.

I sensed Philippa staring after Scarlett, so I got up, unable to bear the charade of chatting along as though this was simply a jolly day out for the four of us. I could feel all the muscles tensing across my back as I pretended to be looking out of the window. 'It's a really busy high street here, isn't it? I wonder how many independent wedding shops manage to make a living.' I could hear the conversational fluff coming out of my mouth, non-descript and dull.

Philippa came and stood next to me, emptying her flute of Prosecco. 'Is Scarlett upset that Abigail is getting married? She seems a bit prickly today.'

I scrabbled about for my best acting abilities. 'I think she's delighted for Abigail, but it's probably made her feel a bit left out – or left behind – at any rate. And it's always an adjustment when your friends start getting married.'

Philippa said, 'True, though I didn't feel left out when you did because Ian was always so welcoming. Looking back, he must have felt like a gooseberry himself sometimes because we had so much history together. I think the trickiest time is when your friends start having babies, because they're suddenly so much less available.'

That familiar feeling of shame rose in me, a flutter of panic that I was deliberately deceiving the one person who knew the whole truth about me. I told myself that there was no way she would use it to punish me. Would she? It didn't bear thinking about.

Before I could respond, Scarlett appeared in a green chiffon dress. Abigail and the shop owner were raving about how the groom's dark green tie would complement the theme and her 'bouquet could even have a ribbon of the same colour'. The thunderous look on Scarlett's face suggested that she didn't share their enthusiasm.

'That colour really suits you with your dark hair,' I said.

'Thanks,' Scarlett said, sulkily.

Philippa raised her eyebrows. 'I'm getting the sense there's something you're unhappy about?'

There was a pause, then Scarlett blinked. 'Sorry. It's been a long week and my period has just started. I'm tired and I've got a lot to sort out this weekend.'

Philippa sighed noisily, glancing at Abigail. I could tell she found Scarlett grumpy and selfish, and frankly, I didn't blame her. 'Abigail? Are you happy with everything?' Philippa asked.

Abigail had always been accommodating of Scarlett and her moods and smiled. 'Yes, I'm feeling super-excited. It's becoming very real! Not long now.'

I had such admiration for Abigail. She was always so sunny, approaching everything with childlike excitement.

Philippa suggested that we all went for a quick coffee, but Scarlett was sending me 'Let's get out of here' signals, so I made up some excuse about having to get back in time for my Tesco delivery before I went bed shopping. Not exactly glamorous, but the best I could do on the spur of the moment.

When we got a good distance towards the car, Scarlett all but exploded. 'Abigail tells me that Philippa thinks she's made a mistake and is hoping – and I quote – "to use the romance of the wedding day to get back with my dad". Did you know about that?' Without even letting me answer, she demanded, 'Why didn't you tell me?'

I glanced over my shoulder and unlocked the car. 'Get in,' I said. Like someone hanging off the window ledge of a burning house, I was barely clinging to my decision to not voice any opinion that could alienate Scarlett. 'I didn't tell you because I didn't know,' I said, hearing the fury vibrate through the deliberate calmness of my tone.

Scarlett banged the dashboard. 'Come on! Do you expect me to believe that? Philippa tells you every little detail of her life.'

I relinquished my hold and gave her both barrels. 'Have you ever stopped to think about anyone else in all of this? Either of you? About what impact this ill-conceived love affair – if that's what it is, rather than just an older man having sex with someone half his age – might have on anyone else? Your best friend for a start? Dad? Me? My friendship with Philippa?'

Scarlett wrapped her fingers around the door handle. 'I'm not listening to this. We love each other. He's the only person in my whole life who has made me feel that I'm not failing in some way. That I'm not living up to expectations.' She waved her hands about in an imitation of me: '*Oh Scarlett is Scarlett, you know what she's like, here, there and everywhere, living entirely in the moment...*' She did a nasty impression of my laugh, which should have made me angry at her meanness. Instead, I just felt so sad. Sad that I'd made her feel as though she was failing when, in reality, I had often admired her.

Nowhere in my family blueprint had lurked a future where my daughter was quietly building a bonfire of resentments that would accidentally be ignited by my desire to ease Philippa's concern about poor lonely Andrew. I could barely get my head round how a simple request to introduce him to a running club had dominoed into a spectacular catastrophe.

I tried to argue back. 'That's not true. I've never had a problem with the way you live your life. In so many ways, I'm in awe of you for not being motivated by money and for seizing every opportunity that comes your way.' As I said the words, I knew that was only half the story. I did admire her, but, self-ishly, I also longed not to worry about her. I didn't want her to be at the mercy of a temperamental landlord or unable to pay the rent if her flatmate decided to move out.

There was no distracting her. She was like a wild sea intent on breaching a breakwater that had tricked people into thinking they were safe and sheltered. She pushed the door open and stuck one foot out, hurt and accusations pouring from her. 'That's just not true. I'm sorry for not being that daughter you can boast about. For not having a fiancé like Guy, who you can parade up and down and everyone can think that I've done well for myself. But, you know what, I have done well for myself. I've finally met the one person who makes me feel that I'm pretty enough, smart enough, successful enough, fucking nice enough. Who isn't rolling his eyes and waiting for me to "grow up". This is who I am, Mum. Like it or lump it. But Andy and I aren't splitting up any time soon so you and Dad better get used to it.'

The door slammed. I sat, winded and wounded. I'd always known I was a terrible mother.

13

JACKIE

Ian was upstairs in his office when I got home. There was plenty of time for him to take grim satisfaction in the details of my disastrous day, so I didn't rush up there. I made tea and sat veering between multiple versions of 'How dare she think that of me?' and 'Is that what she took away from all those years of me telling her how proud I was of her? How kind she was? How funny?' Did all children gravitate naturally towards the stuff we got wrong, the things we forgot to praise, amassing it as proof that they weren't loved as much as other children and over-looking all the positive input?

Maybe at a subconscious level, she knew what I'd done. I couldn't allow myself to entertain that idea. No. This was Scarlett lashing out because we hadn't gone all Cinderella about this nightmare relationship and she wanted to punish us.

My heart ached, as though I'd had a full-on fist to the chest. The injustice of her words. The fear that Andrew might sweep her away, steal thirty years of caring, rendering it void. All that listening to the minutiae of who said what in a friendship spat. The making sure she had a good breakfast before her exams. A hot-water bottle in the middle of winter, because hers was the bedroom with three outside walls and it was lovely to get into a cosy bed. Could Andrew swoop in, gather up all the fruit of our love for her and cancel us out to the point that we might never see her again?

I was sitting with tears pouring down my face, when Ian walked in. He was engrossed in his phone, so it took him a moment to register my distress. 'What? Why are you crying?' he asked as though there were so many possibilities rather than one obvious one. As I assembled the gist of what Scarlett had said about how we'd failed her, he rushed in. 'She's gone and told them, hasn't she?'

I shook my head. 'No. No she didn't.' I sobbed through explaining how Philippa had seen the photo of Scarlett and Andrew together. 'The worst thing was she was happy because he looked well and she didn't need to feel guilty. And then Abigail told Scarlett that Philippa wanted to get back with Andrew and as soon as we left, she blew up, accused me of keeping things from her.'

Ian was shaking his head, doing that man thing of wanting to leap in with a solution, instead of allowing me to unload all the sadness, all her awful accusations that I so desperately needed him to rebut as Scarlett's deranged ramblings grounded in anger, not reality.

He slammed his phone down on the table. 'Why are we having to deal with all this? I cannot believe how selfish that pair are. I feel like driving straight over to Andrew's and punching his lights out. He should know better than to take advantage of a young woman who's only a few years older than his daughter. Revolting.'

My shoulders slumped. 'My God, are we really going down the route of the big man storming over to slug his daughter's lover? How would that help anything? Surely we're beyond that "get your hands off my daughter or I'll give you a thump"?'

Ian turned on me. 'Of course I'm not going to go and beat

up Andrew. For God's sake, I'm a civilised human being, not a bloody thug. But I'm so angry, that's what I feel like doing.'

'Glad we've clarified that,' I said, irritated that Ian had defaulted to ranting about wanting to clout Andrew, rather than giving me a hug and expressing a bit of understanding for how upset I was. I wasn't interested in what he'd like to do to Andrew – he of all people should know that what Scarlett had said would have hit home. Ian's macho posturing went nowhere towards reassuring me that he believed Scarlett was just sounding off and nothing she said was true.

'So how do you suggest we handle it? Shall I just let her stew in her own juices? Or should I try to get her over here for dinner so we can straighten everything out? The wedding is only five weeks away and I'd like to smooth it all over before then. I don't want to be the family snarling at each other in all the photos.'

Ian was screwing up his eyes as though what I was saying were the ramblings of a madwoman. 'That's the least of our worries. You don't honestly believe that we're going to be able to go to this wedding and watch Andrew escort Abigail down the aisle with Scarlett trailing after them? It's sheer lunacy. Scarlett cannot be chief bridesmaid – or any bridesmaid. She needs to stay away. Let Philippa have her day without Scarlett ruining it for her.'

I flopped down onto a chair. 'Talk about damned if we do and damned if we don't. We can spoil the wedding now by forcing Scarlett and Andrew to come clean, or we can let it all come out afterwards, thereby ruining everyone's memory of what they thought was the perfect day.'

Ian folded his arms. 'At least we're not complicit if it all comes out beforehand.'

'But Andrew really wants to allow Abigail to have her day, for the attention to be on her, without all the circus surrounding his relationship with Scarlett. I kind of get that.'

Ian rubbed his face. 'Frankly, they should have thought all this through. Scarlett's always been impulsive, but Andrew, for goodness' sake... What a man of his age sees in a thirty-year-old who lives hand-to-mouth and who would struggle to name anyone in government beyond the Prime Minister, God only knows. And even if they have this all-consuming attraction...' Ian shut his eyes as though he wanted to banish a hideous image from his brain. 'Surely they could see that acting on it would end in tears. Scarlett's never been able to adjust her behaviour to accommodate potential consequences, but Andrew is old enough and ugly enough to know better.'

I got up to make tea. 'I know Scarlett is all bravado and stub-bornness, but there must be a bit of her that's terrified? I mean, who knows how long they've been together versus what they've told us – but it can't be more than six or seven months. That's not long to be one hundred per cent certain that the other person is worth wrecking every other relationship for. Maybe she got swept along with it all and doesn't know how to exit.'

I knew what it was like to make bad decisions. To feel like you were out of options. To start down a path that you knew would only lead to disaster but not have the capacity to nego-tiate retracing your steps. Scarlett would never admit that she was lost, that she'd embarked on something that had become so out of control, that she'd just put her head down and pressed on. But I couldn't bear the thought that she was waking up and worrying in the small hours, watching the minutes, then the hours flick round on her alarm. I wanted to be the person to hold out a hand, to say, 'Hang on tight, we'll work this out together.'

Ian waved his hands about in frustration. 'That's the logic of a normal person. Scarlett is like a child in a sweet shop. She sees something she likes the look of and runs towards it without considering anything else. It's always been the same. "I've been offered a twelve-month contract, but I turned it down because I fancy three months in Thailand over the winter." "Yeah, the husband of the family I'm working for offered to employ me on the sales team at his company, but they've got this lovely new red setter puppy I want to help train.""

Even though I agreed with Ian, I still wanted to defend Scarlett. I hated the clinical coldness in his words, as though he wouldn't hesitate to throw her to the wolves in his quest to do the right thing.

I knew in that moment that I couldn't guarantee that I wouldn't raise my hand on the witness stand if Scarlett was on trial – 'the truth, the whole truth and nothing but the truth' – then lie my backside off. Not for murder, maybe.

But before I got any further down how morally corrupt I might become to protect my daughter, Ian said, 'I'm going to tell Philippa. She can decide what she says to Abigail, but I'm not turning up to that wedding without bringing her up to speed.'

'You can't do that.' I was shouting now. Scarlett's face, her eyebrows knitting together, the determined set of her shoulders as she stormed out of the car were high definition in my mind.

Ian put his shoulders back as though he'd made a decision. 'I haven't forgotten what Philippa did for us, and you shouldn't either. I didn't know which way to turn back then and she was a bloody life raft. I'm not paying her back by letting her be the last one to find out.'

There it was again. The debt we owed to Philippa. She never referred to it, never made a big deal about it. But, none-theless, it had hung in the background between us all these years, as fine, yet as strong, as spider silk.

Ian pressed on. 'Anyone could see them together. Someone from the running club who knows someone who knows Abigail or Philippa. Andrew loves eating out and Scarlett is always up for a good nosh. No doubt he's wining and dining her, showing off to his new girlfriend.' I'd never heard Ian sound so venomous; he was not a man who indulged in spiteful observations. 'People who live round here are always going up to London, anyone could bump into them randomly in a pub or a restaurant.' Ian grimaced. 'People love to gossip. It's much better that she hears it from us.'

'No. No. Let's not rush into anything. She might not even be home from town yet anyway.'

'This is well overdue. I'm going to sit outside her house until she turns up if she's not back.'

Then he grabbed his keys and disappeared out of the front door before my brain could process the speed at which we'd moved from a discussion to Ian's car backing out of the drive.

I couldn't let this happen. And if it was going to happen, I couldn't leave it to Ian. He'd be so blunt and forthright, make it so much more incendiary than it needed to be. I could soften the blow, make it seem less definitive, more of a blurring of boundaries rather than a full-on relationship. I snatched up my mobile and rang him. He didn't pick up. I imagined him watching my name appear and that self-righteous jut of his chin as he refused to be derailed from what he, Ian Dalton, knew to be the correct course of action.

There was no way I could let him loose on Philippa without being there to mitigate and moderate. I ran out to my car and screeched down the road. A ticker tape of scenarios was flashing through my head, not least that me driving too fast and dying in a fatal accident would be the cherry on top of the shit-show bun.

I made myself scan the road junctions twice, look properly with exaggerated care as I approached zebra crossings. I opened the window to let some fresh air in. The fury I felt with Ian was making my whole body emanate heat. He'd commandeered the moral high ground before we'd given Scarlett and Andrew proper notice of our intentions or allowed them time to take control and direct the narrative. I should admire him for his standards, his commitment to integrity and honesty. But in that moment I hated him.

With a mixture of shame and pride, I recognised that I'd been holding off telling Philippa because I wanted to protect Scarlett. It wasn't the wedding I cared about. Or Abigail's right to a joyful day. Or some misplaced loyalty to our long friendship with Andrew that made me, despite everything, not want to rob him of that milestone of walking his daughter down the aisle. No, purely and simply, I'd been playing for time, hoping that Scarlett would grow bored with a man whose cultural frame of reference was so different from her own. I'd hoped to brush it all under the carpet. No harm done. No one need know.

It had worked once before. But I'd been ridiculous to think I might be lucky enough to pull off the same trick twice.

14

JACKIE

Ian's car was already parked outside Philippa's house, but there was no sign of him. My stomach dipped as I pictured him sitting at her kitchen island, already halfway through life-changing revelations.

As I walked up the drive, I prepared myself for her anger. Or her disbelief. Or maybe her quiet sadness. Philippa was so even-tempered, so logical, that after all these years, I still couldn't predict which way it might go. The one thing I did know without a shadow of a doubt was that she was loyal. She'd stuck by me, covered for me, defended me, when I could barely put one foot in front of the other. Always made excuses for what I did. I didn't have her down as vindictive, but who knew how she might react, if only with outrage on Abigail's behalf?

I would find out now.

I stood for a few seconds, my finger hovering over the bell, wanting my ordinary, uneventful life to continue for a moment longer. I pressed my ear against the door, just able to make out the murmur of voices, but nothing that sounded angry or hysterical. Maybe that would come later.

I rang the doorbell, the noise jangling alongside my nerves.

Philippa came to the door, all smiles. 'Hello! Lucky me, seeing you twice in one day – did you get your new bed? And two Daltons for the price of one. Have you got an AirTag on Ian? He was just passing and popped in. I'm making him a coffee, do you want one?'

I nodded, unable to articulate anything as the relief flooded into my system that Ian might have been bluffing, or simply bottled out.

One look at his face told me otherwise. As Philippa bustled about, digging her cafetière out of the cupboard, opening a fresh bag of coffee, holding up two packs of biscuits – 'I've got low-cal boring or double chocolate splurge ones' – my heart broke incrementally. I was mouthing a mixture of pleas and threats to Ian every time her back was turned. When she popped into the utility room to fetch some more milk, I whispered, 'If you do this, Scarlett won't ever forgive you. And I don't know whether I'll be able to either.'

He didn't manage to reply before Philippa came whirling in, setting everything down on a tray. She plonked herself opposite us on a stool at the breakfast bar, sitting back with a cheery 'What's new?' expression.

I glanced at Ian, who raised his eyebrows.

The smile slipped from Philippa's face. 'What? What's the matter?' she said, reaching for the coffee pot, automatic pilot overwriting the weighted silence.

Ian inspected his fingernails. I willed him to make up some old nonsense, to save himself, us, Scarlett at the eleventh hour. But it wasn't to be. He looked Philippa straight in the eye and said, 'Andrew and Scarlett are in a relationship.'

It took every ounce of self-control for me not to burst out with 'Dress that up, why don't you?'

I couldn't bear it, that bald fact without any context, turning everything we'd all taken for granted on its head. In the framework of our families, Andrew was a middle-aged adult and Scarlett would always be a child. There was a tiny part of me that grudgingly applauded Ian's courage, but a far greater part that burned with anger that he was putting Philippa's right to know above Scarlett's right to decide when to make it public.

I waited. We both waited.

Philippa's eyes flicked towards me, as though she was expecting me to laugh, nudge Ian's arm and tell him off for being an idiot. 'What?' she said.

I'd imagined this moment so many times. The pause before the words sank in. The horror and disgust on Philippa's face. Tears, anger, blame. I'd considered that she would probably say some horrible things about Scarlett, that later she'd be embarrassed about and apologise for – 'It was shock. Sorry. You know I don't think like that.'

'Scarlett is having an affair with Andrew?' Her voice was low, thrumming with suspicion. 'As in your daughter is having sex with my ex-husband?'

Her question made it all sound even more tawdry than it was and her naming of Scarlett first suggested she was already shifting the blame onto her. Ian must have thought so too because he said, 'I'm really disappointed in Andrew.'

Philippa ignored him and said, 'How? How did this even happen?' Her eyes were boring into me as though I'd engineered it, encouraged it.

'I'm sorry,' I said, though none of this was my fault. 'I know this is going to be really hard for everyone. Scarlett invited him to the running club, like you asked, then I don't know what happened, how it went from there. She hasn't explained it to us, but they're in some kind of relationship.' Adrenaline was coursing through my body, making my legs jiggle on the bar stool, the metal stand tapping out its own rhythm on the slate floor.

'Like I asked? I never asked Scarlett to take Andrew to the running club. You suggested it!'

I backed down. 'Maybe I did. I was just trying to help you be less worried. None of us could have foreseen this happening.' Despite my conciliatory tone, I was immediately annoyed that she was already apportioning blame as though my game plan all along was to matchmake Andrew with Scarlett.

Ian stepped in with 'I don't think the details of the running club and whose suggestion it was are the crucial issue here.'

I wanted to shake him. I wished I had come on my own, weeks ago, instead of Ian barrelling in here and shooting from the hip without a plan of how to mop up the fallout. How could he not see that this exchange was part of an intricate dance of assigning and accepting blame, even if it wasn't justified? In an illogical way that Ian would never be able to fathom, the 'who' that appeared to be the stumbling block didn't matter. What mattered was whether I was prepared to take some unwarranted responsibility in order to earn some forgiveness. Having thought I would, for the sake of keeping my friendship with Philippa on a firm footing, I couldn't deny that the flare of injustice was burning brightly.

Then the question that I'd been dreading: 'When did you know?' The words came out staccato, as though she hated me.

I was grappling about for something that wouldn't make me seem such a disloyal friend. A fuzzy response along the lines of 'We had a bit of an inkling that they were getting quite close a few months ago, but we didn't believe it would turn into anything serious.' But Ian wasn't having any of it.

'We found out at the end of May. On Jackie's birthday, actually.'

'Ian! We didn't know for sure, we just knew that they were spending a lot of time together.' I was lying. Full-on lying. But the iciness in Philippa's words was making me panic, that sense that fifty years of friendship were hanging by a fraying thread. That she had absolutely no interest in why I might have delayed telling her. That she was not going to be mollified by my excuse that I hoped it would all blow over and didn't want to cause trouble for the sake of it.

Ian didn't contradict me out loud, but his face was screaming 'Bullshit!'

Philippa slumped against the back of her stool. Her tone had an artificial ring of 'If you just tell me the truth, everything will be fine' as she said, 'Jackie, how long have you been keeping this a secret from me? Did you know when I was talking about getting back with Andrew and you kept persuading me to go on dates?'

I nodded. 'But let's be clear, I wasn't keen for you to date other people to keep you out of Scarlett's way. You haven't been happy with Andrew for a long time, and it was my firm belief that you'd be better off with someone new.'

She leaned her forehead on her hand. 'I don't know what's a bigger betrayal. Andrew and Scarlett – God, the very idea makes me sick – or you knowing about it all this time and giving me fob-off answers whenever I've asked about Scarlett.' She looked at me with such incredulity that I felt myself shrink down onto the stool.

'I didn't want to lie to you – of course I didn't.'

Before I said any more, she tilted her head on one side and said, 'But you did lie, though.'

'It wasn't like that. I wanted to protect you. I didn't think it would come to anything.'

She leapt off her stool. 'So you were hoping just to keep quiet and I'd be none the wiser?'

'I was in a difficult position. Andrew didn't want to spoil Abigail's wedding. They were going to tell you afterwards. Abigail – and you – were so looking forward to her big day... I didn't know what to do for the best, what would be the least awful for everyone...'

Around and around we went, with me trying to make Philippa understand that I hadn't intended to deceive her and

Philippa pouncing on everything I said, twisting my words to paint my actions in the worst possible light. Ian sat in silence and I wanted to scream at him: 'Look, look what you've done. I hope you feel that your commitment to "I simply can't live with this deceit a moment longer" has achieved what you expected. And you get to walk away. You've delivered your message and now you're sitting here like a turnip, without uttering a word to help.'

In the end, I started crying. 'After being friends for fifty years, you honestly think I wanted this? That I would ever do anything to hurt you on purpose?'

Philippa stared at me. 'I don't think you'd do anything to hurt me on purpose, no. I just expected that you'd have my back the way I've always had yours. Even if you didn't want to tell me yourself, I'm pretty sure you could have imposed an ultimatum on Andrew.'

She ran her finger around the rim of her coffee mug as though she was formulating another stab at my integrity.

'When would you have told me? You obviously didn't want Ian to come here today.' She leaned towards him. 'Thank you for not letting me be the last one to find out. I'm still struggling to imagine sitting on the top table, with Scarlett and Andrew pretending that they haven't been shagging each other for the last few months.' She threw her hands up in the air, spinning around to face me. 'I mean, would they secretly be squeezing each other's hands in the photos, waiting for Abigail and Guy to depart for the airport before beckoning me over for "a quick word"? How could you even consider letting me blunder blindly through such a special day, knowing what you know?'

Ian got off his stool and said, 'I think we should leave you to digest this. I know it's been a shock and I'm so sorry we had to be the ones to tell you. I really didn't want to be in that position.' He leaned forward and gave Philippa a hug, the sort of hug he'd

delivered thousands of times over the years – warm, affectionate, platonic. 'We'll all find a way through this. We will.'

I was really crying now. 'I'm sorry. I'm really sorry. I was
stuck between a rock and a hard place. Let's talk in the week,' I
said and went to hug Philippa. She didn't push me away, but
her hands rested limply on my waist and her body arched away
from me. Nothing like our usual tight squeeze when I always
had the sensation of a two-way exchange of love, with no
restraint.

She muttered, 'I guess we all live and learn who we can
trust and who we can't.'

In that moment, the chill of vulnerability engulfed me. A
sudden fear translated into a need to safeguard myself that was
so strong I had a sense of almost hating her for the power she
held, that I'd gifted to her. I'd trusted her with the most devas-
tating moments of my life. Now I wished that the person who
knew everything about me didn't know a single thing.

15

SCARLETT

I'd never been in love before. I thought I had, but I was wrong. For the first time ever, I wanted the other person's happiness more than I wanted my own. I didn't realise that people actually felt like that. I'd thought it was just something they said, a soundbite that they came out with so as not to appear selfish. Up until now I'd been drifting along. I'd fooled myself that various men I'd been out with might be the one, assessing them in terms of what they could bring to my life – entertainment, extra income, great sex, adventure. A kind of shopping list to make embarking on a long-term relationship a bit less of an impulsive gamble and a bit more of an informed bet.

I realised now that I'd never loved them in a way that meant I stopped and considered how I could make them happy beyond anything more significant than picking up wine en route home on a Friday night. Yet suddenly, I found myself deriving so much enjoyment from what made Andy happy. Not for any gain, for what I could get out of it, but for the sheer joy of seeing his face light up, the uncomplicated delight of pleasing him. Not in a subservient way that gave him control, but in a way that strengthened us. That stopped me looking at the differences, the complications between us. That made me feel grounded, keen to hear his views, his take on my work, mistakes I made, dreams, ideas I had, his celebration of my tiny triumphs.

I dared tell him things I would never have bored anyone else with – seeing a nuthatch on the common, finding framed pressed flowers I loved in a charity shop, the vibrant colours of the ivy on a house we often walked past. I realised I'd never considered myself important enough to share that level of detail with a man before, prided myself on only talking about meaningful things. Andy took pleasure in my pleasure. I trusted him, blossoming under his encouragement, as he dismissed my apologies for 'being a nature bore'.

'I find it brilliant that you have a passion, that you open your eyes and observe the world around you. How much better than sleepwalking through the world, never noticing anything. I love it,' he said.

And just like that, the impatience that my friends, my family had with me on a walk, as I stopped to examine the veins in a leaf, photograph spiders' webs, get excited about the feathery crystals of a hoar frost on the park railings morphed from an annoying quirk to a quality.

So that evening when Philippa called Andy to say she knew about us, it was a revelation. I expected to be all guns blazing for a biting retort to whatever accusations were levelled at us. Instead, my heart trembled as I watched Andy get to his feet, his shoulders sagging, the outline of him in the doorway as he walked through to the kitchen. The tall, slim frame, the dark waves of hair curling over the collar of his shirt, the way his head tilted to the right when he was concentrating. I could feel the sadness in him as he said, 'I know. Of course I know what it looks like, but that's not what it feels like. Yes, she was a child, but she's not now. She's thirty – older than when we met.'

Loving the right person for me but the wrong person for everyone else was such a strange alchemy of remorse and elation. Nevertheless, regret was gaining the upper hand when Andy was explaining to Philippa that he hadn't meant to fall in love with me, and that of course he hadn't spent the last fifteen years lusting after me. 'Do you really believe I was secretly ogling a teenager in a bikini? I know you're upset – it is shocking, for everyone – but I also expect you to know me better than that.' His words contained such respect, such an understanding of what Philippa would feel, that I didn't want to be the cause of this strife for him.

I heard him say, 'Please let me tell her.' A pause. 'I'm not going to dress it up. No, that's where you're mistaken. It's not a mid-life crisis. I'm not going to go into detail because I don't think it's helpful. All you need to know is that I wouldn't be doing this if I wasn't in it for the long term.' He scraped a chair back, a thud as he sat down. More scraping. Pacing. The tap running. 'I am well aware of the consequences. I have thought it through.' Then a disbelieving 'But I'm her father. Of course she's going to want me to give her away. No. No. You can stop right there. I'm doing it and that's final.' But there was still that calmness about him, that although events might buffet him about, he would never descend into panic. Who knew that the character traits of steadfast and reliable would be such a turn-on?

He clicked the kettle on. 'Scarlett is Abigail's chief bridesmaid. That's not up to you.' The cutlery drawer rattled. 'This has got nothing to do with Ian and Jackie. Yes, but that was by accident. Believe me, neither of them wanted to find out like that. You're punishing the wrong people. If anything, they are just as devastated as you are. I don't think Abigail would want that. She loves Jackie and Ian. This isn't their fault. It's not what you or I think is right; Abigail has to make the decision.'

This was what maturity looked like. Not storming in and demanding to know what was being said, what Philippa was threatening. Not even semaphoring from the doorway to demand a clue, but being so grown up that I didn't give in to the fear flooding my body, the panic that threatened to translate into swearing and stomping about. Instead, I sat, my ears straining, my mind racing about to fill in the gaps in the conversation.

Andy's voice ratcheted up a notch in tightness. 'Of course we wouldn't act like that. We're not adolescents, for God's sake.' Another pause. 'I'm going to forget you said that.' Anger, controlled but noticeable. His tone took on that air of wrapping up a conversation. 'I'd appreciate it if you'd give me a few days to arrange to meet with Abigail.' Another huge sigh. 'No, I won't leave you to pick up the pieces. She's my daughter too. None of this affects my love for Abigail. Of course it doesn't.'

He walked back in, his eyes dark with strain, blowing out big gusts of despondency.

We stood hugging each other, his face pressed into my neck. Tension radiated out of him and I wanted to fix it, wanted to make everything better. I longed to see him laugh at my impression of one of my employers or valiantly plough his way through a tofu concoction I'd seen on Instagram, and pronounce it 'an experience'. But the halcyon days were behind us now.

'How did she find out?' I asked.

'I guess it was inevitable. I should have told her myself.'

He should have known by now that I wasn't a woman who could be fobbed off.

'Who told her?' The potent mix of fear and fury was threatening to bubble over into something that could not be dressed up as a rational discussion. Heat was rising in my face and I pulled away from him.

His voice was low, resigned. 'Your dad went round to tell her.'

A gasp of shock shot out of me. 'Dad? I thought it would be Mum.' I didn't know why it being Dad made the betrayal feel so much worse. Mum always had something withheld about her, something hard-edged, as though she'd dispassionately assess any situation, and definitely consider, though not necessarily act on, what was best for her. Dad, though, Dad was a big old softie. Even now, at thirty, I was sure that if I called him to pick me up because I was stranded somewhere at 2.00 a.m., he'd shoot out of bed saying, 'Stand somewhere that's well lit and I'll be there as soon as I can.' To be fair, Mum would probably come too, but I'd have to suffer a ten-minute interrogation about why I hadn't planned ahead/thought things through. I realised that I'd half-expected Mum to dob me in, that she'd be torn between her friendship with Philippa and her loyalty to me.

But Dad. Dad turncoating on me was like seeing the last buoy from my old life come adrift from its mooring. I'd had total faith that however much he disapproved of my relationship with Andy, however repellent he found it, he would ultimately, reluctantly, be on my side. Actively dumping me in the shit was not what I associated with my father.

'I'm not going to let that lie. He's going to get a piece of my mind when I speak to him.'

Andy grimaced. 'Your dad is very moral. He wouldn't have done it lightly. Sleep on it. Don't go storming in and say things that are difficult to row back from. Your dad is a good man. And he loves you. Very, very much.'

'Snitching to Philippa is a funny way of showing it,' I said, my tone aggressive to disguise the distress that was making my eyes prickle. My dad. My dad had prioritised someone else over me.

'Don't speak to them today,' Andy said. 'Let's get a better sense of the lie of the land with Abigail first.'

I nodded, agreeing solely for the purposes of appearing to be a mature adult who could take a beat to consider the right course of action. But the desire to stab that *Dad* contact on my phone and let rip was thrumming through my entire body.

However, Andy filling me in on Philippa's side of the conversation, her insinuation that Abigail might not want him to walk her down the aisle, obliterated Dad as a target for my rage. 'She thinks Abigail might ask me not to go to the wedding at all,' he said.

I tried so hard never to say a bad word about Philippa, but bad words were all I had to direct towards her in that moment. Tempered by good words about how Abigail absolutely adored Andy, that she'd always been a daddy's girl, and anyway who would she think of replacing him with? I even dropped the F-bomb, which I apologised for, a knee-jerk reaction after years of schooling myself never to say it in front of my parents and their friends. His lips carried the shadow of a smile.

'Philippa will calm down. She always goes off at full tilt when things go belly up, but she gets a grip quickly,' Andy said.

I fought a pang of jealousy – unsuccessfully – at how intimate his knowledge was of her reactions, the sort of understanding that you couldn't rush, that built up over many years. I wanted to leapfrog that step, to be the woman of whom Andy said, 'Oh, that's just how Scarlett is. She can be a bit foul-mouthed, but her heart's in the right place.' I wanted him to *know* me. Properly know me. To celebrate all that he loved about me and shrug his shoulders at everything else, seeing my faults as peripheral inconveniences to all that was funny, caring, rebellious and joyful. I didn't want to have to select a version of myself to present. None of my carefully curated options had led to satisfying relationships before. No man had ever understood that my feistiness was the flip side of fragility. That being capable and self-reliant didn't mean that I would reject an offer of help. That relishing my own independence didn't stop me longing to be included, considered, cared about.

With Andy, I never had to pick a personality. I could just be and he accepted it. And it made me kinder, easier to be around. I wasn't trying to push different facets of my personality, to provoke him into a reaction, to see where the limits were, what I could fight against, where I could prove myself. All that posturing and bravado seemed so pointless. I didn't want to create any tension between us, which was just as well, given how much drama we'd caused elsewhere.

'What else did she say?' I hoped in years to come one of the things that Andy would know about me was that if I had trouble heading my way, I was the opposite of the proverb 'Never trouble trouble until trouble troubles you.' I prided myself on rushing towards conflict in a horned helmet to make sure my aggressors knew I wasn't easily cowed.

He did a long intake of breath. 'She also feels that you shouldn't go to the wedding, and that your parents shouldn't either.'

The rage was immediate. 'That's not up to her! That's up to Abigail! She can whistle if she thinks I'm going to slink away with my tail between my legs.'

It was incredible how all those years of considering Philippa as a second mum, someone I could easily have turned to in a crisis, fell away in an instant. Someone I'd trusted my whole life transforming into an adversary in mere moments.

I carried on, aware that I was having to work hard to stop my voice trembling. 'Mum is Philippa's best friend. She'd be devastated if she couldn't see Abigail get married, she loves Abigail.'

I kept pushing him for more details, unwilling to admit quite how closely I'd been earwigging but infuriated by the sense that he was shielding me from the worst of it. 'I'm not a child. I can deal with the harsh truth of what she said.'

For the first time, he became exasperated. 'Of course I don't think you're a child.' He gestured to me, then to himself. 'I shouldn't have dragged you into this. Perhaps it really is as disgusting as people say.'

I stepped towards him. 'No. No. Don't say that. You're always the one saying that life brings unexpected joy, that we have to be open to recognising it when it presents itself, that sometimes we have to go against received wisdom and be brave. You can regret it if you like. But I don't regret a single second of this. Not a second.'

He pursed his lips and shook his head. 'I bloody love you, Scarlett.' He kissed me and I allowed myself to fold into that moment, the rightness of us amidst the wrongness of it all.

'So what's next?' I asked.

'She's giving me until the end of the week to talk to Abigail, so I need to arrange to see her as soon as possible. I'll call her tomorrow.'

He looked so full of worry that I had a split second when I wished that we'd never got involved, that he'd never had to confront his daughter with things that daughters simply did not want to think about. And there lay the fundamental difference in our situations. Although my parents disapproved of us with every fibre of their beings, I was fairly confident that they would eventually accept whatever made me happy. They might not agree with me being with Andy, they might have felt obliged to take a stand and tell Philippa – a new wave of anger burned as I thought about Dad sneaking on me – but they would be invested in resetting our relationship.

'There's nothing as precious as family,' Mum said, a phrase she used to gloss over any gripe I had with her or Dad, which had the effect of making me want to inflate a careless observation about my life into a full-blown argument. Still, it was a sentiment that had underpinned our family for as long as I could remember. I had to believe that would still hold true.

But Abigail was a different matter. She was embarking on a new life, had someone other than her parents watching out for her. And now, because her mum and dad were separated, she could keep one and cut out the other. She didn't have to put up with what, in her eyes, would be Andy's awful behaviour. He'd done his job, brought her up and she no longer relied on him.

I'd kept putting her reaction to the back of my mind, telling myself that she'd be repulsed at first, but... Actually, I didn't get any further than that. I couldn't see how she'd ever accept it, let alone be pleased for us.

A wave of tiredness washed over me. I marvelled at how I'd catapulted from the responsibility of making sure a couple of cockapoos didn't dash into the road to the pivot around which so many people's happiness revolved.

Andy pulled me into his chest and we stood, puzzling over how to turn our support for each other into something other than destruction beyond our immediate boundaries.

'Have you heard anything from Abigail?' he asked.

I tipped my head back. 'She sent me a text to see if I was free for a drink in a fortnight's time, the bank holiday weekend.'

'Are you going?'

I let my head drop onto his shoulder. 'I haven't responded yet. I might wait until you've had the conversation with her. We're going to have to clear the air before the big day anyway.'

I thought guiltily about how much money she'd spent on my bridesmaid's dress. How carefully she'd planned the colours to contrast with those of Guy's little nieces. 'I'm not having any other grown-up bridesmaids. Just the person I've known all my life.' I'd felt a burst of pride that despite all the women she'd met, all her mates from college and work, I'd hung onto my spot as the best best friend. And now I didn't know whether she'd want to be friends with me at all, let alone the main witness to her 'Until death do us part'. Surely our long history had to count for something.

Yet, unusually, I'd been a coward. With just five weeks to go before the wedding, I would ordinarily have been asking how she was, making jokes about whether she was getting cold feet, but I hadn't. I'd gone quiet, none of the usual WhatsApp banter she would have expected. Everything I half-typed felt duplici-tous, but I could tell she was puzzled by my withdrawal. She probably thought I was being weird because she'd got her life together and I was still living like a student.

Without any discussion, I stayed at Andy's that evening, as though we were afraid that our bravery, our determination might evaporate if we lost sight of one another for a single moment. A melancholy enveloped us, which made us gentle with each other.

'Are you up to this?' He cupped my face in his hands and kissed me.

'I am.' I tried to shore up my voice, but there was a flutter in my throat as I said, 'I am worried how Abigail will react though. What do you think she'll say?'

Andy avoided my gaze as though he could make a good guess but didn't want to air it. 'I don't know.' He shrugged. 'I'm desperate to avoid this overshadowing her day.'

'What if she doesn't want me there at all?' I asked.

Andy squeezed my hand. 'Let's cross that bridge when we come to it. She might not want me there either.'

'She will.'

'I hope you're right. I've always been so fierce about the men she's been out with, so protective of her. I didn't expect to be the man who hurt her.' The pain in his voice made me wince.

Quietly, I said, 'I didn't expect to be the friend who hurt her, either.'

We didn't have an answer for each other. We were both on course to hurt one of the people we loved the most. The ramifications of us choosing each other hovered on the border between terrifying and life-affirming. Everyone's reactions to us were a direct contrast to how Andy had made me feel, as though I'd finally pinpointed my place in the world. A drawing pin in the map that bubbled with exciting possibility, a freedom to be bold but still belong, with a safety net of security.

That night, after we'd made love, with a tenderness that felt different, a desire to acknowledge that there was so much more to us than sexual chemistry, I lay watching the sky grow gradually lighter. I was consumed with the worry of where this unexpected love would take us. And then occasionally, I'd be distracted from the what ifs and catastrophic outcomes, falling into the cliché of a thousand boy band songs to study every millimetre of Andy's face as he slept. I was memorising the curve of his lips, the way the last few hairs on his eyebrow grew in a different direction from the rest, how one side of his hair flicked out and the other curled under.

I ran my finger down my phone screen, with its five missed calls – two from Dad and three from Mum – plus the text message *Scarlett, we need to talk. Please call us as soon as possible.* I allowed myself to think the unthinkable: it would be so ironic if my love for Andy made me leave rather than stay.

16

JACKIE

When I came downstairs the next morning, my eyes had acquired several layers of baggy flesh from crying all night until water leaked into my ears. Ian was sitting at the table, reading the newspaper and the sight of this normality, of doing what he always did on a day when my whole world had imploded, made me understand how easy it was to cross the fine line from love to hate. The vindictive thoughts that crowded into my head were so disproportionate. I was fantasising about surprising him with divorce papers and a list of what I'd be taking with me when the house was sold. In that moment, they seemed so valid, I had to stop myself logging into Rightmove to start searching for cosy cottages by the sea.

'Have you spoken to Scarlett yet?' I asked, knowing that it was unlikely at 7.15 a.m. on a Sunday but intending to make a point about the urgency he'd created, that owing to his choices we needed to warn our daughter that her cover had been blown. I also wanted to do that thing that seeped into the long marriage dance: ask a question that was not going to deliver the right answer in order to increase the range of topics to shout about.

Ian was wise to this strategy and cut me off at the pass with a logical plan. 'I'm going to call her at nine o'clock. She won't be up yet and I won't get any sense out of her if she's just woken up.'

I ignored his answer, wanting to punish him with my anger, but instead I was reduced to peeling off bits of kitchen roll to stem the tears that were refusing to stop.

Ian got up. 'Jackie, I hate to see you like this. Please.'

'You made it happen.'

He shook his head. 'I didn't, love. You know that's not fair. I accept that I've moved things on a bit, but I am not the cause of this. Philippa will think about it and realise that you were in an impossible situation.'

'How were you expecting her to react?'

He sighed. 'The way she did. She would have found out at some point. And the longer we left it, the more betrayed she would have felt.'

I waved my hand at him. 'Spare me. I cannot sit through you justifying your unilateral decision to blow everyone's life apart.'

'I did not blow everyone's life apart. That was down to Scarlett and Andrew. I simply decided not to go along with the lie.' I'd never heard Ian sound so furious. He was a man who never yelled. The volume of his response made me jump, then made me retaliate in kind until the cords in my throat vibrated with the exertion.

'Well, Mr Non-Collaborator, you also need to crack on with giving Scarlett the heads-up that a pile of stinking shit is heading her way. Or does your conscience stop at looking after Philippa and Abigail, rather than your own daughter?'

The expression on Ian's face reminded me of a dog curling its lip before it launched a full-scale attack. But he turned round and started to walk out of the kitchen, saying, 'I'll deal with it, of course I will,' his voice once again calm and moderate as though his former outburst had shocked him.

I, on the other hand, was too far gone in my rage – or maybe my hurt – to acknowledge we needed time, with no one speaking, to digest what had happened and regroup. Logic had left me. I wanted to provoke a reaction from him that I could throw myself against like a desperate deer trapped behind a fence. My whole body was rigid with the desire to up the stakes to a height from which we'd be lucky to return.

I chased after him into the hallway. 'It must be so bloody wonderful to be so perfect. To never cock things up so spectacularly that whatever you do for the rest of your life that is the one thing that people remember about you. "You'll deal with it." Of course you will. Did you forget to add, "Just like I always do"?'

Ian came to a halt at the bottom of the stairs, put his hand on the newel post and swivelled around to face me. 'Jackie, this isn't about you.'

With all my senses rearing up like angry bears, I heard his words as dismissive, as though he alone knew the truth of every situation in our family and I was endlessly on the periphery, frantically trying to gather together clues, to react in the right way and prove my worth. Maybe he intended to reassure me that he didn't see any link between what had happened all those years ago and the current situation. Or maybe he intended to lob his own artillery shell into whatever warped battle was going on here.

Just briefly, the words I'd vowed never to say twisted into a poisonous dart. I closed my eyes. No. Not ever.

Nonetheless, I opened my mouth to retaliate, assembling lesser remarks that would still land, spike first, to pierce this assumption of superiority. Even after he'd seen Philippa's reaction and her wrath, witnessed the damage to our friendship, he was still exuding the conviction that he'd acted in the only way possible. I'd felt like that once. Total certainty that what I was doing was right when I couldn't have been more wrong. And here I was, still paying the price, all these decades later.

Ian put his hand up to silence me in a manner that made me want to rush towards him and sink my teeth into the flesh of his palm. 'Don't. No good is going to come from discussing this now. I suggest we wait until I've spoken to Scarlett and we've calmed down a bit.'

He carried on upstairs.

I clung onto the last shred of sanity that was stopping me from charging after him. With great effort, I resisted the temptation to engage – nearly – every possible tactic to taunt him into a row that would excavate the marital burial ground where every last resentment went to die. Or ferment.

I turned around and walked back into the kitchen, feeling adrenaline drain away and a flood of despair take its place. There was only one other time in my life when I'd felt more disconnected from my husband.

I strained my ears as I heard Ian's footsteps in our bedroom. His methodical nature, his resolve not to call our daughter until 9.00 a.m. was more than I could stand. I was on the verge of flying up the stairs to demand that he phoned Scarlett *now* when my mobile rang, making me start. Scarlett.

I didn't even manage to say hello before she launched in. 'Well, thanks a lot for telling Philippa. What part of "wait till after the wedding" didn't you hear?'

I'd had years of training myself not to react to Scarlett's brusque manner, to ignore her until she was prepared to talk to me in a civilised way. But today, I needed an outlet for my bad mood and I simply couldn't be bothered to be the bigger person.

'I didn't tell her. Dad did. I didn't want him to, but he wouldn't listen to me.' I shouldn't have blamed Ian so whole-heartedly, but in the family narrative, I was always the bad guy. The one spoiling things by worrying too much or deeming something too expensive, or apparently 'sucking the joy out of everything' by wanting to pin down details of family events. Not unreasonable ones in my view, such as what time Scarlett and a random partner might arrive, or whether or not they were expecting food. And, frankly, I wasn't prepared to take the rap for something I hadn't agreed with and for which I was already up to my neck managing the fallout with Philippa.

Scarlett grunted. 'Did you try to stop him?'

I couldn't bring myself to attempt to correct whatever version of events she'd decided on in her head. 'Oh grow up, Scarlett. The issue here is not what we have or have not done. You've chosen to embark on a relationship that was always going to be contentious and we're not going to take responsibility for the consequences.'

'I'm not expecting you to.' To my surprise, her tone had dialled down a notch, as though she did understand the magnitude of what she'd done. Maybe I should have snapped back more often. 'I just hoped that you'd allow us to dictate our own timeline.'

'Are you okay, though?' I asked, a distant part of my brain remarking on the fact that she was much less hostile and accusatory than I'd expected. Andrew's steadying influence maybe? Or the fact that Ian – the golden parent – was responsible for this debacle, not me? Despite everything, I wanted to ask if Andrew was all right, how he'd reacted, whether he and Scarlett were still united in their determination to stay on what surely had to be a sinking ship.

'Yeah. Just waiting to see what Abigail says. Philippa suggested that she won't want me to be chief bridesmaid. Or one at all, possibly.' Her voice sounded resigned and sad.

'It's not up to Philippa.' Even now, I wanted to insulate Scarlett from the hurt of Abigail's reaction. 'I mean, it would be a bit understandable in the circumstances...'

'I know.'

There was a silence.

'Andy is going to meet her tonight to tell her.'

For a moment, I was transported back in time, to when Scarlett competed in drama festivals in primary school and used to say, 'What if I forget my words?' and my response was always, 'It will be just a moment in time that no one will ever think about again and we will all still love you anyway.'

Unfortunately, this wasn't going to be a moment in time. Unless Scarlett and Andrew realised that this was a hiding to hell sooner rather than later, this was a drama that was going to run and run. But with great clarity, I knew that whatever happened, Ian and I would still love her anyway.

'Will you let me know how it goes?' I waited but she didn't reply. 'I know you think we're judging you, darling...'

Before I got the rest of the sentence out, she said, 'You are. Everyone is.'

'That's not what I wanted to say. I wanted to be really clear that we can cope with whatever the outcome is, that you can always talk to us. Don't ever feel isolated, or that we won't help you.'

The pause on the other end was so long, I wondered if we'd been cut off.

'Scarlett?'

A murmur indicated she was still there.

'If this does turn out to be a mistake – and I'm absolutely not saying it is, though I'm not going to deny this is a difficult path you've chosen – don't get so entrenched that you feel you've got no choice but to continue with it.'

If only I could be honest with her. If only I could tell her that any mistake she might make would pale into insignificance if she knew the extent of mine.

And that there was always a way back.

17

No one was coming for me. How little my presence in anybody's life had mattered. I'd been forgotten about, washed away like footsteps in the sand. The realisation carried with it a mixture of liberation and profound loneliness. For months, I'd been sleeping on red alert, attuned to every rustle, every footstep in the corridor, every thud or rattle against my door in the early hours. I paused before I stepped out for work every morning, wondering if this was the day someone would be waiting to surprise me, the day my manager would beckon me in: 'There's someone here to see you.' A policeman. A psychiatrist. Him. Her.

Did I want that? Would even a policeman or a psychiatrist be a relief? A chance to release this guilt and shame and perhaps one day make amends. The idea of being able to explain – not justify, of course – but to offer my side of the story seemed fanciful, the far-fetched product of a mind yearning for peace.

Every day, I forced myself to focus on the future, listing what might help me rediscover joy. Joy. A word that conjured up sunshine and snowdrops and snatched kisses and dancing in the kitchen – and love – in all of its sparkling, unwieldy, infuriating forms.

I had no idea how to navigate from where I was to touching distance of contentment, let alone joy. And whatever future, whatever daffodil-filled garden or cottage covered with roses I compelled my mind to envisage, there was always a dark shadow at the centre of the scene. Perhaps I'd already used up my precious allocation of joy, in this life anyway. Maybe that ghostly clutch at my heart would be my punishment every time I saw a pram. Or observed an intimate gesture of love, a glove picked up, a scarf tucked in, a lingering glance backwards after a goodbye. Or witnessed two women leaning into each other, their eyes glittering conspiratorially, their words a secret code mastered over many years. Perhaps I'd never experience those things again.

I only had myself to blame.

18

JACKIE

Three weeks after that hideous Saturday, I still hadn't received a definitive answer about what was happening with Scarlett. Our exchanges were totally unsatisfactory, with any attempt to probe – 'Have you managed to speak to Abigail?' – responded to with infuriating vagueness.

'We're working things out. Don't worry.'

The flippancy of that: the last time I hadn't worried about Scarlett was before she was conceived.

Some days I'd gone into the office rather than work from home, purely to limit the amount of time I could spend tapping out, then deleting, texts to Philippa and Scarlett. But, as luck would have it, today my iPhone decided to torture me by flashing up a photo memory of this September day last year, Philippa's birthday. We'd rented a cottage in Whitstable and Abigail, Philippa and Andrew had come down for the day to celebrate. It was beautiful end-of-summer weather, a mixture of warm sun with a sharp breeze. We decided our location was so fabulous that we'd do a lunch outside on the little beachfront patio instead of going out. You couldn't keep Andrew out of the water, and although it was chilly, he'd insisted on going for a swim and taking a selfie bare-chested while the rest of us sat wrapped up in our coats. We were all crowding behind Andrew, laughing as he did his impression of Popeye.

I stared at the screen, oddly furious with myself, with everyone in the photo, for not foreseeing this catastrophe. The naivety of us, frivolously caught up in the moment, with no sense of what lay ahead. Well, only Philippa, who'd been saying for a while that she and Andrew had been having a few discussions about what retirement might look like. That sometimes she felt that the marriage had run its course, that now Abigail was grown up, they should perhaps accept their different views of the future. 'We don't have to fall out. We'll always be friends, but there's no way I'm going off trekking around South America. I get stressed about missing the last train back from London and whether I'll need the loo.'

I hadn't taken her seriously, shrugging and saying that all long marriages were a compromise. If she didn't want to go with him, surely he could go on one of these group holidays made for – what was that horrible phrase? – silver surfers?

Philippa and Andrew were exactly that: Philippa and Andrew. They came as a package. And now they didn't and the whole of the universe had spun out of kilter.

I studied my arm thrown so casually around Philippa's shoulders, a gesture repeated thousands of times through the years, without stopping to consider whether she would shrink from my touch, shrug me off. Unlike now.

The difference a year made. Her birthday again today. Twenty-one days since the whole debacle and I still hadn't seen her. I'd rung several times and she never picked up. Eventually, I'd texted, overthinking every single word I typed out. Usually I flung out any old message, often resorting to that long-friendship shorthand that didn't bother dressing anything up with words like 'I wondered', 'Would you mind'. Instead I was straight in with 'Can you?', 'Do you want?', 'You going to...?',

'Pick me up some...' I usually managed a please or thank you, but I also didn't give it a thought if I pressed send too soon before I'd remembered my manners.

And now, for the first time, I was crafting messages, fretting over my choice of words, trying to find the right path between conciliatory towards Philippa but not overtly critical of Scarlett. Whatever I thought privately, I was not going to express publicly. I already sensed that my daughter would be considered the main antagonist. That she would carry far more of the blame and shame than Andrew, the man who most definitely could not use youthful inexperience as his excuse. But alongside those considerations, I had to work hard to stop desperation seeping in. The chilliness between us was like an open wound, the first thing I thought about in the morning and the last thing my mind picked away at before I fell asleep.

Philippa had ignored my messages, my *You probably need a bit of space, but please know that I never wanted to hurt you. Give me a shout when you feel ready to speak to me. Love you.* I could see she'd read them, though, and it killed me that she knew how anxious I'd be but wouldn't even send me a holding message, a 'not now but soon'.

I was shackled to my phone. Picking it up every five minutes, willing a forgiving response to appear. Or if that wasn't possible, any reaction, so I could stop wondering what she was thinking, where she stood now she'd had a chance to process, and presumably to talk to Andrew and Abigail.

Some days I'd felt as though my heart was breaking in a way I'd never suffered with any boyfriend. A misery so deep, it was visceral. And edged with disappointment that after banking so many good deeds big and small over the years, that when complex allegiances had prevented me from acting solely in Philippa's interests, she'd chosen to think the worst of me. To blame me for something that was out of my control. When Kenny Rogers' song 'You Can't Make Old Friends' had come on the radio, I'd sat at the kitchen table and cried. It was unthinkable that she might sever all ties with me.

I didn't have to explain anything to her – she'd lived my history alongside me. She'd known my mum was obsessed with dieting and laughed hysterically instead of getting offended when she used to greet Philippa with, 'You've filled out.' She'd charmed my dad into checking the tyres and oil on her heap of a Vauxhall Corsa when she'd passed her test. Long after we'd left home, he'd still nip out whenever she went to visit them to ensure everything was in order.

When I said, 'Let's not do a brandy and Babycham' to signal that opening another bottle of wine would be a bad idea, we were both immediately transported to throwing up in my parents' avocado bathroom aged fifteen. Philippa in the loo, me in the bidet, after we'd investigated the contents of their cocktail cabinet when they were out. And that was before we'd gone through all the child-rearing years, the bacteria-infested ball pits and animal petting farms made bearable by her company. We'd been each other's safety valves throughout our daughters' teenage years and beyond. It was down to her that I'd moved back to the small market town in Surrey where we'd grown up. 'I know it feels like a backward step returning here, but it's a fresh start in other ways – no one has to know anything about what happened.'

Yet today, I had no idea what she was doing for her birthday, despite texting to say I was available for coffee and cake, lunch or dinner if she didn't have a better offer. Maybe she'd gone out with Abigail. I flipped open my laptop and logged onto Instagram. Abigail would definitely have taken a selfie of them both. But the last post was of her emptying the bins at Guy's café. #AllHandsOnDeck.

Like a dieter seeking out a hidden chocolate biscuit, I scoured social media for clues. Facebook delivered what I was searching for – a photo of Philippa celebrating at the house of a woman we knew from our kids' secondary school. A jolly group of mums from Abigail's year. I no longer remembered why I'd always been included in their events, even though Scarlett was in a different school year. But I was. Not any more.

The hurt was instant. A jealous pang of exclusion, no less intense at fifty-seven than it had been at fifteen, just more shameful, as though considering a friend 'your territory' was something that you should have grown out of. I hadn't actively deliberated about whether Philippa was my territory because everyone else was so far down the pecking order there was no need to. We were a solid duo, universally accepted as best friends among the people who knew both of us. It wasn't even that we went everywhere together, it was more that we embraced the opportunity when we could for the sheer joy of the after-event debrief.

I stared at the screen, clocking the faces of all the people who might be potential replacements as her wing woman.

Ian came in while I was leaning into my laptop, resorting to playground insults in my mind. *Oh, bet she's having fun sitting next to Alison. Please do tell me about your bunion surgery. Of course, Fran, my sole reason for being here is to hear about your lactose-intolerant granddaughter, especially the effect it has on her bowels.*

'Why are you hunched over the screen like that? You'll give yourself arthritis of the neck.'

I did what I'd been doing for the last few weeks: responded to an innocuous comment with a sour remark. 'I'm just looking at the friends that Philippa has shipped in to replace me. Having a lovely time on her birthday, despite ignoring my offer of taking her out.'

Ian didn't look contrite. Nor did he say – again – 'She'll come round. It's not you she's angry with. She loves you. She'd miss you way too much. Give her a couple of weeks and she'll be round here with a bottle of Picpoul before you know it.' He simply sighed and went upstairs.

I carried on snooping about on Facebook, seeing if any of the others had posted photos on their feed, a sick feeling of jealousy in my stomach that they might usurp me, sliding into my best friend slot.

Ian reappeared in the kitchen doorway and stood still in that irritating way he had, not speaking but hovering, waiting for me to stop what I was doing and give him my full attention. Reluctantly, I looked up.

'I've booked myself into a hotel to give us both a bit of breathing space. I've got some big meetings I need to prepare for and I can't concentrate here, this whole thing is really getting me down.'

'What? You're going now? On a Saturday?' I made a noise that sounded like a laugh but was at the opposite end of the spectrum from anything approaching amusement. 'The whole thing is getting you down? That's rich coming from you. I thought embracing your integrity and honesty would make you feel so much better. But instead your solution is to jump ship?'

'Jackie, please don't. I am really sorry that you're upset. I'm sorry that Philippa reacted like that. I'm sorry that Scarlett's furious. I wish none of this had ever happened. But me getting sacked for non-performance isn't going to help anything. I've got so much to do. I'd have to work this weekend anyway. This Friday, we've got the whole American contingent flying over to brainstorm how to boost profits and I'm on the spot to present for the whole team. I can't let them down.'

He walked towards me. His gait was slow, as though he was dragging himself through life. None of the energy that I associated with him, the man who couldn't sit still, always tinkering about in the garage, fixing bits of broken fence or jetwashing the patio. He did have bags under his eyes and the wrinkles on his forehead were so deep they were diagonal – the face of an old man who'd seen too much.

My fury dissipated a fraction. 'I don't want to be this angry. I really don't.'

He stepped closer until he was standing right at the side of me. I wanted to lean my head into his stomach, to have him make everything okay. Or at least tell me that it would be. To give me hope that, in a year, we'd look up over dinner one evening and say, 'Wow. September already. That was a tough year, but we've survived.'

He kissed the top of my head. 'I just need a few days to prepare properly. I can't afford to mess this up.'

I didn't move, didn't speak, as he turned and walked out. Out of a petulant desire to punish him for forcing the issue on a timeline that he alone had decided, I didn't want him to know yet that I was softening. I wasn't so stupid as to believe that none of this would ever have happened. One way or another, the news was going to hit and it was never going to be pretty.

As soon as I heard his car reverse off the drive, I wanted to run out to the street and wave wildly to make him come back. The loneliness of being in the house on my own, without the person I'd relied on for the last thirty-three years, engulfed me. It was as though my home knew the difference between Ian going out for a curry with the lads and Ian making a conscious decision to put some distance between us, in a way he never had, even after I'd failed him so badly.

I picked up my phone to text him, to tap out some conciliatory words that would allow him to concentrate on work, that would offer a semblance of a bridge between us.

But my eye was drawn to a message from Philippa.

I don't know how to say this because it feels vindictive, and I promise you it's not meant to be, but I don't think you, Ian and Scarlett should come to the wedding. Feelings are inevitably

running high at the moment and I don't think it's possible to
navigate it all without spoiling Abigail's day, which has to be
the priority. I'm sorry to send this in a text, but every time I
think about it, it makes me cry, and with the wedding a fort-
night today, I wanted to give you as much notice as possible.

I gasped. The shock made my stomach jolt. I stared at the
screen. She'd chosen her birthday to disinvite me from the
wedding. I'd listened to every last detail from the moment Guy
had presented Abigail with that ring. I was supposed to be
making her wedding cake. That was my special gift to her. 'You
know that I will mix every last bit of it with love.' Abigail had
WhatsApped me so many photos of ones she'd liked the look of,
from rose petal-strewn creations to towers of Victoria sponge.
We'd eventually settled on a simple two-tier cake studded with
pressed, edible flowers in a nod to their love of nature and all
things organic.

Were they still expecting me to rock up to the venue with
my cake and hand it over at the door, shouting instructions
about keeping it somewhere cool? Who would look after Philippa's elderly mother now, sit with her, take her to the loo? I
wondered who she was replacing me with. Whose eye Philippa
would catch when help was needed. Who she'd quietly beckon
to the ladies' for a mid-wedding breakfast vent about Guy's
haughty mother.

And Abigail. Did she really not want us there? Had
Philippa had this discussion with her or had she decided unilat-
erally to boot us out? I could understand why Abigail wouldn't
want to run the risk of seeing her father lock eyes with Scarlett
when they thought no one was watching. Or witness a brush of
their hands as they passed each other, gazes averted. How repulsive the idea of her father having sex at all might be, let alone
with her best friend. But Ian and I hadn't caused this or encouraged it. Philippa had to be leading the way on this one.

This was not a conversation I was going to have on text. I picked up the gift I'd been intending to drop round later anyway and headed out.

As I reversed onto the road, all the things I'd been longing to say, the hundreds of small injuries long friendships sustain and recover from, were flowing through my brain. The times when she'd let me down, trivialising extremely stressful periods at work, dismissing my very real worries about how lonely Scarlett might be in London – 'We were all lonely at that age.'

By the time I reached her house, I was defaulting to the inconvenient wisdom of my husband: 'Hang on a minute, what do you want the outcome to be?' The desire to hurt her back in the way she'd hurt me paled into insignificance compared with my need for her to be my friend again. My anchor in all the ebbing and flowing of other lesser people – the ones who floated alongside me through a short stage of life but whose absence I barely noticed when the tide pushed them down a different fork.

I strode up the drive and rang the bell, fearing for a moment that she might peer out of the window and refuse to open the door.

She appeared immediately. 'You got my message then?' she said, as she stepped aside to let me in.

I strained to decipher whether her voice held warmth, despite her disappointment in me. Or embarrassment that, unlike her, I was brave enough to get eyeball to eyeball instead of hiding behind a text. Or was it hostility? I didn't know.

I thrust my present at her and said, 'I was coming round anyway, to give you this.'

She looked down as though she'd completely forgotten it was her birthday, then muttered a thank you, while I resisted the temptation to ask if she'd had a lovely lunch because I wouldn't be able to keep the resentment out of my voice.

I waited to be shown into the kitchen, a strange formality

already blooming between us. I took a seat, fighting against the feeling that I no longer was in the category of friend who could make herself at home, who could bustle about putting the kettle on or say, 'You got any choccies?'

Philippa stood pressing both her hands on the kitchen island. Immediately, her eyes filled with tears. I got up and pulled her into my arms and we stood there, sobbing like a couple of idiots. 'Abigail is so upset,' she said. 'She's threatening to have Guy's father walk her down the aisle and to not let Andrew sit on the top table. When I spoke to her yesterday, she was on the verge of banning him from the wedding completely.' She swiped at her face. 'This is supposed to be the happiest day of her life and two of the people she loves the most have ruined it for her. It's just so selfish of them.'

I totally agreed, had always been of the opinion that there were plenty of people, not just one single person in the world that we were capable of falling in love with. Nevertheless, I still struggled to smother my desire to defend Scarlett. To not shift eighty per cent of the blame onto Andrew, with the mitigating circumstances of immaturity and the ability to be easily influenced accounting for Scarlett's twenty per cent. Even though, when I looked deep into my heart, I was aware that Scarlett knew her own mind and did exactly as she pleased.

'I'm sorry it's turned out like this. I haven't managed to speak to Scarlett recently,' I said, realising that perhaps I should have turned up at Scarlett's (Andrew's?) door to make sure that she was okay, just like I had with Philippa. I was trusting Andrew to take care of her. Even though I was so furious with him, I was certain he would. With a rush of surprise, I recognised that the constant thrum of anxiety that buzzed away in the background around whether Scarlett was safe walking home at night, whether she was underselling herself in the work she did, whether she was lonely at weekends, had calmed. Although I disapproved so completely of what they had done, I knew that

Andrew – a mature, capable grown-up – was looking out for her. I decided not to share that revelation with Philippa.

Philippa walked over to the kitchen roll and blew her nose. 'I still can't believe it. Andrew flat-out denies that they were having an affair at Christmas, but I'm not convinced.'

'No. No. Definitely not,' I said, without even stopping to mine my memories for giveaway signs.

'How do you know?' she asked. 'How can you be sure?'

'Neither of them would have done that to you. Andrew has never ever shown any sign of being unfaithful to you. He's not even particularly flirtatious.'

'I keep thinking about them going on all those long runs. Just feel like they were plotting behind my back and laughing at how I was feeling guilty about ending my marriage when all the time I was falling nicely into their trap.'

'That is not what happened. That's hindsight kicking in, but it's not reality.'

Philippa pulled her lips into a shape that strongly suggested she'd made up her mind about that and wasn't going to be dissuaded. Her face crumpled. 'But the thing that hurts the most, that absolutely kills me, is that you've known about this for so long and you let me make a complete fool of myself. I don't think I've been more upset by anyone's behaviour ever.'

Backwards and forwards we went with accusations from her, apologies and excuses from me, without a resolution. I asked for a glass of water. My throat was dry, as though I'd used all the liquid in my body for tears.

Eventually, I tried to move the conversation forwards. 'So, do you really not want Ian and me to attend the wedding? What does Abigail say? What about the cake? And your mum?'

Philippa tucked a tissue into her sleeve. 'She's adamant that Scarlett can't come. She's going to have Janine as her chief bridesmaid instead.'

'That's such a shame,' I said, breathing out to steady my

voice. My poor daughter. I wanted to be at that wedding so there was at least one person in the room who had her back in her absence. I hated the idea of everyone talking about her, maybe even taking glee in her exclusion. Over the years, her outspokenness had earned her affection and disapproval in equal quantities. Abigail, however, had always understood her, her black-and-white thinking, her disdain for pomposity and self-aggrandisement of any sort.

'I'm sure you didn't expect Abigail to shrug her shoulders and shuffle the place settings on the top table so Andrew could sit next to his new girlfriend.'

There was no disguising the hostility in Philippa's voice and although I sympathised, the cattiness put my back up.

I got to my feet. 'No. I didn't expect that,' I said, a harsh and defensive edge in my own response. My mind jumped to the fact that Janine was about six inches shorter than Scarlett and I could well imagine the face of the woman in the wedding dress shop when called upon to rustle up alterations at this late stage. Good. It would appear that I wasn't immune from my own dose of bitchiness. It was astonishing how quickly all impartiality faded when children, even adult ones who'd royally messed up, were in the mix.

Philippa ran her fingers up and down the smooth edge of the granite island. 'Abigail would probably be okay with you and Ian coming. I'll talk to her again.'

Childishly, I wanted to say, 'Forget it. If you two want to punish us for something Scarlett's done, crack on. I don't need a pity invite.' I couldn't stand this feeling of begging about for Philippa and Abigail's largesse to include us. The words, 'And you can whistle for muggins here baking the cake,' were sitting right at the front of my mouth, an alphabet soup of unkindness.

Instead, I said, 'I've got to go. Will you let me know whether Abigail still wants me to do the cake?' Petty, mean-spirited me wanted to stipulate that I wasn't going to waste my time if we were banned from the wedding. But the me who was so proud of Abigail, in absolute awe of how hard she'd worked to qualify as a midwife, wanted to apologise for Scarlett, to tell her that I completely understood why she wouldn't want any of us there.

I said goodbye to Philippa, sensing that as the minutes had ticked by my presence had reminded her of my betrayal and distilled her anger into something even more potent. I tried one last time to argue my case.

As I left I said, 'I can see why you felt let down that I didn't come straight to you as soon as I'd found out. But if the boot had been on the other foot, say, Abigail with Ian' – the very thought made me sick – 'do you think you wouldn't have tried to get her to see sense and knock the whole thing on the head before you came rushing to me? It's impossible to do the right thing.'

'I would have come straight to you. I would have taken the view that Abigail had to take responsibility for her own actions but that you didn't deserve to be lied to.'

I raised my hands in surrender. 'Easy to talk the talk, but much much harder to walk the walk. Let's hope you're never put to a similar test of integrity.'

I knew in that moment I'd made a mistake.

Her face hardened. 'I was. Thirty years ago. I think I proved myself to be an excellent friend.'

19

SCARLETT

I'd had worse Sundays in my life. I was sure of it. It's just that I couldn't remember when. The look on Andy's face when he came home from dinner with Abigail scared me. This man, with solutions, with ideas, with drive and optimism, looked so broken.

'She left after the starter. Blew up at me because I didn't send Philippa a card for her birthday yesterday. She's asked Guy's father to give her away. She doesn't want me to go to the wedding, says it will just be a distraction because everyone will be talking about us.'

I didn't say anything. Every sentence I thought about uttering seemed far too flimsy for the weight of what had happened. I didn't even dare approach him, afraid that he might confuse offering comfort with a demand for my own reassurance that this was still a price he was prepared to pay.

I'd feared this might happen, embraced the possibility in the dark hours when my mind scratched away at how much pain we'd caused and were likely to receive in retaliation. But I'd honestly believed that after I hadn't put up a fight about being stripped of my bridesmaid duties and being banned from the wedding, Abigail would load the blame onto me and somehow allow Andy his role. The one that he deserved because he had been – and still was – a great dad. I was frightened to imagine the extent of his heartache. Terrified to examine whether he thought I was worth it. Because that, in the end, is what it came down to. Was I enough? Did I merit him withstanding the fracturing of his relationship with Abigail, a gamble on the uncertain prospect that time would build a bridge and bring them back together?

The only way I was surviving the memory of the short meeting I'd had with Abigail was to blank it out. Anger wasn't her style; she'd gone for the quiet, unfathomable disbelief. The 'I'm not sure our friendship and your relationship with my father are compatible'. A whole history of partying, sharing secrets, plaiting each other's hair, sitting in comfortable silence, being the port in any storm, erased in that one afternoon. My kind and gentle friend, who always saw the best in everyone to a degree that I found remarkable, wasn't seeing the best in me now. Just the cuckoo in the nest who'd done a despicable dirty on her family – a betrayal that refused to feel like a betrayal.

No matter how hard I forced my brain to accept what a terrible thing we'd done, I still felt as though I'd stepped into a narrow shaft of sunlight in a dark room when I spotted him coming along the street. But I couldn't blame Abigail for not wanting to hear my explanation, that the place where I'd finally come to land after all these years of whirling about like an autumn leaf was with her father.

Nonetheless, her absence weighed on me, a dull ache like a bruise that I kept pressing on. It was bizarre how much I missed someone that I only saw every six weeks or so, sometimes much longer when life ran away with us. Still, it was astonishing how often I thought of her, wanted to ask her something – nothing important, the name of a poet we'd seen on Instagram, a pub we'd stayed at in Edinburgh, whether it was her grandmother or mine who grew hydrangeas. She was a standard-bearer for my history. And now she'd finished with me, if that was the right terminology for the end of a friendship.

Briefly, I considered how so little import was given to the ending of friendships, that there wasn't even a comparable term to divorce. Whatever the name for it, it was brutal and agonising.

Andy flopped into an armchair.

'Drink?'

He nodded.

I poured some wine and handed it to him, sitting on the arm and stroking his hair back from his face. 'I'm sorry.'

'You've got nothing to be sorry for.'

'I am sorry, though. I'm certain – absolutely certain – that Abigail loves you. Do you think Philippa is in her ear on this?'

He blew out, the air ruffling his fringe. 'I'm not sure. It's complicated by the fact that you're her friend. I think if you were just young but we didn't know each other's families, she might find it more bearable. Who knows?'

'Are there any circumstances in which she might change her mind?' I wanted to suck the words back in as soon as I said them.

He smiled then, his eyes softening. 'If we split up, do you mean?'

I nodded, not wanting to know the answer.

'Moot point.'

I wasn't brave enough to dig any further.

He tried so hard to keep the depth of his sadness from me, telling me that he'd felt more alive in the last few months than in the past ten years. That despite all the upheaval, he believed there were good times ahead. That, undeniably, this was all very tough, but he was up for the fight if I was. He never put me under pressure, made it clear I had a choice to leave – 'I won't hold you to it, though. I don't want you to saddle yourself with an old man if you get a better offer.'

I swatted at his hand – 'I'm not looking for a better offer. I want you. I love you.'

He grabbed my fingers, squeezed them as though reminding himself that, despite all the angst, there was so much love between us too. A ferocious amount that made us want to stand up to the world and all the naysayers.

Over the next few days, however, I witnessed a grief so intense, the way he had to clear his throat before he could say Abigail's name, the lines around his eyes tight as though if he let his face relax, misery would melt his features. I practised the words all week. When he came through the door after work on Friday, he looked so dejected that his whole body seemed weighted down, nothing like the athletic and energetic man who'd embarked on this ill-fated love affair with me six months ago. I knew then that tonight was the last time we'd ever make love. The last time my heart would ever feel the ecstasy of loving completely while preparing for the agony of loss. The only time I'd ever love someone enough to leave them.

20

JACKIE

The week that Ian was staying in a hotel gave me an insight into how long the evenings would be if I lived on my own permanently. Even on the days that I went into the office, I was home by six. The four and a half hours before bedtime seemed to last forever, in direct contrast to how they flew by when Ian was here and I was still hanging out washing at eleven o'clock at night. But there was also a certain freedom in eating Marmite on toast instead of feeling obliged to cook. In watching cheesy romcoms with corny titles such as *Love and Gelato*. In being able to listen to my audiobook without having to take off my headphones every time Ian spoke. I could see the attraction of being single but also that the allure might tarnish considerably in six months' time.

Undeniably though, I viewed his absence as a hiatus, a reset when he'd concentrate on work, move back home and we'd start that slow thawing until spilling the beans to Philippa against my wishes became something that was only dredged up in the worst of future rows.

On Friday, the day of his presentation, when I expected him home in the evening, I made his favourite fish pie as the first rung on the ladder to a truce. So much easier to smooth the path to peace with food rather than offer or accept an apology out loud.

I'd just taken it out of the oven when he texted me.

'I've booked a few more days in an Airbnb – things didn't go well today and the whole team will be working long hours to get back on track. They're relying on me to steer us through this and I can't afford to be distracted.'

I felt like driving round to his office and flinging the fish pie in his face. What a wonderful thing to create unholy chaos and then book yourself some peace and quiet to concentrate on your own priorities while everyone else flounders about in the aftermath.

I rang him.

His voice was flat and monotone and, despite everything, I felt a burst of concern. 'Are you all right?'

'A bit battered. We're on the verge of losing a big supplier, because one of the team tried to screw their margins down to the wire and they've called our bluff.'

'So you do actually need to work, this isn't just some ploy to get me used to living on my own before you divorce me?' I laughed as I said it, as though it was unthinkable.

'No. I need to work.' Matter-of-fact. Devoid of warmth. I heard voices in the background. 'I've got to go.'

He hung up. I was left with a sense of him saying the right words, yet me not feeling the slightest bit reassured.

In the old days, I'd have packed a toothbrush and some underwear and driven over to Philippa's with a bottle of wine and all the cheese in my fridge. But, instead, I sat scrolling through my phone, assessing and dismissing my other friends as possible sounding boards. I couldn't trust them with the intricacies of my marriage and family.

The following day, I'd reached a stage of unsettled that had me eyeing my car keys and pondering the wisdom of storming into Ian's office – would it even be open at the weekend? – to double-check he was where he said he'd be. He'd never given me any reason not to trust him, but my view of what I could take for granted was no longer so robust since the Andrew-Scarlett fiasco. I weighed up that course of action versus a salted caramel ice cream spree, another episode of *Slow Horses* and the rest of the bottle of Shiraz. And as though I'd manifested her into existence, in the early evening, a WhatsApp message arrived from Philippa.

> *I guess you've heard the news. Abigail is very happy for you and Ian to come to the wedding and would be really grateful if you could still do the cake. Let's catch up soon xx*

I frowned at the screen. What news? That Abigail was happy for us to go to the wedding? I puzzled over the friendly, almost expansive tone. It was a direct contrast to the monosyllabic or non-committal texts I'd had in the last couple of weeks any time that I'd sent a little message with a 'How are you doing?/Let me know if I can help with any organising even if we don't come to the wedding.'

I'd eaten humble pie, apologised profusely, begged forgiveness. Yet only now was there any sign of a defrosting towards me. I rang her.

Her tone was neutral but not unfriendly. 'Hi. That was quick. Were you doomscrolling?'

Philippa never understood how I could spend so much time reading about politics and scrutinising the opinions of random strangers on X.

'No, I don't need to doomscroll. Real life is shit enough,' I said, in the hope of making her laugh. Which gratifyingly she did.

I didn't want to ask outright what the news was, didn't want to admit to the fact that I was the last person to find out anything at the moment. Even to the extent that I wasn't sure what my husband was doing or thinking or whether he'd in fact left me but just hadn't told me yet. I felt a spike of sadness at that realisation; pride had never entered into my relationship with Philippa before. It had always been the opposite: plumbing the depths of our humiliation in order to find the humour.

Except that one time. Neither of us had ever managed to see the funny side of that. Nor had we tried to.

So I opted for a cheery 'Delighted that Abigail is on board with us still coming. I've got all the ingredients for the cake, so I'm glad I haven't been made redundant.'

'No, she's very keen for you to do it.' There was a funny pause, as though that sentence had more to it. 'You do know that Andrew and Scarlett have called it a day, don't you?'

'What?' Was I imagining that tiny note of triumph? I was torn between sacrificing my pride and begging for details, and tossing the phone down and screeching off to London to check my daughter was okay. All underlaced with a scorching rage that Scarlett had brought all of this trouble to our door and hadn't bothered to tell us that the landscape had shifted, if not back, at least substantially away from where we thought it was.

Philippa said, 'I think they finally came to their senses. Thank God. At one point, Abigail had just about banned Andrew from the wedding. And although I'm still livid with him for being such an idiot, when all this has blown over, I think Abigail would have regretted not having him there.'

I urged myself to see her point of view, to not read any slight on Scarlett into her words. Even if it was justified, my hackles still stood on end.

Philippa seemed to be relishing her role as the deliverer of news and if there was any chance of our friendship regaining its previous comfortable footing, I accepted that I'd have to allow her a crow of victory. 'I mean, it was only a matter of time before Andrew realised that a man of his age and a thirty-year-old wouldn't have enough in common to sustain them.'

Spitefully, I wanted to point out that it was Philippa's perception of how little she had in common with Andrew that led to their break-up in the first place.

All the time she was speaking, I was wondering where Scarlett was, whether she'd had to work this Saturday, maybe walking the dogs on the common, crying tears that she would hate anyone to observe. I told myself off for assuming that Andrew would have dictated the outcome. But he had so much more to lose and I was pretty sure, like me, he was discovering that blood was thicker than water.

Suddenly, I couldn't bear it any more. I needed to hear her voice, needed to know that she was okay, that it had been as much her decision as his. I'd always perceived Andrew to be a kind and decent person, but then he'd probably say the same about Ian and me, and we'd definitely fallen a bit short on that front of late. Divided loyalties appeared to be poison to the qualities of kindness and decency.

I signalled my intention to close down the conversation. 'Now I know how the land lies, I'll crack on with the cake. I'll be in touch, but I'd better check on Scarlett now.'

I mentioned Scarlett as a trap, waiting to see if Philippa would make a snide comment. But she said, 'Thank you. Can't wait to sample it. You've always been so good at baking.' No snide comment. But no compassion for my daughter either. It was staggering how many years a friendship could exist, solid and unquestioned, yet how swiftly it could be reduced to a fragile edifice, vulnerable to misunderstandings and suspicion.

As soon as I finished on the phone, I rang Scarlett's number. Just voicemail. I couldn't wait a moment longer to speak to her so I got into my car and drove up to her flat, uneasy and anxious. A million miles from the elation that I'd imagined feeling at this news that I'd wished for. Ian had often joked that there was no pleasing me, that I hankered after one outcome only to realise that I wanted something different when I achieved it. I'd never told him that I hated it when he said that, that those words always touched a nerve, peeling back the covering of the years to reveal a layer of shame.

As I drew up outside, it occurred to me that she might have done what she always did in times of emotional crisis. It wouldn't surprise me if she'd disappeared off on what she called a 'sabbatical' but what Ian dismissed as 'avoidance of real life'. Surely she wouldn't have taken off without letting us know but then again, she might not have wanted to witness our reaction to her 'news'.

I was relieved to see a light on. At least her flatmate might be able to offer an indication of where I might find her.

I rang the bell. After a long wait when I wondered what to do next, the door opened and Scarlett stood there in a T-shirt and pyjama bottoms, her hair hanging limply, dark circles under her eyes.

'You've heard then?'

'I have, love.'

She stepped aside to let me in.

'Who told you?'

My stomach flipped with fear, though fear of what, I wasn't quite sure: of hurting her; of making things worse; of igniting her anger so that I had to leave before I'd understood what had happened.

'Philippa.'

'That figures. I bet she's bloody cock-a-hoop.'

I shook my head. 'Not at all. She just wants what's best for everyone. We all do.'

Scarlett let out a little snort of scepticism. 'At least you can go to the wedding now and tell me how shit Janine looks in my dress.' Then she turned away abruptly and filled the kettle. Without turning round, she said, 'I loved him. Love him.'

I sat down, fearful that I only had one stab of saying the right thing that would lead to Scarlett confiding in me rather than shutting me out. I'd never heard her say that she loved any man before. She had a knack of being friendly with everyone and no one, never really building what I would consider meaningful relationships with anyone, apart from Abigail. But Abigail had been more like a sister – they'd spent so much time together growing up. The people she socialised with in London seemed transitory, with names popping up frequently, then disappearing from conversation. If I asked, 'How's Freddie? Have you seen that friend that worked in the café, Lena?', names I'd committed to memory to prove I was interested in her life, she'd pull a slightly puzzled face as though I was being weird for even mentioning them. 'I think Freddie went back to Australia. Lena's got some job in Harvey Nichols. Or it might be Harrods.'

The one thing I did know about Scarlett was that she never invested in anyone. She always gave the impression that her friends were interchangeable and the boys she 'got with' even more so. So love, that very big word that she'd announced to us, all those months ago, had at some unconscious level made me take her seriously, while desperately hoping not to have to.

'Can you tell me what happened?'

She swung round, her face crumpled with abject despair. 'I couldn't make him choose, Mum. He kept pretending he could handle it, but it was killing him. And I couldn't stand how much I'd upset Abi, though I don't know what I expected. But I can't figure out what to do with myself. I'm never going to be able to go to work on Monday. I can't stop crying. Me! I never cry. I'll have to pretend I've got food poisoning, but my employer finds other people's illnesses highly inconvenient, so I'm not going to be able to spin that out for very long without losing my job.'

'Oh my poor girl. Come here.'

For the first time since Scarlett was a teenager, she folded into me. We stood, clinging to each other while her heart broke and mine struggled not to join in.

'He understood me, Mum. For the first time in my life, I didn't feel like there was somewhere else, somewhere just out of reach, round the next corner, that would be better, that I was missing out on. I was happy, exactly where I was.'

What a thing to be brave enough to give up. And what a thing for a mother to have the unsettling thought that such an unsuitable man might have been perfect for her daughter.

21

JACKIE

The phrase 'papering over the cracks' had never seemed so appropriate. Ian returned from his sojourn at the Airbnb two evenings before the wedding. I was expecting a slightly less dour version of him given that Andrew and Scarlett were no more. He had at least replied to my text delivering that information with a brief but perfunctory phone call. But, if anything, he'd shrunk into himself, flopping wordlessly into an armchair and flicking through the TV channels. I hovered between concern and irritation, especially as I was flapping about in my reinstated role as wedding cake maker, fretting about the thickness of the buttercream and whether making the layers seventy-two hours before the big day meant that they'd be as dry as a mummified dishcloth.

'How did the meetings go? Did you make progress?' I asked, though I'd barely listen to the answer unless there'd been a catastrophe and it was likely that Ian would lose his job. I'd done too much listening to Ian's corporate dramas over the years – the pressures from the American parent company to increase savings, the decision of a supplier to work exclusively with a different hotel chain, his most reliable colleague disappearing to a competitor. Now when he explained the intricacies of his work woes, my brain took itself on a day trip to somewhere less boring, but it still felt polite to enquire.

He did a frustrated sigh. 'Still not sure of the outcome. I guess they'll let us know when they're ready.'

I waited a suitable amount of time before I moved on to the topic that interested me. 'Have you sorted out your shirt and tie for the wedding?'

'Not yet. That whole "Will we, won't we be allowed to go?" nonsense has done my head in. If it wasn't for me, Abigail and Philippa would still be bumbling along in total ignorance – they should be falling on the floor and thanking me that someone had the courage to tell the truth, not dithering about whether I'm persona non grata.' He opened the fridge and ate a sausage roll straight from the packet, scattering crumbs onto the floor.

'For goodness' sake, get a plate,' I said, relieved to be able to snap about domestic trivia rather than the much greater irritation that Ian had somehow written himself into the hero role. I couldn't resist reminding him that there were other allegiances he might consider exploring, thereby hopping onto the moral high ground myself. 'I feel so sorry for Scarlett. I did offer for us not to go in a show of solidarity, but she was adamant that we should.'

Ian huffed. 'I think it's more important to support Abigail and Philippa and prove that we're neutral, that we haven't taken Scarlett's side. They are the innocent bystanders in this.'

I'd done that mother thing of starting to gloss over the facts and choosing to back my child regardless. Plus Philippa was pissing me off with her little jabs at Scarlett, which directly diminished my sympathy for her.

'I hope you're not going to curry favour with them all by badmouthing Scarlett. We need to be united in that. I'm not exactly looking forward to being the mother of the scarlet woman – pardon the pun.'

Ian shot me a look that suggested he thought it was rich for me to expect any leverage in how he behaved, given how cross I'd been with him for his part in the whole fiasco. I was wrestling with this obstinate, antagonistic version of my husband. It was becoming apparent that in the family hierarchy of contrariness and feistiness, we'd both muted our own belligerence to accommodate Scarlett's fiery character. I'd recovered some of mine after she'd finally moved out; I missed the bloodletting of a good spat. Ian, though, had adopted the habit of either not engaging, making a joke to defuse the situation or stating his point of view then not discussing it any further, with an aggravating 'I've said all I'm going to say.'

'Don't be rude to Andrew, though, will you?' I said.

'Why are you worried about him? Look at all the aggro he's caused. Couldn't keep it in his pants even with someone he'd known as a baby, half his age. Then, surprise, surprise, it all gets a bit difficult and he dumps her, leaving her in an absolute state and total mayhem in his wake. So no, I won't be toasting the father of the bride and clapping him on the back.'

I never worried about Ian in social situations – he was adept at smoothing things over, keeping conversation bubbling along, with just the right amount of tact and teasing. Now there was something so tightly coiled about him, as though the amount of anger I was witnessing was merely the oil spitting in a pan before the whole damned lot burst into flames.

There was so much more I wanted to say. So many things I was tiptoeing around, doing a hokey-cokey dance in and out, wondering whether to douse them in petrol and fetch the matches or do the sensible thing and bring a bucket of sand.

In the end, the wisdom of years won out. 'Can you at least be civil? It's Abigail and Guy's day. Let's stay focused on that.'

He nodded, but his eyes narrowed and I had a moment of understanding of what it would be like to have lived all these years with an unpredictable husband, one you couldn't rely on to be solid and dependable. I didn't know how other women did it. Reluctantly, I had to recognise again the enormous effort Ian had made over the years not to keep reminding me about my own unpredictable behaviour. I'd been married for thirty-two years to a man I'd never doubted. He hadn't had that luxury of certainty. Maybe he'd decided it was time for a taste of my own medicine.

We arrived at the church early. Philippa was craning around to watch everyone coming in, and I caught her eye. She gave me a beaming smile and waved. I mouthed 'You look lovely' and she blew me a kiss. Some of the tension dissipated as I settled into the familiar movements of our friendship. I stood there, determined to believe that although there'd been some unkind thoughts between us as we both fought to protect our daughters and ourselves, we could steer our relationship back on track. I refused to accept that a few months of distance could compete with five decades of holding each other dear.

Ian slipped his hand into mine as the music signalled Abigail's arrival. I overrode my instinct to whip my hand away and forced my fingers to relax in his grasp, to signal that we were a couple who could have fundamental differences of opinion but we could also agree to disagree.

As Andrew escorted Abigail down the aisle, I smiled at him to let him know that I wasn't here to make trouble, to ruin such a special day by giving him a piece of my mind. He nodded in brief acknowledgement, but didn't smile. And immediately, resentment flared within me, that I was the one extending an olive branch and he wasn't prostrating himself with gratitude at my magnanimity and snatching at it with both hands. Then I got a grip and told myself that it wasn't about me and he was probably overcome with emotion about his daughter getting married and trying not to cry.

As Guy and Abigail said their vows, I stared at the back of Philippa's head, the stillness of that wide-brimmed navy hat. I wondered whether those words were scorching regret into her heart, making her long to find a way back to Andrew, to revisit what had led them to each other in the first place. Perhaps she'd realised that the grass wasn't greener now she'd tried out the ilk of Noah and his allotment. Maybe she could see her way to agreeing to trek up Machu Picchu if it meant she could slot back into the easy dynamic of established coupledom.

If they reunited, would that make it easier for us to re-establish our friendship? If she'd 'won' against my daughter? Any gatherings of the two families would be out of the question forever. Even if Scarlett fell in love with someone else. Even if Philippa and Abigail chose to brush over that liaison as a regrettable aberration that would allow us all to pretend that it wasn't that big a deal. Even if we all rewrote it as a few shared dinners that went a bit far, I would never be able to trust Scarlett to go along with it. She might want to, for my sake, for Ian's sake, even for the sake of her friendship with Abigail, but her natural honesty would burst through eventually, and not in a calm, tactful way. No, the occasions of our families combining for high days and holidays were over. Starting with today.

At the reception, in a converted barn on a local farm that Abigail and Guy had agreed to with Andrew's encouragement, I was surprised to see an old-fashioned receiving line. It seemed oddly formal for such a modern couple.

I glanced at Ian, who was muttering under his breath. 'I'll go first,' I said, simply because I didn't want to be next if Ian refused to shake Andrew's hand.

Philippa was at the head of the line. We hugged – a gesture

I monitored for any stiffness or reticence, but she relaxed into my embrace.

'Did you have a little cry?' I asked.

'Just about held it together. I was determined not to ruin my make-up. Sylvie spent ages disguising all my wrinkles this morning. I think she did a good job.'

Sylvie. The name landed. I didn't know whether it was intentional, but it hurt as if it was. Another of Philippa's friends – historically way down the pecking order in my view – had helped my best friend get ready on this once-in-a-lifetime day. After she'd told me, 'No, no need to come round. I'll probably be less emotional if I'm just here on my own.'

I plastered on a smile. 'You've got great skin. They're laughter lines, anyway. You look fabulous.'

Quick as a flash, she said, 'If they're laughter lines, I wish I could remember what I've found so funny.'

I made myself take the comment at face value, Philippa rebutting compliments as she always did, majoring on self-deprecation. I mustn't assume she was implying that she hadn't had much to laugh about lately.

I moved along to Andrew and we did a half handshake, half embrace as though we didn't know what the new rules were for greeting each other after a lifetime of hugging without a second thought. 'You smell nice,' I said, relieved to have come up with a comment that didn't carry a burden of implication.

'Just a cheapo from the Marks and Spencer range. Bergamot.'

The aftershave that Scarlett always wore, eschewing perfume as she did as 'too flowery and sweet'.

'I thought I recognised it.'

He nodded. And leaning into my ear, he whispered, 'I know you don't want to hear it, but I loved her. Still do.'

I stepped back, terrified that Ian would choose that moment

to stop complimenting Philippa on the décor – 'This looks fantastic!' – and tune in to what Andrew was saying.

I flicked my hand out dismissively as though it was all water under the bridge. I moved on to congratulating Abigail and Guy. My face flushed as I registered the conflicting feeling of satisfaction that my daughter hadn't just been a mid-life crisis plaything. Which was swiftly followed by a desire to urge Andrew to stick to his commitment to exit stage left so we could all start to rebuild our lives.

I kept a wary side-eye on Ian, who adhered to the polite society rulebook and shook hands with Andrew but quickly shuffled along the line. I heard Andrew say, 'I appreciate you coming today, thank you.' I summoned up a smile for Janine, the stand-in chief bridesmaid, feeling duty-bound not to be over-friendly. She was gracious and sweet, complimenting me on my dress. I dug deep to be bigger than the mother who turned loyalty to her own daughter into a criticism of someone else's. Still. That deep green dress that was perfect for Scarlett's dark colouring swamped Janine's delicate features. I was ashamed that gave me a little starburst of pleasure before I remembered I wasn't an eight-year-old in the playground and smothered it.

My phone buzzed in my handbag. As if she'd read my thoughts, Scarlett had texted: *Is it okay? Is Dad behaving? Can you send me a picture of Abigail (without her knowing)?*

I admired her restraint. In her position, I would have wanted to ask, 'Has anyone mentioned me? Does Janine look awful?' But Scarlett would superglue her fingers together before weakening enough to text me the big thing I was sure she was dying to know – *Has Andrew mentioned me? Is he okay? Do you think he'll get back with Philippa?*

I sat at a table with the simple vases of penstemons and fuchsias, admiring how beautifully Abigail and Philippa had decorated the room. Scarlett would have loved all the natural wood centrepieces, the eclectic glassware that Abigail had sourced from charity shops, tapping straight into Scarlett's approval of the vintage and mismatched. I hated the idea of her sitting in that flat of hers, excluded and isolated, heartbroken over both Andrew and Abigail – and for what? So everyone who'd had a part to play, directly or indirectly, could carry on as though nothing had happened, clinking champagne glasses and sucking back starters decorated with tiny fennel fronds and three pomegranate seeds.

Abigail was moving on to a different life stage, automatically becoming closer to Guy than to Scarlett, which would already have represented a challenge to their friendship. But now Scarlett had fallen even further behind, having to heal herself before she could contemplate a new relationship. Would it be counterproductive to tell her what Andrew had said? Let her know that he was thinking of her, even if the rest of them had erased her from the day? Would that merely be a short-term balm for her heart, when the best possible option was to forget about him, believe he was just using her and turn that love she had for him into disdain?

My chin wobbled as I had a sudden image of Scarlett as a baby, four months old, those dark eyes of hers staring up at me, the centre of her universe and able to fix anything. If only I'd known that was the easy bit of parenting. Now, the problems were bigger, more unwieldy, with many more moving parts. The desire to fix, to make everything right, to elicit that smile of relief remained the same, but the tools at my disposal were drastically reduced.

I bent over, pretending to look for something in my handbag on the floor while swiping at my eyes. When I thought I'd pulled myself together enough, I straightened up, glancing around the room for Ian.

With relief, I saw him talking to Guy's dad, Peter, who hadn't been at all what I expected – a golfer type with a florid face, very hail-fellow-well-met. A contrast to Guy, with his serious, pensive nature, his reserve suggesting a certain diffidence or at least real discernment about whom he entered into conversation with. Yet another example of how our offspring would be who they were destined to be, rather than blended carbon copies of their parents.

With dismay, I saw Maureen, a woman that Philippa had been with on a charity committee years ago. Philippa had been trying to shake her off for ages but regularly caved in and met her for a coffee. Every time, Philippa tipped her head back in mock horror, saying, 'I'm seeing Maureen tomorrow,' before slumping onto the table in dramatic despair.

'Why? Why don't you keep saying you're too busy so she gets the hint?'

'I'm always saying I'm busy, but even if I said I have no available dates for the next five years, she'd get out her ten-year diary and book me in six years from now. It's just easier to allocate a couple of hours than cringe through fobbing her off.'

Goodness knows why Philippa had invited her. Though, knowing Maureen, she'd probably assumed an invitation and Philippa was too embarrassed to put her right. And now she was heading towards me, the feather in her fascinator already buckled and sticking out at an angle.

'Jackieeeee!' she said, as though she was astonished to see me there, Philippa's best friend at her only daughter's wedding. She threw her arms out in a way that made me want to hold my hand up like a stop sign. But manners won the day.

I disentangled myself as quickly as I could.

'I wasn't sure you'd be here,' she said, grinning away.

For a moment, I wondered if she'd figured out that I always hid from her. Then I clicked. She knew. She knew what had gone on.

I was going to take a lesson from my daughter and hold my head up high.

'Why did you think that?' I asked, my eyes wide.

She blinked at me, as though she was puzzled by my question. I watched her bluster, keeping my head tilted to one side with an enquiring look on my face. 'Well, Scarlett having that carry-on with Andrew and you, well, you know, not...' She tapered off.

I eyed the feather on that silly purple fascinator and battled with the urge to snap it off. 'Me not what?' I asked, staring directly at her.

She fiddled with the clasp of her clutch bag. 'Not, sort of, being totally upfront about it.' I was gratified to see a pink tinge creeping across her chest and up her neck. I was astonished that people like Maureen ever had the self-awareness to recognise when they'd put their foot in it. At the same time, my stomach was dropping, hollowing out, with shock that stupid, thick, tactless Maureen might be acquainted with quite a lot of details about my family's disgrace. That Philippa might have discussed my part in the deception with someone who wasn't a close friend, someone she didn't even like very much. Someone we laughed about together, pitied even. Philippa had confided in her. About me. And not in a way that would show me in my best light.

I pursed my lips. 'What do you mean by "not being upfront about it"?'

Maureen was waving her hands about in a panicky, 'don't mind me and my silly nonsense' way. But I wasn't letting this go. I felt as though I was five seconds away from grabbing her arm and squeezing it until she told me.

'I just meant that Philippa was, er, *surprised* that you didn't mention the whole Andrew-Scarlett thing to her, as soon as you knew.' She leaned in as though she was about to tell me a secret. 'Especially as you were aware Philippa wanted to try to repair the marriage, and Scarlett's track record with men was' – she frowned, as if attempting to recall the exact words in order to be extra helpful – '*patchy*, so it wasn't likely to last.'

'Did she tell you that?' I didn't expect Philippa not to speak to anyone about Andrew and Scarlett but Maureen? I was praying that Philippa had told someone else, a much closer, better friend who'd unexpectedly gossiped behind her back rather than this loose cannon of a woman who'd often been the butt of our jokes. This airhead whose words ran at top speed but whose brain didn't appear to keep up, spewing out thoughts that should never have been let loose. Philippa knew that Maureen would revel in my demotion from best friend and delight in being the holder of the knowledge. No. Not the holder of the knowledge, the disseminator. Philippa often came back from meeting Maureen wide-eyed about some nugget of gossip that Maureen had burst out with. She had to have grasped that anything that reached Maureen's ears would snake its way around the local networks, saving her the trouble of telling anyone herself.

A fleeting smugness crossed Maureen's face. 'Oh, she only told me because she needed someone to talk to, someone who was a good listener, who wouldn't judge.'

I needed a winch to close my mouth at that point. The scorch of betrayal seared through me. I could feel a pressure building in my chest that could turn either into laughter without any humour, or sobbing. I wouldn't give her the satisfaction of bursting into tears. I set my face, hard.

Maureen rattled on. 'She was so upset, but I think I helped her make sense of what she was feeling. I haven't said a word about it to anyone, so don't worry. Though I suppose a few people will wonder why Scarlett isn't here.'

'Oh sod off,' I said in a sing-song voice as though I was complimenting her on her outfit. 'If she told you, then I can guarantee that everyone in this room knows.' I picked up my handbag and marched to the ladies'.

I touched up my make-up in the mirror, squaring my shoulders in order to survive the next six hours before I could go home and release the tsunami of tears lodged in my chest.

When I returned to the room and watched Philippa chatting and circulating, one thought kept hounding me, as insistent as the waves on a seashore. If she felt able to share anecdotes that showed me in a terrible light with all and sundry, what else might she feel free to divulge to the people who really mattered?

22

JACKIE

In the week following the wedding, I had bursts of optimism when I wanted to believe that now Andrew and Scarlett had split up, now Abigail was married and the stress of organising the wedding was over, we could all take a great gulp of fresh air and reset. Yet there were many more occasions when I itched to phone Philippa up and ask what the hell she was thinking of, telling my business – our business – to Maureen the Motor-mouth. Still, there were moments when I almost excused her by telling myself that people who are hurting do hurtful things. That, although there had been no malice on my part, I had prioritised Scarlett over her. How could I not? She, of all people, knew that I had to put Scarlett first. Part of me wanted to get my own back and point out a few of her shortcomings, but, most of all, I longed to rewind to our easy friendship, that distant land where we linked arms and created a solid wall against the world.

When I'd told Ian about Maureen, he'd shrugged. 'Why don't you have it out with Philippa? What have you got to lose? Realistically, I can't see how you're ever going to be really close friends again anyway, so you might as well have your say.'

The bluntness of his words made me want to lash out, apportion responsibility, paint myself into the blameless corner. But something had changed in Ian. He no longer gave out the energy of a man who loved his wife and daughter unconditionally. As a consequence, I was no longer so confident that I could be my unadulterated self and expect him to put up with it. I'd always been able to withdraw a little, disappear for a few days on my own to recharge, knowing that I could re-present a revitalised version of myself. Ian had never minded, never taken it as an insult. Just accepted that was who I was and, if the truth be known, probably encouraged these short absences as a kind of circuit breaker, for both my personality and our marriage. Now I saw him as a man who wanted to rewrite the rules of the marital agreement that had been set long ago. I hovered between lifting my chin and saying, 'Too late, mate. This is who I am and this is what you signed up for,' and doing everything I could not to rock the boat.

I wanted to discuss it with Philippa, pick it apart, have her tease me, advise me, even tell me to stop my whining. But, like Ian, she had floated out of reach. In ordinary circumstances, it would have been unthinkable that we didn't get together for a debrief after the wedding as soon as we could. But when I suggested catching up, she sidestepped me, citing 'so much post-wedding admin to sort out, be in touch when I come up for air'. Three weeks after the wedding though, I received a text that previously would have been unremarkable: *Fancy popping over to look at the proofs of the wedding photos? Tuesday evening work for you?*

Perhaps she'd forgiven me. Perhaps we could consign all this to history, brush ourselves down and move on.

Tuesday evening, I turned up, bang on eight o'clock, with an expensive bottle of wine, fidgeting on the doorstep, wondering if I'd have the guts to lay everything out on the table.

Philippa's welcome was warm. So far, so good. Everything

had an air of normality, except the second-guessing that was going on in my head. Was I prepared to gloss over the fact that she'd gossiped to Maureen? I didn't know why I couldn't just let it go given the enormity of all the other things we had to 'get over'. But every time I thought about it, it felt like a poisonous seed in me that might increase in toxicity over time. I realised I'd still expected her to present what had happened as a difficult situation for me, for all of us, not tell everyone what a terrible friend I was.

I plonked myself down at the kitchen table, trying to remember how I used to be.

Phillipa cracked open the wine and passed a photo album over to me. 'Honestly, they say the camera never lies. I look like my face needs a good iron.'

I laughed. 'You looked lovely, don't be silly. I loved that outfit and you even managed to pull off the hat. Very Holly-wood.' I flicked through the pages. 'That's a fabulous one of Abigail and Andrew,' I said, pointing to them walking down the aisle. His name seemed to stick in my mouth and I hoped I'd sounded natural rather than strained.

I studied the photos of Abigail and Guy with the respective sets of parents, trying to read Andrew's face, to store up infor-mation, not necessarily to tell Scarlett but to equip me to help her navigate this painful episode. That was if she ever deigned to discuss it with me beyond a perfunctory 'I'm glad Abigail had a good day'.

'Did you love every minute?' I asked. 'I thought the whole thing was brilliant. Abigail looked so happy and whenever I saw Guy, he looked as though he'd won the lottery.'

Philippa nodded. 'Apart from the beef that I thought was a bit tough, it all went very well.'

I continued examining the pictures until I came across one of Ian, grim-faced, standing next to Andrew. Before I could stop myself, I said, as I always would have done, 'Oh look, there's Ian having the time of his life.' I pointed to his surly expression.

Philippa raised her eyebrows. 'I don't think Andrew is at the top of his Christmas card list any more.'

'No. I think you're right about that. You two seemed to be very civil though?'

'I concentrated on putting our daughter first.' Her tone had an edge to it.

I looked up and smiled. 'Quite right too,' I said, with a little wisp of dread prickling at my stomach.

I became aware of my fingers fumbling to turn the pages, of Philippa's eyes boring into me. And suddenly I just wanted this to be over, to know one way or another whether we could ever get back to the kind of friendship that didn't have me over-thinking everything, feeling that I was constantly on the back foot with something to apologise for.

'Is there something you want to say to me? I hate all this tension between us. You must know that I never meant to hurt you, that maybe I should have made different choices, but I genuinely couldn't make up my mind what would cause the least amount of damage.'

Philippa nodded. 'I do know that. But still, you did really hurt me.'

That flare of indignation that Philippa had me firmly in the baddie frame, with nothing to reproach herself for at all. 'I didn't feel great that you told everyone what had happened. Especially someone like Maureen, who couldn't wait to tell me what an excellent listener she'd been for my misdemeanours.' As soon as I said the words, I wished I'd swallowed them down, just done the whole mea culpa thing so we could end this horrible, uncomfortable exchange about who did what and who was most at fault.

Philippa had the grace to look abashed. 'She caught me on a day when I was barely holding it together.' She stopped short of apologising and my mental abacus railed at all the bad deed beads sitting firmly on my side.

I flicked open the palms of my hands. 'So where do we go with this? Are you able to forgive and forget, or do you want to divorce me as a friend?' I tried to inject a bit of laughter into my last question as though I didn't consider that an option, but my voice caught. 'I really miss you. I can't bear the fact that you think so badly of me. I know I haven't behaved well, but please, please just put it in the context of our whole friendship. Surely the good friend bit trumps the bad friend cock-ups?'

She grinned. 'Let me see,' she said, scratching her chin. 'I think it does.'

We hugged. I felt as though I'd lost something valuable, which had filled me with regret and guilt for not looking after it more carefully, only for it to turn up unexpectedly in a pocket or under a chair, offering me a reprieve, a second chance to take better care.

'Thank you. So we're all good?'

'No more secrets,' she said.

And the air around us seemed to loosen as we chatted about people's outfits, who we'd liked talking to, until eventually I said, 'I'd better head off, I've got work tomorrow. Will you order me a photo of Guy and Abigail? The one where they've got their heads down, talking to each other in the churchyard? I love that one. So natural.'

She smiled, the face of a mother whose child had reached a successful milestone and was happily embarking on the next stage of life. 'I shouldn't tell you this, but Abigail told me they're going to try for a family straight away.' She rubbed her hands together. 'I might be a grandmother by this time next year.'

'Fingers crossed,' I said. 'Wouldn't that be fantastic?'

I hated myself for the stab of envy that Philippa could relax now, knowing that with a fair wind, Abigail's life was set on a path that would inevitably enhance Philippa's along with it.

Whereas Scarlett was in turmoil and Ian didn't feel as stable as he once was either. I didn't expect Philippa to have much sympathy on either count, certainly not today. Maybe in a few months' time, we could stop pretending that Scarlett didn't exist.

I gathered my coat and bag and gave Philippa another big hug, delighted to smell her familiar perfume up close. I set off along the street, promising to text when I got home and laughing as she told me to stick to the main road, no short cuts through the rec.

I waved until I turned the corner. My phone rang, just as I was heading through a short avenue of trees, the darkest part of the walk, making me jump.

'Hello, love,' I said.

'Where are you?' Scarlett asked.

'I'm actually on my way home from Philippa's, just popped in for a drink,' I said, noting the apologetic 'actually' as though spending time with her was disloyal. I didn't mention I'd gone to look at the wedding photos, which seemed even more of a betrayal.

'Oh.'

'Is everything all right?' I'd never wanted to be that mother who assumed her child only phoned when there was a problem rather than calling out of a simple desire to touch base, yet here I was.

'I'm pregnant.'

23

JACKIE

The word 'pregnant' set off a starburst reaction in my head, as though someone was smashing cymbals together while twirling around with sparklers in both hands.

'What?' I corrected myself quickly, 'Sorry, yes, I heard you.' I managed not to say, 'No need to repeat that particular bombshell.'

We both waited for the other to speak, my brain quickly assessing then discarding all the responses that naturally sprang to my lips – 'How the hell did that happen?' 'I assume it's Andrew's?' 'Surely you've caused enough trouble?' 'Well, you can forget about Abigail ever speaking to you again.' And the one that I really needed to know the answer to: 'Are you intending to keep it?'

When it became clear that Scarlett wasn't going to elaborate unprompted, I said, 'That's quite the surprise. How do you feel about it?', allowing myself a small pat on the back for digging out a neutral question among all the accusation-loaded ones that I would have loved to unleash.

'I wondered if I could come home tonight? If I got the train now, I could be at the station by 11.15.' Her voice was uncertain. 'Is that too late? Would Dad pick me up if you've been drinking?'

I felt that familiar sensation of searching for a reserve of energy that would get me through the next few hours and still enable me to be sharp enough at work tomorrow to handle a complaint about body odour with tact and diplomacy. 'You come, darling. I'll make up your bed and get Dad to fetch you.'

'Thanks, Mum. Thank you.'

I hurried home, bursting through the front door to find that Ian was already in his pyjamas, filling the water glasses to take upstairs. The sight of him was so reassuring, so welcome, that I was hard-pressed to remember why on earth I'd ever flirted with the idea that life without him might be easier.

He turned to greet me, then froze when he saw my face. 'What's happened?'

I filled him in. As he ran upstairs to change out of his pyjamas, his fury was so intense that he looked as though some alien creature was bubbling under his skin ready to burst out in a spurt of noxious fluids. I walked up the stairs behind him, realising that one person had to be calm and, unusual though it was, that was falling to me.

I stood in the doorway as he put his jeans on, saying, 'Don't back her into a corner. Let's hear what she's planning first. We don't even know if Andrew is aware yet.'

Ian nodded while continuing to swear under his breath.

I waved him off at the door, wanting to issue so many instructions about how to deal with Scarlett, as though I had all the answers. Had ever had any answers.

I went into her old bedroom, wondering how she'd felt about having it turned into a guest room, the vibrant green walls she'd insisted on in her teenage years now a classic grey, the heart-shaped hooks that once held a brightly coloured patchwork coat and all manner of scarves removed. Was there some part of us that longed to remain a child with our parents, where we could hand over responsibility? Whether she liked it or not, the buck stopped with her on this one.

As I put a hot-water bottle into the bed, memories of when Scarlett was off sick from school resurfaced, those simple days when I'd fussed about, tucking her in and feeding her toast, knowing that this discomfort was only temporary.

My phone buzzed. Philippa. *Did you make it home safely? x*

I was supposed to text. Tonight was meant to be the first step on the road back to us and I was immediately going to lie by omission, again.

Sorry! Got distracted. Yes, all safe and sound. Lovely to see you. Don't forget to order me the photo please x

It dawned on me that might be the very last normal text I sent her. Perhaps even the very last text full stop.

My heart contracted as I considered that my daughter was carrying her daughter's half-sibling. We were no better than the families in those stories in gossipy magazines: 'My ex-husband hired a hitman to shoot me', 'I married the burglar who broke into my home', 'My boyfriend married my bridesmaid'. I couldn't see a way of Philippa or Abigail getting past this. Unless Scarlett had a termination, didn't tell Andrew, and Ian and I never breathed a word. Another huge secret to keep. Would I? Could I? I didn't know. But if we went down that route, we'd have to be confident of taking it to our graves, because Philippa might not be so amenable to keeping her own mouth shut in the face of a second big lie from me.

Philippa hearted my message just as Scarlett and Ian came through the door.

Scarlett looked pale but composed. My eyes were drawn to her stomach, even though I knew there'd be nothing to see. How I wished that this was a moment of deep celebration, that I'd had Philippa's path of my daughter marrying someone suitable and doing everything in the right order. I was ashamed of my old-fashioned wants. It wasn't even that I thought Scarlett needed a man, but I did wish for her to find a cheerleader, someone who'd be on her side, champion her when we were dead. Selfishly, I hoped that if she was settled with a partner, I would be able to release myself from the guilt that I'd refused to contemplate having another baby, despite Ian pleading with me. Maybe I wouldn't worry about her future so much if she had a brother or sister to look out for her. But today was not a day for going down that much-visited cul-de-sac.

I was desperate to throw my arms around her, demanding to know if she was okay, but a pregnant Scarlett was probably not much different from a non-pregnant one. So instead of rushing at her, I approached her like you would a nervous dog, slowly, low-key, though everything about her being here, in these circumstances, was a huge deal.

I gave her a hug, though nowhere near as long as I wanted to. I already felt steadier for having eyes on. 'Come on, come into the kitchen where it's warm. Can I make you a sandwich? Some toast?' I just managed to swallow down the sentence: 'You must keep your strength up.'

She nodded. 'Toast, please.'

It was astonishing how that simple act of being able to do something practical for her, however tiny, soothed my nervous system.

Ian was pacing, making me tense. I tried to signal to him to sit down and let Scarlett take the lead, but he burst out with, 'Tell your mum what you told me.'

Scarlett raised her eyes in that clear, determined way she had. 'I'm keeping the baby.'

Ian was waving his hands about as though it was the most unhinged thing he'd ever heard. 'She hasn't even told the father yet.'

I frowned. 'Andrew, do you mean?' I asked, wondering how many other men were in the frame.

'Yes, that's the one, that bastard. I'm trying not to say his name.'

'Dad, stop it. Not that it's any of your business, but I'm the one who messed up the contraception. I took my pill too late. I was the careless one.' Scarlett glanced at me for support.

'Yes, stop it, Ian. It's not helping. "I'm trying not to say his name" – really? Don't be so bloody childish.'

He slammed down into a chair. 'You say it's none of our business, but how are you going to bring up a child? You only just make enough money to survive as it is.'

'I don't know yet. But plenty of people manage it. I'll work something out.'

I placed a plate of Marmite toast in front of her, with a cup of tea. 'Are you planning to tell Andrew?'

'Not yet. I want to get my own head round it first.'

'Scarlett! He has to know,' I said.

She squared up to us. 'I will tell him when I'm good and ready.'

Ian said, 'If you don't tell him, I will. He has to take some responsibility. This isn't just on you. Or on us, in fact.'

Scarlett jabbed a finger in his direction. 'Dad, let's be really clear, if you so much as breathe a single word to anyone before I am ready, I am not kidding, you will never see me again. Ever.'

And with that, she snatched up her bag, her tea and her toast and marched off upstairs.

Suddenly, I had absolute clarity about why I might have flirted with the idea of divorcing Ian.

24

SCARLETT

Dad could be such an idiot. I should never have come here. Never have told them. I would refuse to speak to them ever again if they told Andy behind my back. While these furious thoughts whirled through me, I had a vision of the tiny little bean growing inside me, absorbing all this anger and sourness. I forced myself to calm down, recognising with a jolt that I already felt protective, that I was prepared to alter my instinctive behaviour.

I lay there, softening slightly as I discovered the hot-water bottle. That was Mum. She'd never been the sort of mother to go overboard on saying 'I love you', but I'd eventually understood as I'd got older that people show love in different ways. Even so, I was going to tell this baby how much I loved him or her every day of its life. My baby would have to overcome many things in the world but the lack of hearing me proclaim out loud how important he or she was to me wouldn't be one of them.

I pulled out my phone, scrolling through Andy's messages. I should have blocked his number when I took my stuff and moved back to my own flat four and a half weeks ago, after that dreadful Friday night when, as we lay there naked and entwined, I'd broken down and told him I was leaving. We'd stayed up till the early hours, with him begging me not to go and me clinging onto the last fragments of my determination to do the right thing. But as the first light of dawn spread across the September sky, I'd grabbed my things and leapt in a cab before my heart overpowered what my brain knew was the right, the only, course of action.

Since then, I'd read his words on a daily basis. How much he missed me. How much he wished it wasn't like this. How much he should – but couldn't – regret embarking on a relationship with me, because he'd caused me so much pain. I couldn't bring myself to delete his last text:

> But even though I know it was a short time and there were so many (good) reasons not to have done it, I will carry the thought of you with me. Know that I wish every wonderful thing for you. You are such a special person. Properly one of a kind. I will always love you.

I couldn't heal while I was torturing myself, re-reading it all, every morning, every evening, sometimes sitting on the bench on the common while the dogs played, any time I was waiting for a bus, Tube, train. The more I tried to banish him from my thoughts, the more he seemed to slip in through a side door and a longing would envelop me, visceral in its intensity. The time I'd had with him had made me see myself in a totally different light. I wasn't someone to be fixed or changed. Someone who could be marvellous if only I could iron out my dominant personality traits. Instead, he admired my stubbornness, the way I didn't care what people thought about me as long as – in my view – I'd behaved decently, my lack of interest in material things. For those precious months, I'd felt enough. And what a liberation that had been.

He'd helped me distinguish between what I thought of as

independence and what was often a distrust of everyone else around me. I'd started to make myself vulnerable, to allow myself to be helped and looked after without automatically assuming that I'd fast-forward to becoming some weak woman who had to ask for permission to go out for a curry with her friends.

However, perhaps the single thing that I hadn't grasped until now was that love doesn't exist in a vacuum. That once you loved a person fully, loved them in a way that meant their unhappiness dogged your day, that meant your own heart reached out across the city to wherever they were, hollow with despair at their despair, that was where real love began. When even if they begged you to stay, even if they might have chosen you over the other people they loved if you gave them an ultimatum, you couldn't agree. I didn't want to oblige Andy to choose me over Abigail. I couldn't do it to him. Or her. I'd caused enough damage. But I could make a decision about what to do with my own child. *You and me against the world, babe. I've got you.*

The following morning, Dad had already gone to work by the time I went downstairs, having slept surprisingly well in that odd way I often did when I came home. It was almost as though I reverted to being a child, knowing that if the monsters showed up, my parents would take care of them, so I was no longer required to sleep on red alert.

Mum, however, was 'working from home', though when I came up behind her, I saw she was searching online for things in the John Lewis nursery department. At least one person was taking me seriously. She turned round, guiltily clicking off the page, when she heard me.

'At least it's not porn, Mum. You might have been webcamming for OnlyFans.'

She gave a weary smile and I noticed the lines around her eyes. She wasn't old, but I could see that she'd aged since I'd last studied her. When was that? When had I actually viewed my parents as individual humans rather than stable, staid people who hummed along in the backdrop of my life? They occasionally came to the fore at birthdays and Christmas and when I needed advice about how to get tomato sauce out of a white T-shirt or help putting together my flatpack bookcase. But, mainly, I just liked knowing they were in the background, a bit like jump leads, stashed away until required but invaluable in an emergency.

Mum bustled about making me breakfast. As she put down a bowl of yoghurt and fruit, she said, 'I totally respect your decision to have the baby, but you need to be realistic about what you'll be able to do workwise, darling. We can support you a bit, but Dad is hoping to retire at sixty. Andrew is going to have to contribute.'

'I know.' I felt my eyes prickle, as though Mum could see straight through my bravado. 'I just don't know how to tell him, because it's so tied up with his relationship with everyone else.' I tried to make a joke to disguise the sadness swelling up in my chest. 'I'm sure Abigail will be desperate to meet her half-brother or sister.'

Mum didn't even bother to acknowledge my feeble attempt at humour.

'When did you last speak to Andrew?'

'About a month ago. A few days before the wedding. I just needed to know that Abigail had relented, that us splitting up was worth it.'

Mum leaned her forehead on her hand, her fingers gently massaging her scalp as though to release some of the tension.

'Do you love him that much?'

'I don't know how you quantify love, Mum. I mean, how much do you love Dad? Is it more important to you that he's happy or that you are?'

Mum looked down, puffing out her cheeks. 'Do I want Dad

to be happy even if I'm not? Good question. Right now, in this particular circumstance, the thing that matters to me most is that you're happy. That you make the right decision for you. Not for me. Not for Dad. Not for Andrew or Abigail or anyone else, but for you and the baby.' In a much quieter voice, as though she was talking to herself, 'That's all that's ever mattered to me.' Her head snapped up. 'Would you like me to talk to him?'

'Mum! For goodness' sake! I'm not a teenager who's found herself pregnant after too much vodka and a fumble behind the rugby club. I don't need my mother to talk to my ex-boyfriend about what he's going to do about your daughter who's up the duff!'

She put her hand up in apology. 'Sorry. Sorry. I just want to help. And I'm worried for you. The longer you leave this, the less time you have for everyone to adjust to the idea before the baby arrives.'

And in her words, I caught a tiny glimpse of motherhood. A relentless cocktail of love, selflessness, worry, delivering advice and wrestling with another human being whose own opinions rarely coincided.

I took a deep breath. 'Is it worth it, Mum?'

'Is what worth it?' she asked.

'Having a baby. Being a mother. All the shit that goes with it.'

She leapt up and grabbed my hands. 'Oh my goodness, I cannot think of anything in the whole world I could have done with my life that would have brought me more satisfaction. I know I didn't get it all right. But I always did what I thought was best for you.'

And despite having decided long ago that what my parents thought about my life and the way I lived it was irrelevant, I leaned into my mum, feeling less lonely than I'd felt in days.

She hugged me, stroking my hair. 'Don't let anyone ever tell you any different. I always did my best.'

25

SCARLETT

On the day of my twelve-week scan, the bleakness at going to the hospital on my own obliterated the excitement I felt about seeing concrete evidence of my baby. I'd always considered myself above the cheesy social media posts of couples grinning like idiots on their way to an ultrasound, as though they'd done something so clever the whole world should be applauding. Instead, I longed to feel Andy's hand in mine, that commitment that wherever this adventure took us, he was right beside me. And although I'd probably have small stabs of jealousy that this wasn't the first time for him, I was pretty sure they'd soon be balanced out with the relief that he knew what he was doing when I didn't.

Mum had offered to come with me. Since I'd told her, she'd really surprised me. I'd never thought she was particularly maternal; she was always kind to my friends but never went out of her way to engage. I'd always gravitated elsewhere for sleepovers, parties and revision sessions, drawn in by other mothers with their easy manner and plentiful supplies of cake, and later, wine. Ironically, I'd spent a huge amount of time at Philippa and Andy's. They were so much less uptight than my parents, who tended towards patrolling and swear-word monitoring. Now every time I saw Mum, she repeated a variation of 'I know the circumstances are a bit tricky but I honestly can't wait.' And she'd pull her shoulders up around her ears and do a little dance of delight. She was more excited than I was about the baby, which made me feel a bit of a failure.

Ungraciously, I found her enthusiasm off-putting when there was so much I still had to process before I could share her joy. So I simply couldn't face her gushing about the gorgeousness of babies during my scan. Guilt made me irritable when I'd told her last week that I'd rather go on my own and it wasn't worth her taking a day off work.

'Sorry, I didn't mean to impose at all. Of course, you have to manage the way you want to. I was getting carried away about seeing my first grandchild.'

'You can come to the next one. This is something I need to do by myself.'

The truth was, I dared not rely on her, on anyone, in case I couldn't rediscover my backbone. It felt like a slippery slope when, ultimately, I was going to have to find a lot of grit to get through what lay ahead without becoming a burden to my parents.

I'd heard the intake of breath on the other end of the phone and cut off the recurring question before she even articulated it.

'No, I haven't told him before you ask.'

'Oh darling.'

'Mum. Mum. If there's anything to report, I'll let you know.'

So I didn't pick up when she called that morning. I already felt as though I might burst into tears and I didn't want the ultrasound woman writing me off as an unfit mother. No one was ever going to think I wouldn't be enough for my baby. I instructed Alexa to select an easy-listening station to send calm and cheery vibes to my little one. I sang along at top volume to

Simon and Garfunkel, Billy Joel, Abba, proud of my 'fake it till you make it' as a sliver of buoyancy returned.

Then, with perfect timing, Stevie Wonder's 'Isn't She Lovely?' came on and I sat, numb, unable to direct my thoughts anywhere other than to repeat to myself that love was exactly what our baby was made from. The pull to tell Andy, to let him know that I was growing a bit of us, a homage to what we'd had, even if he couldn't, shouldn't, be part of it, overwhelmed me. Like someone who'd lost three stone on a diet and was totally convinced they would never get a craving for ice cream again, I scrolled through my phone to his number, frantic with longing.

It rang five or six times. That frenzy of desperation to hear his voice started to spiral into something that was causing sobs that didn't even create tears, just deep whimpering when he answered. 'Scarlett!'

I swallowed. 'Where are you?'

'I'm at work. I've just come out of a meeting. Are you all right?'

The sound of his voice felt like home. A home where even when things weren't okay, they would be okay. And suddenly I was crying and blubbering out the news that I was pregnant. Nothing like the composed, mature communication of my imagination in which I explained my plan to go ahead with the pregnancy and the non-necessity of his involvement.

'I miss you so bloody much,' I said, wailing so dramatically that I started to laugh.

'I'm on my way,' he said.

26

JACKIE

Five days after her scan, Scarlett warned me that Andrew would be telling Philippa and Abigail about the baby the next morning. In the four weeks since I'd known, there'd been a couple of birthday dinners when Philippa and I had been with our extended group of friends, but I'd managed to avoid direct one-to-one contact. On the evenings when we'd been out, I'd watched her talking with the others, her easy laugh, the way she said outrageous things, quite blunt in her manner but also compassionate and charming.

A couple of times, I felt as though she'd announced she only had a year to live, that I was impressing all the things that made her unique onto my brain. Grieving while she was alive. Except she wasn't dying. It was our friendship that was. Fifty years and so much history. But this was too big. She wouldn't forgive me for keeping a secret a second time despite the many hours I'd dedicated to finding a solution when I should have been asleep.

Instead, I found myself studying all the other women, wondering which one would be my replacement. Tanya? Sandra? Ellen? Would they remember the anniversary of her father's death, go to the cemetery with her? Make collages of photos dating back to the seventies and eighties for everyone to ooh and ahh over when she had a big birthday? Add detail to her teenage memories, present the glittering gift of a recollection she'd never have brought to mind without my prompting?

Not one of them could do that. But even my unique best friend skill set wouldn't be a match for the one thing absolutely guaranteed to harden her heart: there would be a new kid on the block to rival Abigail in Andrew's affections. And I'd hidden it from her.

Of course, me telling her wouldn't have changed the outcome, but it was all about allegiance. She would choose her daughter and I'd chosen mine. We had to pick a side, which was incompatible with picking each other.

The night before the big reveal, I was stuck in no man's land, my huge expanse of friendship with Philippa on one side and an extensive wasteland on the other. I was hoping to avoid enemy fire but recognised the miraculous odds that would have to fall in my favour to survive. I longed to go round, stand on her doorstep and tell her everything she'd meant to me. The part of me that accepted this was the end of the road for us also wanted her to know that I would always love her, more than I would love any other female friend ever, past, present or future. Thank her too, not just for what she did back then, but everything else since. I wanted to be the bigger person, to say without any agenda that I was sorry about how all of this had worked out. But, of course, she would never believe me, because although all of that was true, I did have an agenda. I wanted her to promise that she would never reveal the truth about me.

But I couldn't do any of that without breaking Scarlett's confidence. The irony wasn't lost on me that secrets became increasingly powerful the longer they remained guarded. So instead of paying homage to the dying throes of my relationship with Philippa, I channelled my distress into bickering with Ian about his lack of interest in Scarlett's baby. 'He or she will be your grandchild. I know the circumstances aren't ideal, but the baby is still your family.'

He nodded. 'I know.' Then refused to engage any further, leaving me pouncing on everything from the way he slurped his tea to how he used his fork in a fruitless effort to provoke an argument as a vehicle for venting my misery.

I clattered plates and cups about as I unloaded the dishwasher, not caring if they chipped as I slung them into the cupboard. I ordered a new rug that I'd coveted for ages but deemed too expensive. Totted up how much money I could take out of my pension if Scarlett needed some help. Ran outside shouting at the squirrels to get off my birdfeeder. Descaled the kettle, snipped off the hair that was tangled round the hoover rollers, bled the radiators. I didn't dare allow a single idle moment in case my thoughts overpowered me.

But despite collapsing into bed worn out, I still lay awake with my heart hammering as I visualised what the morning would bring. Ian snored gently and I veered between faith that if he was managing to sleep, maybe I was catastrophising, and fury that he had not yet understood the magnitude of the loss that was facing me. Maybe I hadn't either; a little spark of hope persisted that Philippa would revisit the defence I'd produced when we'd discussed why I hadn't told her about the affair. With time, she might recognise that, again, my hands were tied.

The next morning, Ian disappeared off to the office and I worked my way through various Zoom calls. I forced myself to focus on discussions about paternity and adoption leave, prompting me to wonder whether Scarlett was entitled to anything from her employers. I couldn't imagine that she would have done anything as sensible as insisting on a contract. For all I knew, they handed her a stack of notes at the end of every week. She probably kept them rolled up in an elastic band in an old baked bean tin.

At eleven o'clock, my stomach contracted with dread as my phone pinged with a WhatsApp message.

HOW COULD YOU DO THIS TO ME AGAIN?

There was my answer, the death knell of all hope.

To which the only response, although it broke my heart, was *How could I not?*

27

I'd wanted time to pass. Now six months had. I'd dragged myself through the days, the weeks, yet suddenly time seemed to have flown. All that time and no time at all. I was a completely different person, though I bet I hadn't changed as much as she had. I wondered if that flare of pain would ever abate when I thought about it.

I'd watched the holidaymakers with their deckchairs, umbrellas and cool boxes give way to emptier sands, the summer breeze shifting into a winter chill. The buzz of the high season had fizzled into something quieter, the sense of community heightened as the crowds thinned. And with it, an increased visibility and vulnerability. More questions about where I was from, what brought me here. More curiosity from those who were too run off their feet during the summer to notice one more person who wasn't from Yorkshire.

I didn't invite conversation; it was too hard to remember who I was now, who I'd had to become. But that desire to belong, to share, to connect, sometimes overwhelmed me. I rolled out a filtered version of how I'd ended up so far from home. On a good *day, I dreamed that I could eventually belong here. On a bad day, I knew that I'd never belong anywhere ever again.*

28

JACKIE

SIX MONTHS LATER

It was three-thirty in the morning, but I still hadn't been to sleep. I snatched up the phone when the call came. 'Scarlett! What's happening? Are you okay?'

'It's Andrew.'

'Is she all right? Is the baby here?'

'Yes, yes, he's here. All fine. They're just doing the checks at the moment. Scarlett's throwing up a bit because of the pethidine, but she did brilliantly. He's a beauty.' There was no mistaking the pride and love in his voice. 'A decent weight too, eight pounds.'

'Exactly the same weight as Abigail,' I said, wanting to acknowledge that this would be a day of mixed emotions for Andrew because of the strain this baby had put on his relationship with his daughter. Poor little thing. Barely a few minutes old and already a source of tension, though I liked to think my own joyful reaction would act as a counterbalance.

'Indeed. She was a beautiful baby too. I can see her in Rowan,' he said, his tone resigned and sad.

'Rowan? Is that the baby's name?' I asked, adding, 'I love that' in case he thought I was being critical. I did love it.

He laughed. 'You know Scarlett and her love of nature. I had to draw the line at Forest and Cedar.'

'Well done, that's probably a good call. When can we visit?' I added. 'If she wants us to?' I hesitated. 'If you both want us to?' Though obviously I was going to see my daughter whether he was in favour of it or not, but there was plenty of time to be rude.

'Of course she does, we both do. Visiting time is four to eight.'

I wanted to say something big and profound and conciliatory, but the words stuck in my throat. Instead I said, 'Thank you' as though he was an admin assistant communicating basic information, rather than the father of my grandchild.

'I know you have great reservations, Jackie, and I don't blame you. But I promise I'll look after them.'

I nodded, although he couldn't see me. 'I know that.' From the day he'd found out about the pregnancy, Andrew hadn't wavered. He'd proved himself to be what I already knew: a decent man. He'd moved Scarlett into his flat immediately, which had the unforeseen consequence of us seeing her much less. Ian point blank refused to go there. 'I'm not sitting around making polite conversation in a flat that he used to live in with his first wife.' Inevitably, my continuing to visit Scarlett there led to us quarrelling about it.

But today, as Andrew and I said our goodbyes, Ian propped himself up on one elbow. 'Congratulations, Grandma.'

Right then in that moment, after so many months of Ian refusing to discuss anything to do with the baby, reticent even to talk much about Scarlett, my heart lifted as I detected a hint of pleasure in his tone. It was probably relief that Scarlett was all right, but I was grateful to him for not spoiling my joy.

Later that morning, I took myself off to Asda, to buy some

fresh fruit for Scarlett in case the only offering on the maternity ward was the choice of minced fish or corned beef hash that I'd had when she was born. I took a detour into the baby section, desperate for an opportunity to tell someone, anyone, that I had a grandson. That I was going to see him that afternoon. That they'd named him after a tree – 'my daughter is really into the environment'. And that I was going to love him beyond all reason.

I studied the minute sleepsuits, unable to remember Scarlett ever being that small. Out loud, I said, 'Today is a day for looking forwards.'

As I stood debating between the tiny T-shirt with a giraffe on it and the hoodie with tiger ears, I heard a familiar voice. I spun round to see Philippa with Tanya, further along the aisle, discussing whether a pack of bibs and a fold-up changing mat would be more useful than a hooded bath towel, before exclaiming over a pink bodysuit with a matching hat. 'I think I'm going to go with this. The daisies are so cute. She loves flowers so that seems like a safe bet.'

I stood frozen for a moment, the pain of not celebrating with Philippa, this milestone we'd dreamed of, making my chest constrict. But I wasn't going to run away. I wanted to believe that, despite holding a grudge and refusing to take my calls, her anger would have dissipated enough in the six months since that final text exchange to say hello at least.

I was trembling though, scared of my friend, the power she had to hurt me, all those years of love turned inside out and transformed into weapons that knew exactly where to find their targets. I screwed up my courage, dropping the baby clothes in my hands to my side. She might not know yet and I didn't want to rub her nose in it.

'Hello, Philippa. Hi, Tanya.'

Tanya looked mortified as though she really did want to scoot off and hide her head in the fresh fish cabinet. It had been 'interesting' to discover not a single one of the women I'd spent the last twenty-odd years socialising with had trodden a neutral line. In spite of repeated assurances that no one was taking sides, that it was 'a very unfortunate situation' that had nothing to do with them, my extended friendship group had practically vanished overnight. They'd all scuttled off to line up behind Philippa since they'd obviously decided I was in the bad friend slot for not controlling the behaviour of my adult daughter.

'Hello. How are you?' Philippa asked, in the tone of someone who'd bumped into a former neighbour she hadn't seen for a while. But her face coloured with emotion, though which particular one, I couldn't read.

'I'm okay, thank you,' I said, as I struggled not to blurt out all the words jostling to explode out of me. How much I missed her. How I still reached for my phone to send her funny memes I saw about how to distinguish between real friends and friends of convenience. Or jokes about fetching the matches to burn bridges with people who let you down, all designed to reinforce our belief that we could depend on each other, come what may. 'How are things with you? How's your mum settling down in the care home?'

She gave short, vague answers, staring at the baby stuff I was clutching. I panicked, suddenly terrified that I'd be the first one to break the news that Rowan was here, that I was now a grandmother.

I indicated the bodysuit in her hand. 'Are you shopping for Abigail? Is she pregnant?' I asked, smiling.

Her eyes filled. 'This is for my neighbour's daughter. Abigail had a miscarriage last month,' she said, in an accusatory tone as though I'd somehow contributed to it.

I clapped my hand over my mouth. 'Oh Philippa, I'm so sorry. I didn't know.'

'Andrew didn't mention it? Wow. I guess he had other things on his mind.'

I wanted to explain that we didn't socialise with Andrew and Scarlett because Ian was still funny about seeing them together. That Scarlett was still loyal to Abigail, would have considered her miscarriage to be private to her, not something to bandy about without her permission. Instead, I said, 'He probably didn't feel it was his news to share with me.'

But she was already walking away, Tanya's arm around her shoulders. Philippa said something to her and Tanya jerked her head round to look at me in that surprisingly obvious way that people do when they're talking about you. Today, they could crack on and say what they liked. Nothing could chip away at my joy of becoming a grandma. With the exception of one thing.

29

JACKIE

During the weeks following Rowan's birth, I expected a text from Philippa, some acknowledgement – even if it was a harsh and bitter one – that I was a grandma, that my daughter, the woman she had adored right up until last summer, had had a baby. Every day I braced myself for words that would stretch me between opposing poles – obliging me to protect myself with vengeful thoughts while simultaneously producing an urge to ring her to appease.

In fact, she did what she had to do. She ignored me. On a good day, I assumed that any contact with me was simply too painful, a reminder of how this bit of life was not at all how she'd envisaged it. On a bad day, I felt as though her silence was calculating, designed to wound. I was impotent; I'd proved to her that in the end blood was thicker than water. She'd have done the same. In truth, I would probably also have punished her with a façade of not missing her. Maybe for her though it wasn't a façade. Maybe she had genuinely moved on without a backwards glance. I would never know; I couldn't undo what had been done and now there was my grandson in the mix as a constant reminder.

Slowly, as the weeks and months wore on, other bits of life filled the space she'd left. Checking in on Scarlett and Rowan. A busy time at work as the rising summer temperatures went hand-in-hand with an increase both in absenteeism and personal hygiene issues. My continuing frustration with Ian's belligerence also dominated a fair amount of my thinking time. However, I no longer woke every morning burdened with a blurry despondency that evolved into the recognisable shape of Philippa's absence as the day wore on. Instead, missing her became distilled into specific, acute moments. I heard from Scarlett that Philippa had guilted Andrew into looking after their cat because she'd booked her annual spa break, this time in Scotland, with one of our mutual friends. Philippa and I had planned to go that autumn. I'd long accepted that we wouldn't be doing it together, but it hadn't occurred to me that she might take someone else. I was ashamed of how upset I was. How even the gratification of calming a crying Rowan, rocking him to sleep and watching his eyelids clang shut, didn't assuage the hurt that hollowed me out.

I tried to discuss the loss of friendship with Scarlett, how much she missed Abigail, in an effort to feel less humiliation about how bereft I was. Scarlett, however, was consumed by new motherhood, which narrowed her vision to survival and navigating that misnomer of a learning curve. Sheer rock face, more like. She didn't have the energy for missing anyone other than her pre-baby self: the woman who could lie in at weekends and linger over brunch in a café. I wasn't sure why I felt so ashamed of missing Philippa so intensely. There was something immature about it, a bit playground politics, as though friends shouldn't be so important. A sense that there should be more freedom to come and go, and that if you became so anchored to one particular person, it was a personality flaw: lack rather than loyalty.

But alongside Philippa, in a different way, I'd also lost my relaxed relationship with Andrew. If I was ever at the flat when he came home, I'd disappear fairly swiftly, but today he was back early, swinging Rowan up into his arms in the same way that I remembered him doing with Abigail. Easy, confident, radiating security. I'd never felt like that when Scarlett was a baby, never trusted my ability to meet her needs. I didn't seem to have that instinctive understanding of her cries, becoming flustered, especially in public if she screamed. Scarlett was much more laid-back than I'd ever been, but then again, she had the benefit of Andrew's experience, who'd already successfully steered the choppy waters of bringing up a child.

When Scarlett went for a shower, I asked him how Abigail was.

His face pinched with pain. 'She lost a baby just before Rowan was born. She didn't tell me. Philippa did.'

I nodded. 'I'm sorry. That's really tough for you. I bumped into Philippa in the supermarket. She gave me the impression that they'd all been having a very difficult time.'

It was the first time in ages that Andrew and I had connected as a mum and a dad who'd known each other for years, discussing our kids. He told me how angry Abigail was with him, how Guy was mediating between them, showing a maturity beyond his years. 'He's far less flaky Gen Z than I thought. Much less vanilla chai latte and more builder's tea.'

I laughed. I'd missed him. The man who had been Philippa's husband but over time had also become my friend, the guy I could phone to ask for a recommendation for a roofer, or if we could borrow his gazebo.

'How is Scarlett doing?' I said, straddling the odd territory of eliciting information from him as my friend but also my daughter's lover, my grandson's father. I was glad Ian wasn't there and I could prioritise my need for maternal reassurance above all other considerations.

'She's doing brilliantly. I mean, it's a baptism of fire for all of us, isn't it? I'm finding it easier this time around, despite being that much older. Probably because I know that none of these stages lasts forever and that we will sleep again one day. Also how quickly it goes and how much I want to appreciate it in a way I didn't know how to when I was young and ambitious and still learning to manage myself.' He grinned. 'But back to Scarlett. She seems contented, as though she's found her purpose in life, which I have to admit I didn't really expect. She didn't seem at all worried when I went back to work. It will be better when we move house.' He glanced around the sitting room, cramped with the Moses basket, baby seat and drying rack hung with bibs and sleepsuits. He grimaced. 'I'm working on it. I don't know if Scarlett told you, but we've got an offer in on a little terrace the other side of the common?'

I wanted to know more about the house, but I heard the shower shut off, Scarlett clattering about in the bathroom. I had to ask. I rushed out my question.

'Are you happy, Andrew? Or just surviving?' I held up my hand. 'You're not going to tell me even if you're not, are you? But I need to know.'

He put both of his hands on my forearms and looked me squarely in the eye. 'Can you leave aside the more' – he raised his eyebrows – 'not sure how to say it, "disagreeable" aspects of this whole experience for a moment? Perhaps "distasteful" is a better word. You might not believe me, but I am happy. Of course I regret the obvious and I won't rest until I've made peace with Abigail. And I know you'll be looking at me and wondering how the guy whose bucket list included touring South America in a camper van can possibly be delighted by fatherhood when we'd all been waxing lyrical about how much freedom we had now the kids were grown but...' He did a funny half-smile. 'I feel very alive right now. I love him,' he said, nodding towards Rowan. Then, with a bashful expression, he glanced towards the bathroom. 'And her too. Very much.'

Shortly afterwards, I drove home to Ian, asking myself whether something that had a detrimental effect on others was acceptable if previously miserable people became supremely contented. That felt like quite a big question to be wrestling with, so I defaulted to the far simpler concept: was my daughter happy? Was my grandson well-looked after? Did they both have someone to love them? With a resounding yes on all of those fronts, I was going to consider it a win in the face of everyone else's loss.

30

JACKIE

Every year, in November, on the closest Saturday to Bonfire Night, our family and Philippa's had a tradition of having a curry at the same restaurant, a proper old-fashioned gold and red diner. We'd started going after the fireworks display we went to in the grounds of Abigail and Scarlett's school and carried on long after they'd left. We no longer did the fireworks but still relished the tradition of drinking Cobra beer, stuffing ourselves with poppadoms and arguing about which combinations were the optimum blend of spice and sweetness. We'd skipped it last year because Andrew had only just found out that Scarlett was pregnant and no one had the stomach for small talk over the sag paneer.

This year, I wanted to get back to the old traditions and also start establishing new ones that included them all. So, in a moment of madness, I suggested doing our usual curry and inviting Scarlett and Andrew, with Rowan, who, at five and a half months, would fall asleep anywhere in a pushchair.

Ian was horrified. 'You can't be serious? Are we really going to turn up there and have the manager ask Scarlett when she got married, and then question Andrew about where his lovely wife is?'

Although I could see his point, the incident in the supermarket with Philippa had shifted something in me. I refused to apologise for living my life or waste a single second feeling as though I needed to make excuses for Scarlett and her choices.

'I'm not letting a few potentially embarrassing remarks from a restaurant owner dictate where I can eat. We can choose to look at the positives here. She's a great mum, far calmer and more chilled than I ever was.' I paused, then pressed on. 'Rowan is a sunny baby and they seem to be getting along much better than we ever imagined.'

Ian was making all sorts of faces that suggested he was gearing up to rehash the same bloody objections I'd heard a million times in the last year.

I folded my arms. 'Sorry, but I'm using this as a watershed. You can join me or not. From now on, I'm going to stop dwelling on all the things that are wrong: the way they got together, all the grim age difference weirdness. I'm accepting that this is the landscape for us. We can either embrace it or fight against it. But I'd like to forge a solid relationship with Rowan and I don't think it's fair for you to punish a little boy just because you don't like the background story.'

Without waiting for an answer, I left Ian standing with his mouth open, marched into the sitting room and rang the restaurant. I spoke louder than necessary as I booked a table for four and double-checked whether it was all right to bring a baby if we didn't manage to get a babysitter.

I mentioned it to Scarlett when we were out walking on the common, Rowan in a sling, his bright eyes drinking everything in. Scarlett was so natural, so unselfconscious in the way she chatted to him. I'd always been second-guessing myself, wondering if I was doing it 'right', whatever that might be. I wish I'd known back then that I was good enough. As we walked, I asked her how she felt about doing our traditional curry evening and her face lit up. 'With Andy too?'

I nodded. 'If he'd like to come.'

'Was Dad okay with that?'

'Yes, I think he feels it's time to move things on to a different footing, now you're a proper family.' I did an inward grimace at my words, which were vaguely approaching the truth but definitely on the extreme positive spin end of the spectrum.

Scarlett stopped, pressed her lips onto the top of Rowan's head and said, 'Thanks, Mum. I do know how hard this has been for you.'

'It has, love. But there have been huge upsides as well, not least this little chap.'

Her face brightened with the type of joy you can't manufacture, that serenity that comes from deep down within. I felt my heart lift. Unconventional family or not, my daughter was happier than I'd ever seen her.

On the night, I was berating myself for being so nervous about spending an evening with three of the people I knew best in the world. It was fast becoming clear to me, though, that no one was as predictable as I'd thought them to be. I'd always assumed Ian would do anything for me, that the thing that mattered to him was keeping everything on an even keel, working hard to make sure there were no surprises. Since Scarlett had got together with Andrew, and especially since she'd had Rowan, I had the sensation of dragging him along, a bit like a suitcase with a wonky wheel that might or might not follow my lead.

If I tackled him, he simply said, 'I find there to be something inherently repulsive about our close friend becoming intimately involved with our daughter. You, apparently, don't, or have decided to overlook it on the grounds of embracing the bigger picture. Which is your prerogative, but doesn't negate my opinion.'

There was a slight pomposity to his words. A hint that he saw the situation more clearly owing to his superior intellect and that my stance resulted from a lack of integrity. What he would never understand, and I would never be able to explain in a way that he could accept, was that as long as Scarlett was happy, I found it hard to care about the rest. So, he was probably right, but that didn't stop me hating his attitude.

No longer being able to rely on Ian to muster just the right amount of charm to put everyone at their ease in a social situation made me prone to blurting out clumsy comments to fill the silence. So when we arrived at the restaurant, I was tetchy with the pressure of making it right for everyone, of proving that we could find a way to forge ahead with this strange new family dynamic.

Andrew, who would usually join Ian in oiling the wheels of any gathering, had adopted some kind of weird deferential son-in-law stance. He was very much in 'I'll go with the flow' mode, refusing to offer any opinion on wine, sharing menus or anything else that might have made this dinner seem like a normal occasion. In turn, this seemed to discomfit Scarlett, who spent most of the poppadom part of the evening fussing over Rowan. I was pretty sure she was manufacturing a distraction from the stilted exchanges about work, weather (for goodness' sake!), the train strikes and the occasional desperate comment about the people we could see walking past outside. Hat on, hat off, blanket on, blanket off, moving him away from the radiator, wondering whether it was too noisy for him, when, frankly, he just seemed fascinated by his toes.

I tried to carry the chat with questions about where they might go on holiday next year. Scarlett shrugged and said, 'We hadn't really thought about that. I suppose we might stay in the UK, perhaps get an Airbnb by the seaside somewhere. Now

Philippa's intending to move to Deal permanently, I guess that option is off the table.'

I sat up. 'Philippa's moving to Deal?'

Andrew nodded. 'That's one of the things that's slowing up the financial settlement. She keeps changing her mind.'

Again, that blow to my stomach. This huge event, Philippa moving away, announced so casually, as though we were talking of a work colleague I knew a decade ago. That raw, wounded feeling coursed through me. Anger followed soon after. Anger that I hadn't yet accepted that it was over. That we would never be friends again. Some stupid bit of my brain was clinging onto hope that as long as she lived within walking distance, we'd somehow bump into each other and bury the hatchet. When would I come to terms with the fact that it didn't matter whether she lived in Deal or Dubai, I was no longer on her radar?

We mumbled our way through biryanis and kormas and, between bites of chapati, I regretted not appreciating the ordinary evenings we'd previously spent here to the absolute full. I'd taken for granted the easy camaraderie between us all. Ian and Andrew competing over who could bear the hottest dishes. Philippa pronouncing onion bhajis the devil's work. Scarlett and Abigail rolling their eyes at comments from their parents that proved beyond all doubt that we were not down with the kids.

Just as I slugged back another gulp of wine with the aim of loosening the knot in my stomach, I was aware of a rapid movement on the other side of the window, then the door flinging open.

Philippa marched in, drops of rain flying off her hair, and parked herself in front of our table. 'I wondered if you'd all be here, same old, same old, except two people haven't been invited and one of the husbands has swapped his old wife for your daughter. And his own daughter for a spangly new baby boy.'

She was slurring her words, loud in her delivery, causing heads to turn.

Andrew was quick off the mark, leaping to his feet and taking hold of her arm. 'Philippa, not here. Come on. You've had too much to drink.'

She shook him off. 'I'm all right, just thought I'd pop in and say hello to your son.'

She leaned over the pushchair and looked at Rowan, causing Scarlett to snatch him up and away from her.

Philippa gave a loud bark of laughter. 'Jesus, I'm not going to hurt him. He looks like you did at that age.' There was a pause and my heart began to thud. The same sharp burst of adrenaline that I'd experienced when a lorry had narrowly missed me on the motorway.

I also stood up.

She waved her fingers at me in a 'back off' gesture. 'Ronan does look like Scarlett at that age.'

'His name is Ro-W-an,' Scarlett said, her eyes dark, her jaw set in a way that wouldn't end well for Philippa if she dared to say anything horrible about her baby.

'What do you think, Jackie? Can you see the similarity? What is he, five, six months?'

And with sickening clarity, I realised what she was doing.

At the same moment, Ian did too as, suddenly, he was standing beside me, saying to Philippa in a soothing, concilia-tory voice, 'Would you like me to get a cab for you? You don't want to be walking around in this horrible weather.'

She smiled at him, swaying slightly. 'You always were a good man, Ian. You never let anyone down. Unlike some other people I could mention.'

'Don't,' he said. 'You're better than that.'

How much love did I have for my husband in that moment?

That when it mattered, despite the hurt I'd caused, despite everything, everything bigger than we could ever have imagined when we met at twenty-three, he still had my back. And even though I was so sorry for what I did, as the years passed, it had been hard to translate my regret into endless gratitude. It had faded, obscured by the thousand day-to-day irritations that sliced away at patience and thankfulness. But now, wow. My heart was brimming with the same relief I'd felt, when I was finding my way back into life, three decades ago. He'd smoothed a path for me with understanding and kindness and that much underrated quality of just getting on with it, letting what I'd done wither quietly and shifting our attention to the future.

But he didn't know all of it. Not yet anyway.

Out of the corner of my eye, I could see Scarlett hugging Rowan to her and Andrew standing watchful, not quite sure where this conversation was heading.

Ian cupped his hand under her elbow. 'Come on, let me get you a coffee at the bar.'

'Always were the protector, eh? You fool.'

I could barely hear their words over the hammering of my heart, which seemed to be banging directly in my ears. She wouldn't. Surely she wouldn't. I was staring at her, pleading with her not to make things any worse.

She was glassy-eyed as she pulled away from him and leaned towards me, as though her brain had encountered a chicane and hopped onto another train of thought. I didn't know which option was worse. 'You haven't answered my question, Jackie.' She swivelled round to Scarlett. 'Your mum doesn't know whether Ro-W-an looks like you or not at that age. And do you know why? Because when you were four months old, she walked out and didn't come home until you were nearly one.'

Scarlett raised her eyebrows, her face full of disbelief as though Philippa was trotting out deranged comments simply to cause trouble. She scowled at her. 'Oh stop talking shit and go home. You're just drunk.' A note of doubt crept into the very last word as she clocked my reaction.

There were so many ways I could have handled it, that might have given Philippa's words less credibility, less weight. Instead, I sank into my chair, putting my head in my hands, afraid to look up and witness Scarlett's reaction. It would all come out now, the truth, worse than Scarlett would expect even from Philippa's bombshell. How could I ever explain, prevent my daughter from reviewing all of our good family times through a lens of that awful deed? Would she forever see the difficult moments in our relationship as proof positive that I didn't want her, didn't love her, when in fact the reverse was true? I didn't know how I would withstand the vitriol that Scarlett was sure to unleash on me. All the scaffolding, all the armoury I'd put in place over the years to ensure that I'd never return to that deep dark place felt as insubstantial as a cocktail umbrella against a thunderstorm.

I glanced at her, but she was stroking Rowan's head, her focus on him. Of course. She was a much better mother than I'd ever been.

Andrew was the first to move, as though he'd instinctively known that, intoxicated as she was, Philippa was telling the truth. He grabbed Philippa's arm. 'We're leaving. Come on.' Over his shoulder, he said, 'Take Rowan back to your mum and dad's tonight. I'll get there as soon as I can.'

I made pleading eyes at my former friend, willing her to go before she uttered another word. 'I'm coming, no need to pull me,' she said. I expected to feel a glimmer of relief, but my despair was so deep that I was only aware of a heaviness weighing on me, as though anything extra, even that other thing that she could use as a weapon against me, couldn't sink me any further. But I was wrong. As Andrew propelled her towards the door, she turned and shouted to Ian: 'She met another man while she was away, you know, slept with someone else. Guy in the hotel. But I'm assuming she told you about that?'

Andrew bundled her out, hissing objections I couldn't hear as I stared, frozen. Unable to look round at my family, wanting to postpone for a second longer the moment when I'd have to see the disgust on their faces.

As I swallowed, trying to find some words – what possible words? – I expected to see triumph residing on Philippa's face. But the fight had drained out of her. Instead, she looked horrified, confused, as though someone else had shouted out my secrets and blamed it on her.

There it was. The last stitch of the complicated embroidery that wove a friendship together severed for all time.

31

JACKIE

I'd been a fool to think that it was ever possible to move on from mistakes of that magnitude. In the cab on the way home, I had that sense of Ian and Scarlett bonding and siding against me in their joint hurt. Ian sat alternately screwing up his face and raising his eyebrows as though he was trying to bring a different reality into focus. I wanted to touch his hand, to offer up that platitude, those meaningless words: 'It meant nothing, absolutely nothing. A desperate attempt not to think or feel or be so bone-achingly lonely, so frightened that I screwed everything up so badly that I could never make things right again.'

Scarlett sat there, straight-backed in the seat, reaching out to stroke Rowan every now and again, as if to reassure him – and herself – that she'd never be this mother. Even if she didn't yet know the true hideousness of what I'd done, she already knew that she definitely wouldn't do it, whatever it might be.

I made an attempt to take the first steps on the road to my defence. I offered cryptic and vague statements along the lines of 'I know what it looks like, but it's not quite the way it seems' so as not to alert the cab driver to the fact that he was giving a ride to a despicable wife and mother.

Both of them shook their heads, with Ian growling out, 'We'll discuss it when we get home,' in a tone that brooked no argument. I would just have to stew in the porridge of accusation until then. Well beyond then, I expected. I couldn't blame them. There was no mistaking who the baddie was in this scenario.

At home, we jumbled our way into the house, hiding behind making sure we'd got all of Rowan's paraphernalia, hanging up our coats, settling the baby into a makeshift crib on the sofa with Scarlett. Putting off the moment when Scarlett's view of me and what sort of mother I'd been would alter forever. When Ian would have to decide if what I'd done between then and now, the wife I'd been in the intervening years, had accumulated enough ballast to see us through.

The minutes ground past. I went through to the kitchen, where Ian was making tea. I stepped towards him and he jerked away from me. My hands up in surrender, I said, 'It was just once.'

Hurt blazed from Ian's face, his eyes sweeping over me as though he was coming to terms with living with a stranger for all these years.

'Once is a lot when you're married,' he hissed. 'I was so bought into the fact that you'd been ill and hadn't been thinking straight about motherhood that it only briefly occurred to me that you'd have been well enough to shag someone else.'

I'd fallen into the trap of thinking that the gulf between zero and just once was somehow better than the gulf between once and thirty, fifty, eighty times. I opened my mouth to explain, though what I thought would serve as a valid excuse wasn't clear, not even to me.

Ian put his hand up. '*That* part of this can wait. Right now, you need to speak to Scarlett. I don't want the whole view of her childhood to be coloured by this. She was so loved and I don't want her to have any cause to think otherwise.' He sighed and looked down, tears gathering along his bottom lids. 'You were a really good mum in the end.' He passed me a couple of mugs of tea and beckoned me through to the sitting room. 'Come on. I'll help you.'

The generosity of this man – who'd stood alongside me, deserving nothing of the chaos I'd caused – made me love and appreciate him more than I had in years. At the very point when he might decide that the downside to me far, far outweighed the upside.

Ian settled himself next to Scarlett, but I didn't feel I had the right to squeeze onto the sofa with them. I sat in the armchair beside him, already isolating myself from the brutal judgement I knew would come my way.

I didn't know how to start, how to find ordinary words to broach the topic of my extraordinary actions. Scarlett was looking along the sofa at me, mirroring Ian's look of disbelief, but she didn't speak. It wasn't in Scarlett's nature to contemplate her reaction; she was very much a 'shoot from the hip' woman. She was either wounded in a way that had rendered her numb or rehearsing her response for maximum impact. I didn't even have the energy to cry; this felt too big to merit something as banal as tears.

I kept closing my eyes, searching for the sentences that would convince her that my leaving was no reflection on her, her lovability, her value either then or now. I couldn't find the starting point; it was like grappling for the end in a tangle of Christmas lights and endlessly pulling a knotted loop from the centre.

Eventually, Ian reached for Scarlett's hand. He said, 'I know this is all very shocking, Scarlett, but just listen to your mum and approach it with understanding, think of her as someone who was ill, not evil.'

That enormous compassion whipped through me. This man I'd hurt so badly. Who'd been big-hearted enough to open his arms and welcome me back after my long absence, with the words: 'I'm sorry. I brushed it all under the carpet. I was too young and too stupid, kept hoping that if I didn't acknowledge how bad you were that, eventually, you'd keep plodding on until you came out the other side.'

Scarlett's head snapped round. 'I suppose her "illness" extended to some rare disorder of needing to sleep with other men?'

Ian turned his body so it was square-on to face Scarlett. 'We're all going to try to understand each other here, Scarlett. Mum and I will deal with that aspect, but for the time being, you need to absorb what happened with you.'

Scarlett pouted, actually pouted as though she was fifteen again and I'd told her that she needed a bra under her shirt. In the whirlpool of guilt, despite yearning for a crumb of compassion, I also understood that Scarlett was having to deal with a double whammy of revelation. One, that I'd abandoned her, and two, her staid, unchanging parents whose job it was to be the solid beige scenery to her unpredictable life suddenly appeared to have needs and dramas of their own. Eventually, she nodded. 'I'm all ears.'

Ian tapped my knee, a tiny burst of warmth against the coldness I felt through the rest of my body, my signal to plunge in, to start anywhere. I took a sip of my tea, forcing myself to allow memories of that day to resume their full shape, rather than fading into the blurriness that I'd condemned them to over the years. I'd been afraid of holding up a mirror to the fragility of my mind, terrified in case a convergence of unforeseen circumstances might lead me back into a dark hole that this time I might not be able to climb out of.

Finally, I jumped, not knowing whether the truth would fix my family or finish us off once and for all.

32

JACKIE

THIRTY-ONE YEARS EARLIER

'It's my first birthday without my dad. The third without Mum,' I said, through a mouthful of toothpaste. I didn't want to be twenty-seven without my parents.

'I know, love.' Ian's words competed with Scarlett's screams as he jiggled her on his hip. In the mirror, I saw him check his watch, his face tensing as he calculated how late for work he'd be if he stayed to talk. Or maybe he was setting a time limit on how much more gloom he could bear before being released into the freedom of work and colleagues. Chipping into conversations about what he'd watched on TV. What he'd done at the weekend. Anything other than how little sleep he'd had, how the reality of having a baby bore no relation to the joy he'd expected. How his wife kept either shouting or crying.

I rinsed my mouth, wanting to beg him not to leave me, to keep me company in the quest to find the solution that would make Scarlett sleep or at least coo contentedly for five minutes while I had a shower.

Someone had to earn the money. I knew that. Knowing that

didn't stop me hating Ian though. Didn't stop me being so jealous, right down to my core, that he could march out of the door, unencumbered by noise and endless repetition. And, most of all, walk away from the feeling of being responsible for keeping a tiny being alive and content – surely a simple task that mothers had accomplished since time immemorial – and *failing*.

All too soon, Ian was passing Scarlett to me, gathering up his coat and briefcase, kissing me on the forehead and Scarlett on her flailing arm and rushing out. 'I'm tied up at lunchtime today, so I'm not going to make it back. We'll celebrate your birthday tonight. I'll pick up a Chinese on the way home.' He paused. 'Try to go out for a walk, get some fresh air.'

I nodded, laying Scarlett in her Moses basket while I made myself a cup of tea. I filled the kettle, a mixture of irritation and resignation swirling as I contemplated how easy it was for Ian to suggest 'going out for a walk'. And how insurmountable it felt to negotiate the straightforward yet impossible steps to make that happen. I breathed as Scarlett's screams abated to low-level whimpers. The door banged. Scarlett startled at the noise and I braced myself, my stomach twisting and tightening at what I knew was coming.

As she yelled her fury at a world not to her liking, something in me shattered, breaching the barriers I'd been holding in place. Every day I had told myself that things would get better, that I just had to give it time. That having a baby two months after my dad had died had prevented my bonding with Scarlett. The torrent of grief for a love I'd known all my life had somehow swept away the nascent buds of a love yet to establish itself.

I stared down at her. Her cheeks were pink and wrinkled, her mouth a howl of indignation, her eyes squeezed shut against the offences of the world. 'What do you want from me? What? What is the matter now?' I shouted, tears pouring down my face.

I stormed off to the bathroom, threw off my pyjamas and stood under the shower, the water muffling Scarlett's outraged cries, but not enough that I could ignore the visceral pull, the urgency to hurry back to her. My own tears mingled with the spray, my limbs so heavy with exhaustion that lifting my legs to wash my feet required an unusual effort.

I wrapped myself in a towel, picked up a thrashing Scarlett and clamped her to my side while I microwaved a bottle of milk. She sucked at it for a few glorious quiet seconds, then balled her fists in fury, arching herself away from me. I put her over my shoulder, where she promptly vomited down my back, something she'd done a hundred times before. But this time was different. This time triggered a hopelessness so profound that I nearly ran out into the street in my towel to shout for help. I longed to thrust my baby at the first passer-by, to ask them to take her away, to give her to someone who knew how to be a mother.

I took her into her bedroom and put her in the cot, not bothering to wind up the mobile. Nothing ever made a difference. I rinsed my back, leaning into the shower, and got dressed. I told myself that I was only going to do what Ian had suggested and take Scarlett out for a walk because sometimes the movement of the pram allowed her to drop off. Picking up Scarlett's baby bag, I put in some extra nappies. Then I added four clean sleep suits – it was quite common for her to be sick or a nappy to leak. I didn't want to get caught out and be that mother with a baby in a soaking wet suit. I took four bottles of milk from the fridge. She could get very hungry and it was always better to have too much milk than too little. The shame of giving up on breast-feeding flared again, the proof that I wasn't cut out for mother-hood. The health visitor had said that grief for my dad might have affected my milk supply. Ian had shrugged. 'I was bottle-fed and I've barely had a day's illness in my life. Don't worry about it.'

Into the bag went a pen and paper. I might jot down some thoughts, perhaps even start writing a short story to send off to a magazine. Something I could talk to Ian about, watch a flicker of relief pass over his face that I was productive, interested in something again, rather than blankly waiting for the hours to pass until he came home.

I wrestled Scarlett into her coat and clipped her into the stroller, saying, 'We're going to have a nice walk, see some cars and buses and trees. You'll like that.' My voice was loud in my ears, unnatural. I checked twice that I had my wallet. Then I tucked a handful of underwear, my washbag, a clean T-shirt and a pair of jeans into my own bag. My periods were unpredictable these days. It was always good to be prepared with a change of clothing.

I wheeled a grizzling but relatively quiet Scarlett to the door, tucking her pink elephant into the stroller, and covering her with a blanket. Then I hesitated and ran into the kitchen to grab the cash Ian had put aside to pay the guy who was coming to replace the draughty window in Scarlett's bedroom. After all, I didn't want to be stranded with Scarlett, unable to get home.

I blundered out onto the street, convincing myself that I had no particular purpose or destination. That I might end up at the park, or walking as far as the bakery. See, it was great to have time off work to have a baby, to be wandering the streets when everyone else was stressing about getting to the office on time, preparing for meetings, battling with deadlines. But the second tier of my brain, the bit dealing in reality rather than the fairy tale I was telling myself, knew exactly where I was headed. My feet had their own agenda. My hands were complicit, pushing open the door to the doctor's surgery. That shiny black door where the thick gloss paint had run and dried in blobs on the edges of the panels. Someone else not doing their job properly. I wasn't the only one.

There was a queue at the desk and the receptionist didn't

look at me as I entered. I hurried past, tucking myself in the furthest corner of the waiting room out of her sight. I watched as people were buzzed in and out. Mothers who knew what they were doing. One who had three children under five, the oldest girl bringing her little board books from the box of toys. Her mother sat a gurgling baby on one knee and a toddler on the other and read aloud, unselfconsciously mooing like a cow to great squeals of delight from her kids.

Another mother came in with a baby in some kind of posh papoose, the sort of parent that I avoided. Slim, blonde hair with a blunt cut that suggested she'd been near a hairdresser in the last few months rather than tying her hair up with the elastic bands that sometimes came with the post. I buried my head in a magazine, desperate to avoid that assumed camaraderie between women with babies. But she had that confidence, that belief that everyone was waiting for the opportunity to chat. She made a beeline for me, sat next to me and asked how old Scarlett was.

'Four months,' I said, without offering up a reciprocal question.

'Is she starting to sleep a bit longer now?' she asked. Without waiting for an answer, she told me how her daughter had slept for six hours at a stretch for the last week and she felt like a different person. 'I mean, one swallow doesn't make a summer, but at least I can invite a load of people over for dinner and not worry about how tired I'm going to be if I go to bed after eleven o'clock.'

I stared at her, my mind flicking to Philippa, the only person I'd invited to the house in the evening since Scarlett was born. I'd probably made us cheese on toast or pasta. I hoped this woman meant she shoved some pizza in the oven and shook a salad out of a bag, but she had all the air of double-baked souf-fles and jus de this and that. No doubt she'd also been having sex with her husband, waiting with bated breath for the magic six weeks to elapse.

At that moment, Scarlett started to cry and I fumbled in the bag for a bottle. I didn't want to alert the receptionist to my presence by asking if there was anywhere to warm it up, so I gave it to her cold. As her protests gathered strength, the woman said, 'You're not breastfeeding?' Her words didn't feel like a question, more of a criticism.

'I couldn't. Well, Scarlett couldn't. We couldn't seem to get the hang of it. And then, infections, mastitis. I had to give up,' I said, looking down at crusty scales of cradle cap on her head. I repeated to myself the health visitor's words that she would grow out of it, that it was nothing I'd done or hadn't done.

The woman nodded as though she understood, but her face told me I just hadn't tried hard enough.

As her baby gurgled and reached for the keys the woman jangled, I fought the familiar feelings that engulfed me. Maybe the crux of the matter was that I hadn't tried hard enough, full stop. Maybe I was selfish for hating the way the health visitor poked at my breasts, my nipples red raw, Scarlett rigid with hunger and rage. That fear every morning of the long hours ahead, of time passing so slowly. The whole day punctuated by my attempts to appease Scarlett, on a constant hamster wheel of nappies, feeding, changing. Yet I was never sure that I'd picked the right solution for the source of her unhappiness. Within weeks of her birth, Ian was popping home in his lunch hour, which, after factoring in the drive, allowed him about ten minutes at home. With barely time to slug down a cup of tea and piece of toast, he'd leave, his face full of concern. In the evening, he wouldn't even take off his suit jacket before picking up Scarlett, his eyes scanning her as though checking that no harm had come to her under my watch.

My reluctant answers finally made the woman give up on me. Instead, she sang to her baby, tickling her as the verse dictated and eliciting a bubble of giggles, the baby's plump cheeks creasing with delight. I bet this woman's husband didn't choose his words carefully in case she burst into tears or locked herself in the bathroom for the rest of the evening, shouting 'Go away!' through the door and clamping her hands over her ears to not hear her baby's cries. Of course he didn't have to. Her baby was content, eyes roving around the waiting room but always returning to her mother.

Finally, the woman was buzzed in, smiling at me in a way that didn't quite reach her eyes as she said, 'Good luck with her sleeping through the night very soon!'

I brought the pen and paper out of the bag, toying for a moment with the notion of pretending to be a writer, open to inspiration everywhere, so creative that I had to jot down a pressing idea. Instead, I wrote down two telephone numbers and put the paper in Scarlett's nappy bag. There were just two other people in the waiting room – a middle-aged man who'd glared over his copy of *Autocar* at Scarlett screaming and a woman about seventy-five, who'd caught my eye and smiled encouragingly. 'My grandson was so difficult to feed, drove us all mad. Big strapping lad of twenty-two now, though.'

I rocked Scarlett in her pushchair, my legs pulsing every now and again as though I was about to stand up, my mind telling me to sit down. Finally, Scarlett's cries subsided to hiccups, then silence. I peered in. Her little eyelids were fluttering, her hands clenching and unclenching as she snoozed. She gave the impression that she never quite trusted me enough to slide into a deep sleep, never relinquished the need to be ready for action.

With my heart hammering, I picked up my bag, glanced at Scarlett again and said to the lady, 'Would you just watch her for a moment? I need to pop to the loo. Don't worry if you get called in, she'll be fine, I won't be long.'

The woman nodded. 'I'm a bit early anyway. My appointment isn't until twelve.'

'Thank you. Thank you so much.'

I hovered out of sight of reception, waiting until I saw the woman sit next to the pram, smiling at Scarlett as though she was drinking in the sweet innocence of her, in the way that only people who don't have to bear the grinding responsibility of babies could appreciate.

Hardly able to believe what I was doing, expecting a sudden cry, a shout, a hand on my shoulder, I pushed the door open. I hesitated on the other side, blinking as though trying to clear a fog, to connect my thoughts to my actions. I fought to understand how unnatural this was, how alien to motherhood, to instinctive love, to the automatic bond that I should have been able to take for granted.

As I paused, the door started to open again and that moment of indecision was snatched from me. I turned, walking quickly, braced for footsteps, a chorus of voices shouting after me. I kept striding, my own fear chasing me on, the panic that someone would charge after me, broadcasting my shame to a wider audience. That people coming out of shops, standing at the bus stop would watch horrified, craning their necks at this dysfunctional mother who dumped her baby and left without even stopping for a last kiss.

On and on I went, rushing over roads, pushing past people until I arrived at the station. A small voice in my head was telling me to go back, that it wasn't too late, that I could resolve it all before Ian got home, before Scarlett's bedtime. But a much louder, more insistent voice trumpeted about how they would all be so much better without me, propelling me towards the departure board.

There was a train for London leaving in ten minutes. Perhaps I'd stay there for a few nights, get a grip of myself, ring Ian in a few days. Tell him how bad it really was, how I couldn't... Couldn't what? Couldn't do anything, didn't feel anything except desperate or numb. I'd agree that I would see a doctor, after all.

In the meantime, I needed to get away from here, just for a short time, to rest, have some proper sleep. I bought a ticket, expecting the clerk to realise what I'd done and confront me, or make an excuse and slip into the back office, returning with his supervisor. But he yawned, handed me my ticket. 'Platform two.'

Five minutes later, the lights of the station were strobing across the windows, then streaks of sunlight as the train dipped in and out of tunnels.

Whitby. I chose Whitby. Mainly because on the way to London, the woman in the seat on the other side of the aisle was telling her friend how easily her granddaughter had found a job in a hotel there. 'Given her a bedroom to live in and all. Beats having to get the bus to work in winter, doesn't it? All that standing at the bus stop in the rain. Now she just strolls down the corridor. And as far as I can make out, with what she tells me, which isn't a lot, it's a nice enough place, safe and all that.'

But also because I knew Whitby. I'd been there with Philippa for a weekend by the sea as a reward after our O levels, when our parents had trusted us to get the train up and to 'be sensible'. Instead, we'd bumped into a bunch of French exchange boys at the beach and spent the evening up by the abbey snogging Henri and Luc, coughing our way through some Gauloises and drinking cider. Back then, Whitby had seemed like an exotic adventure, a contained recklessness that we wouldn't want our parents to find out about but never represented any serious danger.

Now, though, as the train pulled in and out of stations – Peterborough, Newark Northgate, Doncaster – my whole body was jittery, thoughts crashing towards me like a sudden hailstorm. Panic about what I'd done and what I was going to do

sliced through with jolts of worry about what had happened to
Scarlett, if Ian had picked her up yet. His puzzlement. His fury.
Maybe his relief. That I'd gone, that he didn't have to live with
my discontent any more.

I kept imagining that people filing past my seat on the
train would suddenly swing round to look at me, read the guilt
plastered all over me and start foghorning to the whole
carriage – 'See this woman here? She left her baby in a
doctor's surgery. Who would do that? What sort of mother
disappears like that?'

But no one spoke to me.

I got off the train at York, half-expecting to see policemen
dotted along the platform scanning for a frumpy woman in
desperate need of a haircut, still wearing her maternity smock. I
breathed more easily as my brain accepted that no one was
looking for me, although, by now, surely they must have understood that I'd gone, left Scarlett, possibly for good. It was proof
positive that they didn't need me, that they were in agreement
that they were better off without me.

I crossed the footbridge, searching out the platform for the
next stage of my journey, further north, far away from my failure. I'd bought two postcards of the Tower of London at King's
Cross, posted one to Ian and one to Philippa. The words were
slightly different, but the message was the same: *I've gone.
Don't look for me. I'm sorry I couldn't be a better wife, mother,
friend. Look after Scarlett. Don't call the police, I'm not in any
danger, but I'm not coming back.* They'd arrive tomorrow or the
day after.

It was surprisingly easy to leave a life. Best for everyone.
They could start again now. Perhaps Ian would find a better
wife, who managed to go to the shops for milk. Greeted him at
the door not with a litany of complaints but with the waft of a
casserole from the kitchen. I closed my eyes against the image of
the woman who might have the knack of soothing Scarlett, of

prompting that rare and precious jewel of a smile. I wasn't going to think about that.

It was late when I finally made it to Whitby and I booked into the first bed and breakfast with a vacancies sign in the window that I came across. I accepted the mouldy grouting in the shower and the debris – skin flakes? Toenail clippings? – in the brown shagpile carpet as a fair swap for the lack of curiosity from the owner about where I'd come from and why I was in Whitby.

After a couple of nights there and a couple of days gathering my dwindling courage to walk into every hotel and enquire about work, I got lucky. If there were any blessings to be had, I'd managed to time my escape to coincide with the push for finding staff for the summer season. I found a job as a chambermaid with live-in accommodation in a large hotel near the station. I kept myself to myself, stripping sheets, emptying bins, blanking out any thoughts of the past or future. The hardest rooms were the ones with travel cots, pink teddies propped in the corner, tiny flowery shorts left on a chair.

My mind kept a ticker tape of time passing. She'd be five, six, seven months. Funny to imagine her eating actual food. To envisage Ian having to go into Mothercare to buy bigger sleepsuits. Sometimes, despite my best efforts to distract myself when my thoughts strayed back to my old life, I'd wonder who would talk to her about boys, about periods, about all the things I would never have discussed with my dad. Maybe Philippa would. I hoped that the many years of being a good friend to her equalled enough in the bank for this one last favour. Occasionally, I fantasised that she would have guessed where I'd gone, that she'd rake through all the memories, sieve through what she knew about how my mind worked and come and look for me.

Even though I told myself I didn't want to be found.

33

JACKIE

'Whose phone numbers did you leave in the bag, Mum?'

'Dad's, of course.' I hesitated. 'And Philippa's.'

Scarlett breathed out. 'Please don't tell me it was her that rescued me.'

I grimaced. 'We didn't have mobiles back then. Dad was on the road a lot with his job, so they had to page him – and I know this sounds so old-fashioned – but the pager would vibrate in his car and then he'd have to pull over to call the office from a telephone box.' I realised that I'd taken refuge in an explanation of archaic technology. 'Anyway, Philippa was at home and she raced over to fetch you, kept you safe until Dad could be contacted. Whatever you think of her, she was a brilliant friend to me.' I paused. 'Then.'

Ian spoke for the first time. 'Philippa helped me care for you. She hadn't yet met Andrew, so she often drove all the way to Sussex to help me in the evenings, with bath and bedtime. My mother looked after you when I was at work, but Philippa regularly stepped in at weekends so I could go to the supermarket or whatever.'

Scarlett said, 'I suppose now you're going to say that you had an affair with her.'

Ian scowled. 'No! Of course I didn't. I was absolutely devastated, we all were.'

Scarlett turned towards me. 'Sorry, I forgot. Affairs were Mum's territory.'

I winced as though someone had pinched a tiny bit of skin between two sharp fingernails.

Ian held up a finger. 'That's not part of this story, so stop it.'

Scarlett shrugged. 'So what happened? Presumably you didn't just sit there and say, "Never mind, wives and mothers are two a penny"?'

Ian managed a soft and patient voice. My heart ached for what I'd put him through then and what I was still putting him through now. 'I suppose nowadays we'd have put something on social media, asked people to look out for her, but it didn't exist then. I did go to the police, but they were totally lukewarm in their efforts. The general consensus was that your mother had gone off with someone else, especially when I showed them the postcard she'd written saying not to look for her. They didn't think she was in any danger. I didn't ever believe that she'd run off with another man, though I was prepared to accept that she wanted a different life from the one she had.' He snorted at the irony.

I couldn't meet his eye.

He carried on. 'I felt so guilty for not realising how badly your mum was struggling. Back then, though, we didn't talk about mental health as openly as we do today. I don't know why it felt so hard to acknowledge that there really was a problem, that she was properly ill. My mum kept saying that it would pass, that lots of women got the "baby blues". I was busy building my career and kept telling myself that the best thing I could do was work hard and earn enough to pay for nursery a couple of days a week, to give your mum a break. I'm not making excuses, but we couldn't just stick a symptom into Google or click on a website. It's hard to remember how difficult it was to get information.'

Scarlett leaned towards me. 'I can't believe you literally walked out of everyone's lives?' Her accusatory tone stung.

'I know this sounds stupid, but I thought you'd all be glad to get rid of me. When I was cleaning a disgusting loo or stripping dirty beds, I had this sense that however difficult life was for me, I'd done the right thing, that without me always failing you, never being the mother you deserved, you'd have a much better life. Everyone would. I knew Dad would find a way to keep you safe and happy.' My throat was clogging up with emotions that I could never have separated out. Guilt fused with love, regret melded with shame. All enveloped in a sadness that I hadn't been able to look after my baby girl with the ease that so many other mothers seemed to manage.

Ian stepped in. 'Your mum was really, really unwell. There wasn't the support available then though. Or maybe there was but I didn't go looking for it. I had my part to play. It wasn't all down to your mum.'

The generosity of him. The enormity of his heart. That heart I'd broken once before, that heart he'd trusted me with again. This man whose shoulders came up around his ears if we watched anything on television where the characters gushed openly about how much they loved each other but was capable of showing love on an epic scale. I'd done the worst thing in the world and he'd not only welcomed me back, but he'd never taunted me with it, never flung it in my face even during our worst rows.

Scarlett didn't look convinced, but that wasn't much of a departure from our usual pattern. She seemed to forgive Ian so much more easily. I tried not to believe it was because she had a much stronger attachment to him, but I also wouldn't need a psychotherapist to clarify that for me. 'And you never let anyone even know you were okay?'

'I was frightened that the police would search for me, that I'd get into trouble. I thought they might even prosecute me for abandoning you, so I sent postcards from London before I got on the train to York, saying that...' I hesitated. 'Saying that motherhood wasn't for me and not to look for me because I didn't want to come back.'

Scarlett frowned. 'So if "motherhood wasn't for you", why did you come back?'

Because sometimes, despite bad decisions, bad luck, your own utter stupidity, the universe brings you the person you need to lead you back onto the right path.

34

JACKIE

The festive season loomed, dragging with it definitive milestones, not least Scarlett's first Christmas and my first absence. I closed my ears to the snatches of 'Good King Wenceslas' and 'O Come, All Ye Faithful' that drifted in from the street, to Bing Crosby and Nat King Cole playing in the hotel bar.

A week before Christmas, the deep gloom dogging my days made me slow at work. I was caught between the lethargy of depression and the futility of polishing taps and plumping pillows for people whose lives already seemed golden. I ended up in trouble with the head of housekeeping – a sharp and sarcastic woman who was driven by perfect hospital corners, not compassion for the intricacies of chambermaids' personal lives. Knowing I couldn't afford to lose the job and with it, my accommodation, made me so anxious that I kept going back to check that I'd done everything thoroughly. That slowed me down even more. It also earned me a hissed warning that I was 'on thin ice' right in the middle of the corridor.

One of the other chambermaids, Gwen, pulled me to one side after the head of housekeeping had gone. 'Are you all right, love?' she asked, her apple cheeks – as though she'd been drawn in an old-fashioned children's book – creasing with concern.

I had no energy to dissemble. 'No. No. I'm really not.'

She dragged me into the next bedroom on my list and as we stripped the beds and polished the tables, I told her. Told her everything, too deep in my misery to bother justifying any of it. I didn't care if she hated me, if her easy smile faded, if her soft wrinkles deepened with disgust. She couldn't hate me more than I hated myself.

Instead, she took me in her arms and let me sob until I had no more tears left. 'Go back. Go back. Try to put it right.' Then she took a breath and said, 'I got pregnant when I was sixteen. My parents forced me to give my little girl up for adoption. She'd be forty-three now. Probably a mother herself. And there's not a single day that goes by when I don't wish I'd stood up to my parents, found a well of courage to get me through them difficult days. Too late for me now. But not for you, love. You could still win your girl back.'

I thanked her for her kindness, dismissing her words as impossible. I was resigned to living a half-life where I'd forever miss Scarlett, Ian and Philippa but accepting that I'd been gone too long, that there was no undoing this.

She grabbed hold of my shoulders and stared right into my eyes. 'You're not a bad mum, you was an ill mum and grieving for your dad. Hormones all over the place. The only reason you thought you was useless was because you set yourself such high standards. I bet your baby felt loved, even if you thought you was doing a terrible job.'

Part of me wanted to believe her. But, at the same time, I was frightened that if there was any truth in her words, there was also hope. And allowing myself to dream that I could one day hold my baby girl again, lean my head on Ian's shoulder and feel at peace, might finish me off.

Every day I fought back to a numb place where that possibility didn't exist, yet every day her words ricocheted around my brain, hope rutting against despair, until I felt as though my head might explode.

I volunteered for a double shift on Christmas Day, cleaning mirrors, lobbing towels into the laundry, scrubbing sinks until my wrists ached. But none of it was enough to dull the ache in my heart, to stop my mind circling around what Ian would be doing, what he would have bought Scarlett for Christmas, whether he was missing me, hating me, hoping that, today of all days, I'd get in touch. Twice, I stood by the payphone in the hotel foyer, clutching a handful of fifty pence pieces before returning to my room and climbing back into bed, desperate for the solace of sleep. But sleep evaded me.

At ten p.m., I slipped downstairs again. I would call. I wasn't going back, of course, but Ian and I had loved each other. I still loved him. He was a good man. He deserved to know that none of this was his fault: that feeling that I was falling, that I couldn't breathe, that everything was closing in on me all the time.

As I stepped towards the phone, Sammy, who worked as a sous-chef in the kitchen, was buttoning up his coat, shift over.

'I didn't know you were here today,' he said.

Before I could stop them, the words came out: 'Nowhere else to be. I covered for Gwen so she could be with her family.'

He frowned, opened his mouth, then shook his head, as though he realised that it was none of his business. 'Aren't you a doll? Lucky Gwen.' He paused. 'My mum and dad will be in bed by the time I get home. Do you fancy a quick drink? A little cheers to the festive season at least?'

I glanced down at the coins in my hand. What was I expecting, that I could disappear for seven months and Ian was going to trill 'Merry Christmas' down the phone to me? Provide a sanitised version of how they'd navigated life without me to make me feel better? I had no right to know.

I followed Sammy out. I didn't want to be left alone with my thoughts, to question, to flay off the fragile flesh attempting to grow over my flaws. He led me past pastel-coloured houses in the narrow streets, quiet with everyone else's families tucked cosily inside. The freezing air blowing off the sea bit at our cheeks as we made our way to a pub overlooking the river, where we drank pints of lager followed by whisky chasers. Sammy talked about his siblings: his sister five years younger: 'Honestly, at nineteen, you'd think she was running the Bank of England rather than just filing cheques at Barclays'; his brother, older by two years: 'Hasn't got a clue, my mam still has to wake him up to get to work.' The obvious affection he had for them, that casual sense of belonging was a mirror to my loneliness.

I deflected his questions with short, reticent answers. 'No, no family. My parents are both dead. Yes. They did die young. You get used to it.' As I spoke, the grief in my chest felt like the scenes on TV when old mill chimneys were blown up, landmark buildings crumbling to nothing in a matter of seconds. I wanted to cry, to howl with the injustice of it all, of how I hadn't coped with any of it, of how their deaths had dominoed through my life. Thankfully, unlike my one slip-up with Gwen, I'd got a grip on my dry-eyed poker face again.

When the landlord rang the bell for last orders, I bought more whisky, eager for that deadening of thought, an easy route to superficial hilarity. Instead, I seemed to fold in on myself, moving from sober to drunk without the jolly stage in between.

When time was called, Sammy raised his eyebrows. 'I guess we should call it a night?'

'Come back with me. Please.'

Just for one night I wanted to pretend that I mattered to someone.

35

JACKIE

I repeated Scarlett's words to her, to give me a moment to formulate an answer that was true but also gentle. 'Why did I come back? It's a good question.'

Scarlett was pulling a face as though a response should be easy and instant. I didn't want to discuss how the wretchedness I felt after that night with Sammy was the catalyst for action and reparation. Maybe one day I would share more of that shameful episode with her, but not before I'd allowed Ian the privacy of hurt, of rage, of viewing his whole life through a different filter. I wasn't sure she would understand that reaching rock bottom confirmed that there were only two choices available to me: I had to find the courage to fix what I had broken or continue to blunder into increasingly reckless decisions in an effort to blot out my initial mistake.

'I worked with a woman called Gwen, who saw the good in me, when I absolutely hated myself.' I told Scarlett how that straightforward, unsophisticated woman blessed me with such a valuable gift at the time when I most needed it: she believed I could be better. That simple truth grew in me, like a hyacinth making its insistent way through freezing soil. She refused to allow me to use what I'd done with Sammy as a reason not to try.

'That was just loneliness, love. You put that to the back of your mind and never think about it again.' She'd laughed her throaty smoker's laugh. 'Let's face it, most sex ain't that memorable, so it shouldn't be too hard.'

'Eventually, Gwen persuaded me not to be a coward. To be brave enough to confront what I'd done and at least stop you blaming yourselves. I really didn't want you growing up thinking that I left because of you. That was so far from the truth. I went because I thought you'd be happier without me.'

Scarlett glanced at Ian as if to see whether he was agreeing with my story. 'I just don't get how any mother would think her baby would be happier without her,' she said, tucking a blanket around Rowan.

'I know it doesn't make sense. All I can say is that I was ill and neither Dad nor I realised that it wasn't something that would just go away. I didn't get any professional help until I returned home, but while I was in Whitby, I did manage to get well enough to realise what a mistake I'd made. In January, a couple of days before your birthday, Gwen rang your dad because I was too scared to. I thought he would hate me.'

Scarlett turned to Ian. 'You must have thought that was so weird, a stranger calling you about your wife after she'd been gone for nearly eight months.'

I braced myself in case he said he wished now that I'd stayed away. When he spoke, my heart clenched at the effort he was making not to let what he now knew overshadow how he'd felt then. 'I was overjoyed, Scarlett. We hadn't been able to find out anything. I was beginning to think your mum had gone abroad and we'd never see her again. Sometimes I even thought she was dead. It wasn't like today when you can do so many things to trace people, Google reverse images or trawl the social media sites. It was possible to disappear relatively easily and if the police weren't searching, there wasn't much you could do.'

'And you had her back, just like that?' Scarlett said, as though Ian was the most spineless man in the world, rather than the person who welcomed me home with the words, 'We never stopped hoping.'

'I still loved your mum. I blamed myself for not seeing how hard she was finding it to cope. I was young; we were working out who we were, how to handle each other and also the rest of life,' Ian said.

I didn't deserve this loyalty, this willingness to be accountable for his part in my leaving. He had no reason to defend me except to protect Scarlett's feelings. How lucky I was to have chosen a man who could postpone his own hurt for the good of his child. I couldn't lose him now, yet it would serve me right if I did.

The very least I could do was to urge Scarlett to recognise the strength in her dad, that his kindness was nothing to do with weakness. 'He drove all the way to Whitby that evening to pick me up. Gwen took one look at him and said, "She never told me you was such a handsome chap. You're like a very blonde James Dean."'

I still felt the swell of emotion as I remembered the gentle way Ian had told me about everything I'd missed on the drive home. Scarlett's first words, her little teeth coming through, the way she loved being read to.

'Did I recognise you when I saw you?' Scarlett asked.

Her words speared my heart as I remembered how upset I'd been when I'd picked Scarlett up and cuddled her and she'd wriggled away from me, stretching out her arms to Ian. 'I'm not sure, but we did manage to bond again,' I said, not looking at Ian. I didn't think anything would be gained by telling Scarlett how my fear of spiralling back down into a depression made me nervous of being left on my own with her.

I debated saying Philippa's name out loud, bringing her into the room with us. The truth was, she hadn't yet met Andrew, didn't yet have the responsibility for her own family and generously steered me back to good habits and robust health. She brushed away my apologies for not confiding in her – 'You're back now. That's all that matters' – though I knew I'd hurt her too. Instead of keeping her distance, she threw herself into supporting my efforts to make a second, more successful attempt at being a good mother. I'd tried so hard not to mind that baby Scarlett lit up whenever Philippa walked into the room, a face that was so familiar to her by now, unlike my own.

Tonight, though, I didn't trust myself to talk about Philippa in a way that was a fair tribute to all the positive things she'd done. I didn't want to reduce myself to her level, retrospectively seeing the many times she'd encouraged and praised me as mere deviations from her recent unkind actions. It was terrifying how quickly the difficult events of the last year had destroyed the ballast of the preceding fifty.

Instead, in a small voice, I said, 'Dad supported me really well, as did his mum. I never stopped being grateful that your dad was generous enough to give me a second chance.'

'And you thanked him by never telling him you'd been off shagging someone else while he was warming up my bottles and sitting up with me all night when I had a temperature.' Scarlett's face was contorted with disgust.

'Scarlett!' Ian said, his hand shooting up in disapproval.

My eyes prickled with gratitude that he wasn't milking every opportunity to gang up on me.

Scarlett shook her head. 'I don't know why you're defending her.'

Ian opened his mouth to argue with her, but I said, 'It's all right. I deserve it. Can I just finish what I was saying as far as we're concerned?' I asked, my voice verging on a whine in my desperation to deliver the words that might make Scarlett judge me less harshly.

'I'm going to have to go to bed soon,' she said. 'Rowan will wake me up in a few hours' time.'

'I'll be quick. I wanted to add that it might not feel like it now, but I've always tried to make it up to you. And even if I haven't managed that, I've been so proud of you, so grateful that you were my daughter and I couldn't have loved you more. I'm deeply sorry that I did what I did. No child should have to go through that.' I could almost see an image of a fishing rod waving about in the sitting room, hoping to hook an assurance that I'd been a brilliant mum once the small matter of me abandoning her had been dealt with.

There was a ring on the bell before I had to confront the reality that any such sentiments were not going to be forthcoming.

Ian opened the door and Andrew walked in, puffing out his cheeks. I couldn't help it; the mother in me loved the fact that he marched straight over to Scarlett, sat down and put his arm around her. 'Are you all right?'

Her whole body relaxed, sagging against him. It wasn't a conscious thing; it was that glorious instinctive reaction to knowing that the person with you was cradling your heart in their hands. I wanted to hate Andrew for being the one who had pulled all this misery and upset down on our heads. But he genuinely loved my daughter. My spiky daughter, a prickly mixture of independent and insecure, had found the person who understood her. Her Ian.

I quickly pushed away the surge of dread that Ian might decide that he was done with understanding me now. Nonetheless, I was still surprised, amidst all the turmoil, to feel comfort that if Scarlett chose to cease contact with me, she had Andrew.

I offered him a cup of tea and was relieved to release a bit of tension by taking a breather in the kitchen. I heard Scarlett say, 'Did you know Mum had abandoned me?'

'No. This was all news to me. It must have been the year before I met Philippa. She never said a word to me about it.' Andrew sounded as though this information was also making him reassess his relationship with Philippa.

Suddenly, after keeping my composure all evening, digging so deep to recount my story, our story, in a way that would allow Scarlett to trust that all my doubts about being her mum were firmly tucked in the past, I found myself stifling sobs that came right from the core of me. Philippa was the best friend I'd ever had, the woman who'd kept my secrets all this time without even being tempted to tell her husband. But, most of all, she was the one person who would have listened to me talk about this disaster, teased out complicated feelings, even made me see the silver lining, if not the funny side. I missed her so much.

36

JACKIE

Ironically, Scarlett and Andrew sharing a bed in our house barely registered. It felt far more significant that Ian hadn't refused point blank to share a bed with me. The routine we'd followed without a thought for so many years – Ian lying diagonally so his feet hooked around my legs, me fiddling with the pillows to achieve the exact height necessary for menopausal sleep – felt precious and fragile. Ian huddled as far over on his side as he could without falling out of bed. I reached out a hand as we lay there as formal as a couple of Victorian virgins.

'Hold my hand. Please.'

He hesitated, then stretched out his fingers. I grabbed onto them, trying to transmit my regret, my love, my desire to make everything right, if such a thing were even possible.

Eventually he spoke. 'When you first came back, I worried that you'd been with someone else in the intervening months, but I asked you, straight out. You said no. I remember it so clearly because I had this sensation of relief, that although it had been a terrible time, the circle of our marriage hadn't been broken. The fundamental commitment to each other was still there. That meant something to me, Jackie.'

My stomach knotted. I'd shoved that night so far to the back of my mind that I'd almost lied to myself about it happening at all. The words I wanted to say sounded no different from any excuse that anyone caught out in infidelity might offer up. That it hadn't meant anything. That it was ages ago. That it was all part of when I was so lost that I was flailing blindly in any, all directions, to find a bearing that might lead me to daylight. That was the truth. But still the fact remained that I'd betrayed my husband when he'd been holding our lives together without knowing whether he'd ever see me again. He hadn't betrayed me, though. Hadn't sought solace with someone else. Hadn't been so astonishingly stupid as to think the answer might have resided in any random person that he'd happened upon.

We went round in circles until the early hours – me apologising, not knowing how to answer, terrified that my words would hurt more than they healed; Ian alternating between anger and despair, but also humiliation that I'd told Philippa.

'Why? Why tell her and not me?'

'Guilt. I decided that the fair thing to do was to carry the guilt on my own. That no good would come from telling you, that it would just add more hurt on top of everything else. But I was too weak. I couldn't keep it all in. So I told Philippa because I didn't realise that we would ever arrive at a day when she wanted to hurt me – or you – so much.'

'But if you lied about that, how can I believe that you haven't lied about other things?'

To which I could only answer, 'I haven't lied about anything else, but I don't know how you can trust me on that.'

With Rowan's cries reverberating through the house as he woke for his middle-of-the-night feed, we forced our voices into hissed whispers. Finally, we drifted into the sort of sleep that has nothing to do with resolution and rest and everything to do with respite from reality.

37

SCARLETT

In the period following Mum's revelation, I felt as though I was digging into a feelings lucky dip every morning. One day, I'd be bathing Rowan, my hand gently supporting his head and I'd feel corrosive spite towards my mother scorching through my veins as I stared down at his chubby legs and perfect hands. There had to be something wrong with her, something seriously cuckoo in her make-up, if the woman who was supposed to keep me safe, *love* me had left me in a doctor's surgery with a random old lady.

I'd watch Rowan in his cot, sleeping with his arms at right angles, his chest rising and falling. The idea that I wouldn't be around to witness his curiosity about the world, the wonder in his eyes as he spotted sunlight dancing on a wall or leaves fluttering on the trees, made me feel fragile and naive as though I'd been meandering through life, cavalier and careless. Now I wanted to live forever so I could trail alongside him, shielding him from harm.

Other days, I was far more aware of the superpower of a baby to generate feelings of failure. The occasions when Rowan was spitting out the sweet potato purée I'd slogged over the night before, screaming with his little fists bunched up in primeval rage. The mornings when I'd been up most of the night, caught in a thankless round of feeding, soothing, changing. The afternoons when I just had to wheel him to the park, to speak to another person who didn't throw up over me every time I put on a clean T-shirt.

Could I understand Mum a bit then? Those waves of self-doubt when I didn't know how to stop Rowan crying. When I hated that stupid music class where the babies lay on mats while the mothers shook maracas and dinged triangles. It reminded me of when we'd all play 'London's Burning' on the recorder in a school concert and our parents would lavish praise on our toots and squeals while no doubt wishing they'd been at home eating biscuits. When mothers I met wanged on about how fulfilling they found motherhood and how they weren't resentful about the impact on their social life, I wanted to shake them and say, 'Wouldn't you just love to go out and get absolutely off your face and not have to worry about the 5.00 a.m. feed?'

But would that translate into me parking Rowan at the doctors' and disappearing off on a train for eight months? Or leaving Andy juggling work, childcare and domestics while I got down and dirty with some bartender in a hotel? Definitely not.

My poor old dad. I didn't want to think about my mother having sex with someone else. Or even with my dad, in fact.

I'd rung him at work to see how he was a few days after the showdown. Dad wasn't someone that you could just straight out ask, 'How do you feel about Mum having sex with someone else?' He was the first one to leap up suddenly desperate for a cup of tea if a TV drama veered into *Normal People* territory. I was pretty sure that he wouldn't be unloading on his colleagues or mates down the pub, so I felt some responsibility to enquire

whether he wanted to talk about it, while knowing that I definitely didn't.

'How are you feeling about the whole, you know?' I'd
ventured.

'Yeah,' he'd said.

I wasn't thinking that 'yeah' was an answer, so I'd waited.

Instead he came out with a spectacular non-sequitur. 'Are
you and Rowan all right?' he'd asked.

'Rowan's fine. He's got me,' I'd said, wishing I was mature
enough not to have a little stab but being unable to resist it.

'Don't hate your mum. She loves you.'

'But doesn't it kill you that she did all that? She behaved
terribly, for God's sake. She left you picking up the pieces, not
even knowing what had happened to her, while she was
sleeping with someone else?'

'Yes, it really does,' he'd said, in a tone so heartfelt, so deeply
sad that it scared me, made me want to backtrack. I wanted him
to be angry with Mum, to not let her off completely, but not so
angry that they split up. What would be the point of that now,
when they'd weathered all that stuff? I tried to imagine Dad
cooking a sad pork chop for one and puzzling over how to wash
a wool jumper. Or going to visit one of them and needing to
make proper conversation rather than dipping in and out of
Mum and Dad's framework of family chat.

I bottled out of asking, 'You're not going to get divorced, are
you?' because I wasn't ready to face the answer.

But over the next week or so, the question reverberated in
my mind. I found it impossible to imagine no longer having that
base, that stable and unchanging haven where I could count on
at least two people in the world to be there for me. One afternoon, I couldn't stand the uncertainty any longer and phoned
Dad. Disappointingly, his response fell short of the guarantee
I'd been seeking.

'I don't know, darling. I really don't. I'm still trying to

process it all. Anyway, I need to go, I've got a meeting. See you soon. Love you.'

I spent the rest of the day alternating between fury with Mum that she had pushed my dad so far that he was even thinking along those lines and an odd crossness with Dad that he was being dramatic over something that happened thirty years ago. Even though I knew that I'd be totally scorched earth if Andy decided that the answer to surviving his crotchety sleep-deprived girlfriend was a hot night with a woman he picked up in a bar. But that was because... Well, actually, I didn't know why that would be different. Because they weren't – what was it they often said about me? – highly strung and unconventional. Or simply because I couldn't forego the belief that my parents should behave like proper grown-ups. Anything immature or childish was my prerogative. That probably proved my point.

That evening, I was waiting for Andy to come home, trying not to resent the fact that he was out for dinner with Abigail, whom, on a good day, I recognised as having equal rights to him. In between dreading that my parents might get divorced, I tried not to consider whether Andy ever wished I hadn't, Rowan hadn't, complicated his life. If ever I asked the question, he never wavered in his reassurance that, yes, we'd brought a host of complications 'outstandingly outweighed by the resultant joy'.

Sometimes I was able to recognise that one of the dullest parts of being an adult, especially one in a committed relationship, was not always getting what you wanted. However, I also sometimes defaulted to a petulant child, shouting about how bloody lovely it must be to scarf back a bottle of Barolo with his daughter while his partner babysat his son. Tonight was one of those nights. I didn't want to sit with my thoughts about Mum. Driving myself mad wondering whether she loved me. Whether she'd eventually enjoyed having a daughter or just plodded back to her old life and resolved to not let everyone down again, while secretly yearning for childless freedom to have sex with multiple barmen. I didn't dare consider Dad's role. It was just easier to believe that Mum was the baddie and Dad the poor fall guy for her shortcomings, charged with keeping our leaky family vessel from sinking.

Rowan picked tonight to be tetchy and clingy, probably sensitive to my own unsettled mood. By the time Andy came in, I was monosyllabic and scratchy. 'Hey, do you need a hug?' he asked, and I prickled into him, enviously breathing in the scent of restaurants, of food eaten before it went cold, of night-time air.

'How was Abigail?' I forced myself to ask, instead of out-and-out sulking. Maybe I was growing up. Perhaps motherhood had pushed me to be less selfish, to understand that even when it wasn't convenient, I had to be kind to the people I loved. Or maybe I wanted Andy not to regret choosing me. Even so, I could feel the trepidation in my question as I dithered between praying for it to be all right between Andy and Abigail and bracing myself for hearing what unfavourable things she might have said about me, about Rowan. In reality though, I would also have been a vicious adversary if the boot had been on the other foot.

'I'm worried about her. She just wants a baby,' he said.

'It must be so difficult for her, knowing that you – well, we – have got what she wants and it happened by accident. Before you factor in the other stuff. Poor Abigail.'

We stood leaning against each other, all the frustration and unnerving thoughts of my evening fading away as I contemplated how I'd glided through life, unworried by my biological clock, accepting that I might never have kids but that I'd be happy anyway, that there were so many ways to find fulfilment.

But Abigail, she'd always known that her role in life was to be a mother. She loved her job, found it a huge privilege to bring babies into the world, but that wasn't enough for her.

'I've never seen her so flat. Guy is trying to support her, but I don't think they have the bandwidth to soak up each other's pain. I suggested counselling. She said she'd consider it.'

I sighed. 'I'm really sorry.' How I longed to get in the car and drive over to Abigail's and hold her in my arms until she relaxed against me, let me carry some of her sadness. But, of course, I was the cause of some of the sadness. Yet again, I puzzled at the randomness of the universe, the uplift that had brought so much joy to me at a cost to almost everyone else I loved.

I made Andy some tea, resigning myself to a very short night's sleep. 'Does Abigail hate me?' I asked, not sure if I even wanted to know the answer.

Andy glanced down at his mug. 'She seems to find it easier to paint you as the wanton woman who led me astray then trapped me into fatherhood because your biological clock was ticking. She does not want to hear that I really love my life with you. It makes her feel that everything that went before is worthless, that I was wretched all the time she was growing up. That I didn't love our family years as much as I'm loving having Rowan now and that I just stuck with Philippa out of habit.'

Childishly, I wanted to believe that was true. Didn't we all want to believe that we were the one? That everyone else was substandard and all experiences were just shoddy rehearsals in preparation for our glittering arrival? Then I found my adult self. 'That's so hard for her. I do get why she feels like that. Much as I love Rowan, I don't think I'd want a brand new half-brother foisted on me at this age. Especially if my dad expected me to be all delighted about it.'

'I really don't expect that,' Andy said.

'You love him though, don't you?'

Andy reached for me, the deep lines around his eyes catching the lamplight. 'I do. You never need to doubt that.'

I craved that reassurance because I did have moments when I compared the eagerness with which Andy responded to Abigail's phone calls about whether she should specialise in neo-natal care with his fleeting interest in the increments in Rowan's development. I'd have to suck it up though. I guessed that was what compromise looked like. My skills in that department still required some fine-tuning.

As we got ready for bed, Andy said, 'Thank you for being kind about Abigail. I know you're hurt by her reaction to you and Rowan.'

I smiled. 'I understand her.'

He stood in the doorway. 'We haven't talked about your mum lately. How are you feeling about her? Do you know how your dad's doing?'

I stared at him. 'I don't want to talk about Mum. Or either of them, actually.' Then I spoilt my resolve by saying, 'Dad hasn't ruled out divorcing Mum.'

'What? No way. He absolutely adores her.'

'That was before he knew she was sleeping with half of Whitby.'

Andy's eyes flew open. 'That's not fair to your mum. She's a good person, a great person, and saying stuff like that isn't going to help, especially when you know full well it's not true. You, of all people, should know what it feels like to have done something everyone disapproves of. Of course, she made a mistake. Once. Thirty-one years ago. Does that mean we should all fall on her like a pack of wolves and punish her forever? Personally, I don't think so. I wish I could talk to your dad about it.'

Andy had never snapped at me like that before. I felt ashamed, but also furious that my mother's behaviour was making me argue with him.

Before I could find a response that wasn't simply me lashing out like a teenager, Andy pulled back the duvet and got into bed, saying, 'Rowan will be up soon. Let's get some sleep.'

This full-on adult life was more of a commitment than it had first appeared.

38

JACKIE

In the immediate aftermath of my secrets being thrust into the public arena, I woke with a jolt, flinging out my arm to check that Ian was still there. Every day when I came in from work, I battled with myself not to run upstairs to confirm that his clothes weren't missing from the wardrobe. I often screwed up my eyes, then threw the doors open, gasping with relief that empty hangers weren't jingling in front of me. We skirted around each other, me asking questions about his work, remembering which meetings he'd had. Now I listened to the outcome, rather than nodding as I had previously, quietly having my own thoughts about how the kitchen tap needed descaling and the mystery of how the grout in the tiles got quite so dirty. I no longer argued for complex family dramas over the detective series Ian preferred, as though giving in to *Death In Paradise* would be my pass to a pardon. I became less brittle, the myriad irritations of co-existence – using too many clean towels, empty loo rolls unchanged, tissues left in pockets of trousers – paling into insignificance against the fear of losing him.

Yet, as though my brain was determined to return to a baseline of happiness, flashes of gratitude crept in whenever I wasn't torturing myself with worst-case scenarios. Despite the terror that 'I'd really gone and done it this time' and Ian might divorce me or Scarlett refuse to have anything to do with me, I still sensed the release from the heaviness of hiding guilt and shame. There was a liberation in not having to filter all of life through 'What will happen if they find out who I really am?' They had all found out who I really was. We were now at rock bottom and somehow we'd all have to swim to the surface.

I experienced a retrospective thankfulness for all that Ian and I had shared. I had a frequent desire to take his face between my hands, lean my forehead on his and say in the most heartfelt way possible, 'I love you. I didn't appreciate how much until now. Forgive me. Know what I did was never about wanting someone else. It was about trying to hate myself less by proving that someone liked me. Please don't let that be the thing you remember from our marriage, even if you decide not to stay in it.'

Whenever I tried to talk to him to get an idea of whether he was quietly seeking out somewhere to move to or still weighing my monumental mistakes against my qualities, he simply said, 'It's a lot. I can't give you an answer because I don't yet have an answer. You've had thirty-odd years to process it. I've had a couple of weeks.'

Scarlett had also asked for some time to come to terms with it all. And there was something in me that was so weary, so worn out by three decades of castigating myself that I readily agreed, glad to have a permitted pause before I had to deal with all the big questions that were heading my way. Except I discovered that my need to repair my relationship with my daughter soon assumed an urgency that struggled to respect Scarlett's timetable.

I had no option but to give them the time they needed. Nonetheless, the urge to back both of them into a corner, to throw my arms in the air and yell 'So what's it to be?' hovered permanently on the periphery of my waking hours. In the meantime, I went to work and tried not to shout at my colleagues when their careless mistakes led to me having to find patience I didn't possess. Then I returned home and cooked all of Ian's favourite dinners as feeble encouragement not to choose the nuclear option.

Now and again, I'd text Scarlett with simple messages: *Keep thinking about you and hope you're managing to make sense of it all / You're always in my thoughts and always were / I know you're furious with me and you've every right to be but I have always loved you and I'm sorry you found out like this.*

Almost three weeks passed and my texts went unanswered. My need to see Scarlett and Rowan became so all-consuming that I took a day off work and rang her after I knew Andrew would have left for the office. I barely had any capacity to consider how hypocritical he must find me, all my smelling salt dramatics over his relationship with Scarlett when I'd done something so much worse. Even so, if Scarlett was going to launch into a diatribe about my shortcomings, I didn't want Andrew as an audience.

To my astonishment, she picked up. 'Mum?'

I assumed that my name came up on her phone so I didn't know why she sounded so uncertain. We exchanged 'how are you's and I asked after Rowan. It all felt so pointless, this superficial nonsense when we both knew that there were fundamental issues to resolve.

'Scarlett, just know that I am sorry. That I wish I could undo all of this...'

She sighed, then cut me short, as though she'd decided today was as good a day as any to rip the plaster off the wound. 'Are you at work?'

'No, I'm not. I've taken a bit of holiday. Dad was working from home today.' I wasn't sure why I added that. Maybe to reassure her that we didn't hate the sight of each other.

'I've got some things I'd like to say to you.'

'Both of us?'

'No. Just you.'

'That sounds ominous,' I said, trying to lighten the atmosphere but also to get a feel for where this was headed.

Scarlett ignored my fishing exercise. 'It's the first time it hasn't been raining for ages so I'm taking Rowan to Hyde Park this afternoon. He loves watching the rowing boats. Do you want to meet us up there? By the boat shed?'

My nerve to ask whether this was a last-ever meeting failed me. We agreed on a time, Scarlett's manner perfunctory and clipped. When I told Ian, I tried to imply that there was cause for optimism, that at least she wanted to talk to me. The concern on his face suggested that hope shouldn't be the dominant emotion. 'Shall I come with you? I haven't got any Zooms this afternoon.'

My eyes filled at his kindness, that whatever I'd done to him, he could still prioritise our daughter. 'Much as I would love you to, if this goes badly, I don't want her to have fallen out with both of us. I think she's rather disappointed you haven't tarred and feathered and marched me through the streets, so she'd probably end up having a go at you as well.' There I was again, grappling for an indication from Ian about what he was intending to do. I knew, I absolutely knew, that rushing him was more likely to provoke him into leaving, but my desperation to ascertain my fate kept obliterating my commitment to patience.

Ian ignored my attempt to elicit information. 'So we'd better save a parent to fall out with for another day, you mean?'

'Something like that.' Momentarily, I found that my ability to wear a hairshirt for weeks on end was finite. 'The thing that everyone is forgetting is that I was *ill*. If it was one of her friends, she'd be all understanding and fly off the handle if we suggested any of it – any *single* aspect – had to do with selfishness, or a lack of love.'

Ian's face took on that inscrutable expression that had become so familiar of late. 'I guess that knowing the logic – or lack of it – behind your behaviour and being able to forgive are two different things.'

His words winded me as though I'd been headbutted in the stomach. I had no right to be angry with him, but I still was. Not just with him. With everyone who crossed my path as I made my way to the station. I'd left the house in a fluster by changing my outfit at the last minute and making myself late as I aimed for the repentant but not doormat look. Honestly what a cracking idea for a feature in a magazine: 'How to dress for a potential last-ever meeting with your child before you become totally estranged'. It would make a change from 'Twenty ways to look half a stone lighter without dieting'.

As I marched along, I burned with fury, cursing cyclists on the pavement, the owners who pretended they didn't see their dogs crapping everywhere. Then, once on the train, I redirected my hatred to the people watching videos on their phones with the volume turned right up and a special concentrated rage for the woman behind me who was coughing inches from my ear.

My stomach churned with nerves as I got off the train at Victoria and headed to the park. Surges of adrenaline alternated between provoking a rush of heat that had me ripping off my jumper and making me feel as though my legs might fold up under me. At least I'd see Rowan. I tried hard to dislodge the refrains circling in my brain: 'What if it's the last time I see them?' 'What if she doesn't trust me with him any more?'

I half-wondered if Scarlett would come. If she might change her mind. I kept glancing at my phone, dreading a bald text arriving calling the meeting off. Or worse, her just not turning up at all. But as I reached the park, I picked her out in the distance immediately, despite there being several mothers pushing prams. That familiar shape of her, tall and strong, similar to me, a build we'd joked about in happier times as being the body frame of 'sturdy birds'.

Immediately, I felt the prick of tears and gave myself a stern talking-to. I had one chance to get this right, to turn it around. Looking as though the person I was sorriest for was myself wouldn't get things off to a good start.

'Hello, love,' I said, trying to read her face.

'Hey,' she said, pulling her scarf up around her chin.

I crouched down to greet Rowan, who, bless him, welcomed me with a gummy smile. He wasn't yet old enough to be poisoned against me.

'Shall we walk?' Scarlett asked.

I fell into step alongside her, the bitter wind whipping around my face. I felt as though I was standing in a court room, with the jury about to weigh up my mitigating circumstances against my intentional deeds.

She didn't say anything else. Rowan was waving his hands about, looking at the boats on the lake, squealing excitedly.

'He's such a sweetheart,' I said. 'He's grown too.'

Scarlett stopped dead and turned to me. 'I can't get my head round it, Mum. You're so good with him. Why was it so difficult with me? Was I just a horrible baby? Did you miss me?'

I grabbed her forearm. 'You were a lovely baby. You were not the problem. I was the problem. I was ill; I didn't know how to ask for help. My GP was terrifying – he was in his late fifties without a shred of compassion. A week or so earlier, when I took you to see him because you had a bad chest and tried to tell him how hard I was finding it, he basically said, "Well, no one forced you to have a baby. She'll go to school one day and you'll get your life back. In the meantime, I suggest you bring the baby to me much sooner rather than letting her get this poorly." He cemented the idea in my head that I was a neglectful mother but, honestly, whatever had made you sick had come on so quickly. I'd brought you as soon as I could.'

'So it wasn't that you couldn't love me?'

I stood still. 'I know how it looks. Even now, I can't explain it, love. I was frightened all the time that I wasn't giving you what you needed. I got it into my head that I was somehow stupid, incapable of bringing up a child. And it didn't help of course that my own mum was already dead and my dad had died a couple of months before you were born. I think I had some kind of breakdown, but I didn't recognise it. Dad's mum did her best to help, but she was quite formal and very "stuff and nonsense". I couldn't talk to her.'

We walked on. I ordered myself to be patient. To let Scarlett say what she wanted to without rushing her. I folded my arms to stop myself grabbing her hand and asking, 'So are we okay? Are you going to cut me out of your life, out of Rowan's life? I promise I'll do better, please just give me a chance.'

I directed my attention to Rowan, tucking away his smiles and squeals like treasure for a rainy day.

Eventually, Scarlett said, 'I've been so furious with you, Mum. And with Dad for keeping it from me all that time. Though I'm not quite as angry with him because you weren't honest with him either.'

I swallowed. At no point when I was expecting Scarlett had my daydreams about our future included a scenario when my daughter expressed her disappointment with me for being a liar. 'I understand that. We – I – should have told you before. I'm not going to defend myself, but I do want to say a word on Dad's behalf.'

I glanced at her for an acknowledgement that she would listen. She tilted her head on one side and I took that as my opportunity.

'You were too little to be told the truth when I came home, just before your first birthday. I was still a bit fragile, so Dad was working really hard to keep me afloat, hang onto his job, make sure you were thriving. So the first few years were about surviving, really. Then, after that, we didn't forget about it, but there was never the perfect moment to say, "Oh and by the way, your mother abandoned you when you were a baby, but no need to worry because she's back now." We didn't know how to bring it up without wrecking the relationship that we'd worked so hard to repair.'

'But surely you didn't think it would never come out?'

'We moved from Sussex to Surrey for a new start. We were very naïve, but once the grandparents had died, the only people who really knew about it were Philippa and Dad. It wasn't something we advertised widely.' My voice cracked. 'And I trusted both of them with my life.'

Scarlett pulled a face. 'What a friend she turned out to be.'

Of course, in a contrary turn of events, I didn't like Scarlett criticising Philippa even though I was still reeling from how she'd turned on me.

'Latterly, maybe. But she's been a great friend over the years. She really helped Dad take care of you when...' I didn't want to reiterate the big wrong.

'Andy is a great friend to you, too. He's been arguing your case and nagging me to meet you,' she said.

'Has he?' I asked, accepting that Scarlett would never allow a compliment about Philippa without praise for Andrew.

'He keeps saying that people shouldn't be written off because they've made a mistake, that you have to weigh up the whole picture, that one negative shouldn't eclipse all the positives. He also doesn't think Dad should leave you because of the other thing.'

Not for the first time, thankfulness surged through me that Andrew was old enough to know that none of us ever had all the answers. That sometimes we got things so monumentally wrong that it was only other people's compassion that allowed us to forgive ourselves. I was doubly grateful that he hadn't turned

Scarlett against us and had been willing to accept a humiliating transition period while we battled with our disapproval at their relationship. The irony of owing so much to the man who'd been the catalyst for the secrets being revealed in the first place was not lost on me.

Scarlett picked up Rowan out of his stroller to take him to the water's edge to see if he could see any fish.

'I appreciate Andrew fighting my corner, of course I do, but the forgiveness has to come from you, love. And Dad.' In a small voice, I said, 'I've tried to make up for it ever since.'

Scarlett dropped a kiss onto Rowan's head. 'I've still got my work cut out to understand *how* you did what you did. I just couldn't imagine leaving this one behind. But I do sort of understand *why* you did it.' She blew out a big breath. 'It must have been so frightening to feel so desperate that that seemed like your only option.'

I nodded. 'It was. It was like my mind was diseased; I believed you'd be safer without me.'

Scarlett reached for my hand and gripped it. 'Bless you, Mum.' She looked up and smiled, a spontaneous cheeky grin, carefree and full of life. An expression that I hadn't seen for a while as she'd made the shift in such a short space of time from a footloose and fancy-free woman to a partner in a controversial relationship. She'd barely caught her breath before becoming a mother. 'I'm pretty sure I'll make tons of mistakes. With any luck, you'll live a long time and have the privilege of sitting down with Rowan to convince him that his idiot of a mother really was doing her best, despite appearances.'

Her body language softened. I'd almost forgotten how Scarlett's face lit up with mischief and humour. We'd all been so serious for so long.

'I do love you. And him,' I said.

She stared at me so intently, I had to make an effort not to look away. Whatever she needed to see in me, I prayed she was finding it.

'I know you do, Mum. I know.'

39

JACKIE

Thirty-one years ago when I'd finally come back, Ian had clung to me for a few nights and said, 'Don't ever leave us again. I can't go through it a second time.' But, very quickly, he had refused to indulge my desire for lengthy conversations about the whys and wherefores of what I did. He'd shifted himself onto his preferred ground of logic and concrete actions. He'd made sure that I'd seen a doctor, that I'd had enough support at home and enough distractions outside the house. If I'd ever tried to dig beyond anything superficial about how he was feeling six months, a year, two years after my return, he'd meet my questioning with 'It is what it is. Onwards and upwards.'

So it wasn't a surprise that he was still acting now as though nothing had changed, when everything had. He read his newspaper at breakfast, not speaking much, but he never had. He went to work. So far, so normal. He picked up milk on the way home, complimented me on the dinners I cooked, brought the glasses of water up at bedtime. But the silences between us, that glorious quiet which was previously spangled with companionship, warmth and understanding, now shimmered with distance and accusation. We'd become polite, like waiters and guests in a posh London hotel.

'Would you like a cup of tea?'

'That would be lovely, thank you.'

There was no longer any of that leaning into each other's space, reaching over to claim a bit of the newspaper, the unwritten choreography about who had first shot at a specific Sunday supplement. None of that scooping up of the last roast potato in a gleeful way: 'You snooze, you lose.' Instead, every interaction felt as though we were learning to drive again, internally chanting 'Mirror, signal, manoeuvre' rather than confident in our ability to sing 'I'm Gonna Be (500 Miles)' at the top of our voices and still drive safely on the motorway.

I'd hoped that making my peace with Scarlett and telling Ian about our conversation would push him into a revelation about whether he related to what she said, how he saw our future. Instead, he'd just said, 'Good. That's exactly how it should be. She needs you anyway.'

I'd wanted to say, 'But what about you? Do you still love me? Do you still need me? Can we get past this? Can we resume the life we've been living all these years – the true and real one? Rather than let eight months – and one stupid, stupid night – scythe through our happiness and dictate the future?'

I couldn't get the words out. Wasn't sure I'd ever be able to. I caught myself wishing on more than one occasion that Philippa was around to have a quiet word with Ian, with scripting input from me, to get him to open up. It still gave me a jolt to realise that she was the reason Ian had ever known anything about this. Some days I hated her for it. Some days I felt as though it was exactly what I deserved, my punishment.

On we trundled for a couple more weeks until one day in early December he shrank away from me when I stepped close to him. Anything had to be better than this. 'If you're going to go, can you just do it? I know I have no right to demand anything, but I can't live like this.'

His head dropped towards his chest. 'I don't want to live like this either. I want to trust you, want to believe that...' He waved his hands about as though naming 'the deed' out loud would make it even worse than it was. 'I want to believe that it was a one-off, that you didn't come back to me only because of Scarlett. I don't want you to stay because you're sorry for me, or because Scarlett will be furious. Or because you're terrified of being on your own as we get older, or can't face the thought of selling the house. I want you to stay, I want me to stay, because we love each other. Just that.'

Just that. So simple and yet apparently so complicated.

I put my hands on his shoulders, the most I'd dared touch him in weeks, despite longing for the reassurance of sex, the opportunity to use the familiarity of our bodies to keep us connected while we worked out how to pick our way through this new landscape. 'I am here because I love you. Because you are one of the kindest, most decent men I know and there never has been, or ever will be, anyone I'd rather grow old with.' I clenched my jaw, restraining the emotions that were threatening to get in the way of the most important words I was ever likely to say in my life. 'I'm sorry that I hurt you but also hold huge hope in my heart that you might forgive me,' I said, managing a little pleading smile through my tears.

He pulled me to him. 'Can we never talk about it again?'

I sob-laughed, stroking his face. 'Do you think that would be the top tip on a marriage counsellor's list? Shove it under the carpet and glue the edges down?'

'Probably not,' he said, leaning down to kiss me. 'It's the best I can offer though.'

'I'll take it,' I said as we pulled each other closer, our bodies transmitting the love that we weren't used to having to articulate. All the big things – my disappearance and betrayal, his generosity, the whole maelstrom of marriage and parenting – hovered between us. Yet as his fingers traced my collarbone, slipping inside my shirt, I had the sense that everything that we valued, all that was good and stable and sturdy, was squeezing into the tiny spaces as we relaxed against one another.

A second chance at life with the wisdom to appreciate it while there was still time.

40

JACKIE

NINE MONTHS LATER

Friday was my favourite day of the week. I'd dropped a day at work so I could look after Rowan. I'd get up at the crack of dawn, leap on a train to London and arrive at the terraced house that Scarlett and Andrew had moved to five months earlier. Scarlett would then race off to her job managing a community café that backed onto an array of allotments. It suited her down to the ground; it was the south London equivalent of an Italian piazza. She knew all the locals by name and loved the family-friendly nature of it: the little play area for kids, the vegetable swapping shelf, the old guys who took pleasure in sorting out the pots on the patio, vying with each other to produce the biggest blooms.

That morning, I'd arrived at her house before Andrew had left for work. As time had passed, I'd managed to compartmentalise Andrew into two different personas. One where, eight times out of ten, I could think of him as Scarlett's partner and Rowan's dad without having to issue the instruction to my brain. Another where I still thought of him without any effort as my long-time friend. Right now, it was the second persona I was chatting to, freely and unselfconsciously, talking about Abigail, as though I was simply a compassionate bystander. 'How are things with her?' I asked.

'Not great. She's quite glad to see me and we have time together when she asks my advice and treats me like her dad. But she's never met Rowan and I can't talk about Scarlett to her. That makes me so sad, as they were such great friends.' He ran his fingers through his hair. 'And, of course, it's made worse because she's desperate for a baby. I think she's particularly aggrieved because I had all these plans for retirement – zipping off in a camper van, selling up and travelling, which was what provoked Philippa into booting me out in the first place. Instead, here I am, taking Rowan swimming to the local pool on a Sunday morning and creating a second family twenty miles down the road.'

'I can see Abigail's point of view.'

'I can too,' he said. 'I'm really sorry that she's so upset. And that she's lost her best friend because of me. At the same time, I'm enjoying fatherhood more because I know what to expect. I also know myself better. I'm not that arrogant wannabe hotshot trying to make a name for myself. I've learned that there will always be someone smarter, richer, more connected than I am. And I don't care. I just want my family to be happy. So it's Sod's law that this family being so happy – and I really do love them to bits – has to make my other family miserable.'

Scarlett came in then, so I switched into Andrew as my grandson's dad mode. I still had to make a conscious effort not to make Scarlett feel left out from the many years of our friendship when bizarrely I knew him better. It was so easy to slip into reminiscences – 'Oh my life, that time that we went punting in Cambridge and you got the pole stuck in the mud and fell into the river.' So easy to exclude Scarlett by virtue of being the same generation, with a long shared history.

Ian had mellowed but not melted. He accepted that Andrew had been instrumental in encouraging Scarlett to view my abandoning her as a baby with compassion, the result of an unstable mind, no reflection on her. I'd managed to get all of us together over some lunches, which were mainly jovial with a few awkward pauses. At sixteen months, Rowan was a whirlwind of curiosity and mayhem, which turned out to be a great combination for chasing the elephants out of the room. So much so, that the five of us were planning to spend Christmas together in a few months' time. Ian had resisted the suggestion at first, but Rowan had inveigled his way into that part of Ian that was fiercely family. The draw of unveiling the wooden garage that Ian had been making for Rowan in his shed proved the deciding factor. I didn't celebrate too jubilantly in case Ian examined how enthusiastically I had embraced his carpentry project in the hope of this outcome. I didn't want him to realise that his wife wasn't above a little behind-the-scenes manipulation to reunite the family.

With that thought in my head, Rowan and I disappeared to the park. We spent the day watching ants in the grass, picking up leaves, running his toy cars along benches. At lunchtime we picnicked under a beech tree, grateful for the bonus of sunshine, which had graced us right into September. I read to Rowan, who lay on the blanket, sucking his thumb and watching the leaves speckling in the sunlight before dropping off to sleep. I sent photos of him snuggled up to Scarlett and Ian. Scarlett replied with a kiss-blowing emoji. Ian wrote, *It's been a lot of heartache but what a prize! Love that boy. Have a lovely day. See you tonight. Love you.* My heart lifted still when Ian signed off with 'Love you', a new thing since the emotional Armageddon of last year. And even more so when Ian showed signs of accepting the Scarlett-Andrew situation. I'd surprised myself by how quickly I'd accepted them as a couple. Maybe I just had less moral fibre than Ian. Actually, there was no doubt about that, as I'd already proved to everyone. However, perhaps the upside of my own mistakes meant I felt less able to stand in judgement on others. Or, probably, I just wanted her to be happy and was prepared to be flexible on how that was achieved.

While Rowan snuffled in his sleep, I studied his precious face. Without Scarlett and Andrew, there would be no Rowan. A few years ago, I was coming to terms with the fact that it was unlikely I would ever be a grandmother. I would have missed out on so much joy.

A woman about my age walked past with a little girl a year or two older than Rowan. We caught each other's eye as she smiled down at Rowan, his arm flung across my knees. 'You've done a good job wearing him out,' she said.

I laughed. 'I'll be worn out myself by the time I get home.'

And in no time at all, in that way that women did, we launched into a chat about our lives. How we loved our grandchildren but also how wonderful it was to hand them back to our daughters and not have the permanent responsibility of making sure they turned into decent adults.

Eventually, the girl tugged at her hand, and the woman excused herself – 'Lovely meeting you, we're on our way to get an ice cream.'

I had a sense of belonging to a club, a posse of grandmothers who were able to appreciate the precious hours with young children, in a way that had been hard to do with our own offspring. How I loved knowing that nothing was more important, more pressing, than just being in the moment. I sighed. It was so simple but had been so elusive when Scarlett was little. Even after I'd returned home, I'd still felt the pressure of building a career, running a household and organising Sunday lunches with Ian's mother. Occasionally I'd remembered to throw in some words of reassurance to Ian that I would find time to listen to his work woes but just not right now.

My mind drifted to Philippa. How much she had longed to be a grandmother. Andrew had mentioned that Abigail was trying IVF. Now the rage of Philippa shouting my secret to the world had faded, I found room in my heart to wish her the joy that I was experiencing with Rowan. I missed her – less frequently but with no less intensity. There were so many things that only she would have helped me put into words. The fine line between being delighted to help out and feeling resentful about being taken for granted. My admiration for Scarlett choosing a difficult path in life and having the tenacity to make it work. My suspicion that was only possible if you prioritised your own happiness over the impact of your choices on everyone else.

I missed having a friend with whom I could openly discuss the people closest to me, not always in the most flattering light. Someone I could trust to understand that these were transient grievances, smudges in my affection that didn't come close to chipping a chunk out of the enormity of my love for them. I grieved for the person who knew all aspects of me and had previously loved me anyway, in all my three-hundred-and-sixty-degree glory. Not just the narrow forty-five degrees I revealed to everyone else.

When Rowan finally woke up, we did a tour of the ducks, of the budgerigars in the aviary and a finale at the ice cream van before making our way back to Scarlett's house. Scarlett breezed in shortly after six, scooping up Rowan, who was wheeling a succession of cars around a track in a very specific order that I appeared unable to grasp.

I hung around long enough to have a cup of tea with her, but I was still very conscious of not overstaying my welcome. I was desperate not to be that mother who demanded payment for childcare in attention when Scarlett would rather be sitting with her feet up after a day at work. I did have the impression these days that she tolerated the things that used to irritate her

about me much better. Finally, she'd recognised that occasionally there was merit in my suggestions about vitamin D,
investing in a top-quality frying pan, soda crystals with a white
wash.

I headed home after sticky goodbye kisses from Rowan and
sat replaying all his cute little words and gestures in my head as
I watched the back gardens of the terraced houses flash by out
of the train window. I flicked through the photos I'd taken of
him on my phone. I'd caught him laughing as he toddled after
the tennis ball he'd tried to catch and missed. In it, he looked
like Scarlett – not so much in features, although the shape of his
face and those strong eyebrows were all her. No, the real similarity was in the essence of him, spirited, energetic and – a
blessing and a curse – rebellious.

I was smiling to myself as I walked through my front door.
What a privilege it was to witness the blank canvas of a baby
evolve into a distinct character with dominant traits. I listened
to see if Ian was home. 'Hello? Hello?'

No answer. He was probably still in London at the pub for
one of his many colleagues' leaving dos. I did a tut of irritation.
If there was one thing that annoyed me (for some reason, Philippa's voice popped into my head, teasing, affectionate: 'If there's
one thing? There are a million things that annoy you!'), it was
having to chase family members to know whether or not they
were expecting dinner.

I decided to have a sit-down with the newspaper for half an
hour before starting the frustrating exercise of ringing him and
not getting an answer because he would inevitably have his
phone on silent. I pushed open the sitting-room door, in case
he'd fallen asleep on the sofa reading the newspaper and let out
a gasp of surprise. Ian was lying on the carpet, an empty mug at
his side, with a pool of tea soaking into *The Times* next to him.

I called his name, confused as to why he'd been reading on
the floor but more infuriated that he'd dropped off with his tea

in his hand. That man could fall asleep on a washing line. I wondered what magic product I had under the sink that might get the stain out. That glorious instant of annoyance at my husband's carelessness. That split second before fear. That moment when I still believed that in an hour's time he'd be showered and changed and I would have done my best to scrub the carpet clean. I'd roll my eyes when he apologised yet again. Then we'd be watching TV together, pointing at the screen and saying, 'Isn't that the bloke who was in that thing, the one with, you know, that detective woman? Blonde hair? Irish?' before laughing because neither of us could come up with the name.

And then that moment passed, and just like that, on a sunny September day, I went from wife to widow, with so many words I hadn't said, but thankfully so many I had.

41

JACKIE

Whatever misgivings I'd had about Andrew and Scarlett's relationship seemed like petty trivia from a lifetime ago. After I'd called 999, the next person I rang was Andrew. I didn't stop to consider why he was next, but later I realised that he was the person who would allow Scarlett to react in the way she wanted. That he would be one step removed and Scarlett would have the luxury of embracing her own grief without worrying about exacerbating mine.

He drove straight over, arriving just after the paramedics had told me there was nothing they could do, that Ian had probably been dead for a good few hours already. That it was probably an aneurysm or a cardiac arrest.

He pulled me into a hug. 'I'm so sorry, Jackie. I don't know what to say.'

I hadn't cried up until then.

He held me as the pain seared through me, each sob gathering momentum as each breath brought a sharper understanding of what I'd lost. I leaned against his chest, too despairing even to apologise for the tsunami of tears soaking his shirt. There was something so solid and reassuring about him showing up as my friend, rather than as my daughter's partner. 'I was just leaving a client in Sevenoaks, so I jumped on the motorway. Scarlett's on her way. I offered to go and fetch her, but she told me to come straight here.'

'Will she be all right to drive? What about Rowan?' I asked.

'I went through all that with her, but she was adamant. She's very calm in a crisis. Very capable. It will catch up with her at some point, of course, but I wouldn't have let her get in the car if I thought there was any danger.'

'Thank you,' I said, so profoundly grateful for his steadiness, for considering all the things I wanted to be considered, for showing up in person rather than opting to hide away.

When a police officer turned up – 'normal protocol for an unexpected death' apparently – I was so glad to have Andrew there. The young PC was extremely kind, gently asking questions about whether Ian had been ill and who his doctor was. I still felt as though I might blurt something out that would make her think I'd bumped him off. Andrew sat with me, stepping in when shock made me draw a blank on the name of the GP surgery we used. 'It's the one up by the traffic lights, near the cinema.'

Andrew whipped out his phone and supplied the name, then made tea for us while the policewoman explained that she'd stay until the funeral directors arrived. In between surges of distress that in the next hour or so, strangers would come to my house to take my husband away forever, my mind defaulted to more banal, more bearable observations. Namely that this woman with her neat ponytail and engagement ring was much younger than Scarlett, yet had a quiet authority that suggested this wasn't the first time she'd dealt with some poor person dropping dead.

While she made a few notes, Andrew asked, 'Would you like me to ring round and let anyone else know? It doesn't have to be today, whenever you feel ready for the news to go out into the world.'

I nodded gratefully. 'Yes please. Perhaps in a day or two. I don't think I can cope with other people's reactions right now. And it feels so lame to say, "My husband's dead, but I don't know what happened."'

Andrew cleared his throat. 'Would it be all right for me to let Philippa and Abigail know? Philippa had great affection for Ian.' His voice went a bit thin and scratchy for a moment. 'I did too.'

'Yes, of course. It's a small town, everyone will hear soon enough. We won't be able to have the funeral until there's been a post-mortem.' I started crying again. This morning I'd had a living, breathing husband and now he was lying on a sheet in my sitting room.

To my shame, I was afraid to go in there in case he already looked different. In case that image burned onto my brain, over-writing all the other pictures I had of him. Biting his lip in concentration when he was trying to solve a work problem. How he levered himself onto his elbow in the middle of the night when he could feel me tossing and turning. The teasing face he pulled when my lack of political knowledge stunned him.

'Where is he?' Andrew asked.

I indicated the sitting room. 'I don't want to see him again.'

'That's okay, I'll go in with Scarlett if necessary. I won't pressure her either way. That's a decision she has to make for herself. No problem. You can stay out here with Rowan. He loves being with you.'

Again, that sense that despite everything, all the many ways that Andrew should not have been the right man for Scarlett, he'd mastered the delicate dance of supporting my feisty daughter without ever trying to contain or dominate her.

I ran outside when I heard her car door slam. She lifted up

Rowan and passed him over to Andrew, then flung herself into my arms. Her distress accessed the reserve of strength in me, that desire to protect burned fiercely, competing with the pull of my grief.

An hour later, after I'd tried not to hear the wail of despair as Scarlett said her goodbyes to Ian, a contrast to the contented noises Rowan made as he drove his cars in and out of the chair legs on my kitchen floor, the funeral directors arrived to remove Ian's body. In an act of self-preservation, I didn't watch. I sat at the kitchen table focusing on all the love, all the good memories, all that companionship. I visualised it gathering into a long cloud stretching from my heart to the private ambulance outside and enveloping Ian as he left our house for the last time. I heard the front door open, the instructions delivered in gentle, muted tones that held respect. Nothing like the two men who'd delivered my washing machine a couple of weeks earlier, bantering away as though they were hoping to be discovered for a sit-com. Then the sounds of a trolley rattling down the drive, vehicle doors opening, thudding, a rise and fall of voices, the policewoman asking one of them to spell their surname, the click of a door closing.

I dragged myself down the hallway to the final moments of life as I'd known it for the last three decades, to listen to what would happen, who would call me, within how many days. Andrew came to stand beside me, as though he understood that the words were bouncing off my brain, little rubber darts that I no longer had the capacity to corral to the right target.

I might have thanked them, might have put my hand up in gratitude. Or maybe I gawped blankly, my brain buried in the sludge of devastation. I was vaguely aware of the police officer checking with Andrew that someone would stay with me tonight, of the compassion on her face as she offered her condolences again and left.

Andrew led me back to the kitchen, his hand a comforting

anchor under my elbow. Even Scarlett managed a smile as he walked in.

'You'll get through this, I promise,' he said. 'I'm here for you all, we'll be okay.'

I wished so much that Ian had been there to see what a good man Andrew was.

42

JACKIE

After three days, Scarlett, Andrew and Rowan went home amid a flurry of hugs and 'love you's and 'speak soon's, leaving me to grapple with the wilderness beyond all the constructs of a long marriage. I wondered how long it would take to adjust to the unwelcome fact that I didn't have to consider anyone else. My brain kept bouncing up against the habits of a married lifetime. Two mugs for tea. Peering into the bathroom as I walked past to see whether Ian had opened the window after he'd showered. That moment every morning when I did a mental sweep of what was in the fridge for our dinner. All the routines took place so automatically that it required a real effort to adapt.

I'd been given compassionate leave from work until after the funeral. I'd longed for time off, which was a real lesson in being careful what you wished for. I'd guarded all my leave to go on holiday but had often yearned for a few days off to get on top of life, to do the things that never made it to the top of my priority list. Find someone to repair a pane in the greenhouse, defrost the freezer, match the lids to the graveyard of Tupperware containers (though even thinking that was something that required time off work made me feel like the most boring middle-aged person imaginable). But still, the desire remained. And now I had the time, I was so poleaxed by grief that it was as much as I could do to pour cereal in a bowl for dinner.

There were so few people whose company I could bear. I didn't want to have to make conversation, think about the future, discuss practicalities, look like I was giving serious consideration to some of the ridiculous poems people suggested as suitable for his funeral. I didn't want to have to dig out any kind of filter when my grief was so visceral and raw. I could stomach brief interludes in the presence of the generous friends who turned up with lasagne and soup, not knowing what to say but prepared to listen to my distraught ramblings without rushing in with platitudes. But not the people who popped up out of the woodwork, women I hadn't seen since Scarlett was at school, acquaintances in our road who arrived with casseroles and head tilts and an appetite for the detail of how exactly Ian had died. Which I couldn't provide anyway because I was waiting for the coroner's report and driving myself mad wondering whether he'd still be alive if I'd been at home that day.

Scarlett had only been gone for five minutes when the doorbell rang again. I was regretting not sticking a sign on my front door saying, 'Thank you for your concern, but I'm fine, just need a bit of space to process my loss.' With an undertone of 'So get lost. Please.' Today, I really couldn't tolerate sitting opposite someone else, comforting them as they cried about my tragedy while simultaneously thanking their lucky stars that the finger of fate had fallen on my husband, not theirs.

I stayed at the kitchen table, stock-still, my ears straining for the clink of a crockpot on the front doorstep and the noise of someone walking away. After a few moments, the bell rang again and I gave it the finger, silently. I had no bandwidth for anyone scraping the bottom of the barrel for a memory of Ian along the lines of 'Do you remember that time that his mobile went off during Scarlett's nativity play?' No. No I didn't, because I had five million memories of my husband that were less banal than that. I knew they were trying to be kind, but, honestly, I just wanted to be angry, swear a lot, eat soup out of a pan because I couldn't be bothered to get a bowl. Stay in my dressing gown until lunchtime. Peer at my hair in the mirror and decide I could leave washing it for another day. Or week.

I no longer wanted to observe all the many social niceties that I'd bought into, we all bought into, thinking that living as a decent person, following the rules, paying our way was somehow an insurance policy against a husband dropping dead while we were eating ice cream in the park. I was so furious at the universe, so angry that despite all the horrible people out there that barely anyone would have missed, it had to be my husband, a thoroughly honourable person, who had to die. And because I didn't want to have to rein in my rage, to tease and tame it into something that wouldn't affront your average person popping by with a homemade carrot cake, I wanted to be left alone.

More than once, I'd been tempted to say, 'If we didn't have anything to do with you in the last fifteen years, then you can safely assume that this particular moment in time is not the one when I'd like to reacquaint myself with you.'

I was gritting my teeth, snarling out a silent 'Go away! Just GO AWAY!' when there was a tapping on the kitchen window. I looked up, ready to lose the plot completely that someone had decided to come round the back and invade my privacy like that. But it was Philippa. 'Let me in? Please?' she said through the window, her hands clasped as in prayer.

I'd been through this scenario hundreds of times in my head, though obviously not the exact one of her turning up because my husband had died. I had considered that she might one day contact me out of the blue – and I'd decided that I would be friendly and dignified. Civil enough that we wouldn't have to pretend to be talking on our mobiles if we saw each other across the street.

Instead, I rushed to open the back door and we didn't even pause to do the 'Is this a kissing/hugging moment or do we need to get a few apologies on the table before then?' We threw ourselves into each other's arms and I discovered that despite all the crying I'd done in the last few days, there was plenty more water where those tears came from.

We cried, we swore, we eventually laughed at our swearing. As though she'd never been away, Philippa put the kettle on and got some mugs out of the cupboard, predictably selecting her favourite one – a great big bucket of a mug that she'd brought back for me from a long ago holiday in Devon. 'I can't believe it, Jackie,' she said, her eyes alighting on Ian's glasses that were still in a bowl on the table, his reading pair for the newspaper over breakfast.

'Did Andrew call you?'

She looked down for a moment. 'He thought I should know.'

'Of course. I said he should ring. We were all friends for such a long time.' I swallowed at my use of the past tense, not sure whether I was referring to the fact that we weren't friends any more. Though that was confusing because, right now, there was absolutely no one I wanted in my kitchen more than Philippa. Or maybe I'd been brave enough to acknowledge out loud that we weren't all friends any more because my husband was *dead*. I carried on. 'Ian loved you. He was heartbroken that...' I stopped. I didn't have the energy for raking over who did what wrong when.

'This doesn't feel like an entirely appropriate moment to say this, but I'm not sure appropriateness has been my most pronounced character trait of late.' She clenched her teeth in a show of embarrassment.

I waited.

'Can I just say that I shouldn't have done what I did? I should never ever have told Ian about that guy. That was vindictive and cruel.' Her voice broke. 'Now he's dead, I feel so guilty, because even if I didn't manage to destroy his happiness, your happiness – I mean, thank God you didn't split up over it – I had a good go. It was so selfish of me to let my bitterness spill over into trying to ruin your marriage.'

'It certainly wasn't a marriage-cementer – definitely gave us a few tricky times but probably brought us closer together in the end because we talked about a lot of things that we'd stuffed under the carpet over the years. You could argue I shouldn't have asked you to keep the secret in the first place. Anyway, the truth being out there might even have made us a bit stronger.' I wasn't totally sure about that, but there wasn't any point in making Philippa feel worse than she did; I was just as guilty as she was in thinking that I'd had another thirty years to be a better wife to Ian.

Her face relaxed slightly. She nodded. 'Thank you.'

We sat for a moment, our friendship flapping a feeble tail like a fish that had been out of water for far too long.

Philippa let out a big breath. 'That brings me to Scarlett.'

I sat up straighter, feeling my jaw tighten. Even at this low point of my life, when I needed Philippa more than ever, I was not going to be selling my daughter short. My eyes narrowed. Today was not a day for going head-to-head with the mothership.

'I'm going to start with the easiest bit to apologise for. Again, it was not my place to tell her about what happened when she was little.'

'No, it wasn't.' I was surprised at my matter-of-fact response. Maybe this was a new me. I'd always found it difficult to hold people accountable for their actions as no one ever did anything as awful as abandoning their baby. My natural tendency was to brush over anyone else's wrongs as though they were no big deal, even though I then suffered weeks of imaginary conversations in my head, bringing them to book. 'We had a long talk about it. I think she's forgiven me; she understood that I was ill, not that I didn't love her.'

'Well, that was the case.'

'It was,' I said, noting that I didn't judge myself quite so harshly as I used to, that the flare of shame had dwindled to more of a flicker.

Philippa gave a wobbly smile. 'That's two out of three apologies. How am I doing?'

I'd missed her humour, that knack she had for the self-deprecating comment. Yet I knew that the next stumbling block was non-negotiable. If she was expecting me to deliver up Scarlett on a plate for her to pick to pieces, we'd be back to square one and then some.

I raised an eyebrow. 'Not bad for someone who's probably only uttered the word "sorry" about five times in her life.'

She laughed at that. 'I'm doing my best.'

I knew of old that it killed Philippa to say 'sorry' out loud. She'd make a joke about a tense situation, show she wasn't harbouring any grudges by breezing in all sweetness and light, but I don't think I'd ever heard her articulate a concrete apology before.

She rubbed her hands across her face. 'Okay. The big one. Bear with me. Because I'd had an easy ride with Abigail, I hadn't ever really understood what it felt like to worry. Apart from a few stressful times around exams and stupid spats with mean girls at school, I'd never really needed to tap into that ferocity of protectiveness, to make sure she always knew that I had her back. That's all changed now. I didn't move to Deal so I could stay close while she's having all these problems with infertility.'

I frowned, not entirely sure where she was going with this, how this related to what had happened between us.

She raced on, tripping over her words. 'Boy, have I got my comeuppance. It's totally different, but the amount of times I've had to restrain myself when I've gone with her to IVF appointments and specialists have spoken to her so brusquely, so lacking in compassion... I feel like I could kill someone and laugh while I do it. Guy doesn't want to do any more IVF because he thinks it's putting too much of a strain on them, and although I can see where he's coming from, I would do anything – sell my house, hell, sell my body if anyone would buy it – to make it happen.' She twisted her lips as though she was figuring out the right way to phrase what was coming next.

'Sorry, I know I've just made that sound all about me, but what I'm trying to say is you are a great mother and you couldn't prioritise me over Scarlett. I should have tried harder to understand what a difficult position you were in.' She took a long sip of her tea. 'Obviously it's all still a weird situation and I'm sorry it's taken such a massive tragedy to bring me to this realisation that I miss you so so much and I really don't want you to go through this without me.'

'Thank you. For what it's worth, I never wanted to lie to you and I'm sorry that I couldn't come up with an alternative. It was a total lose-lose situation.'

'I know,' she said.

I reached for her hand. 'I'm really glad you're here.' With a jolt, I realised the absolute truth of that sentence.

'Tell me what I can do to help. Give me a job. Hoover? Cook? Help you sort through his things – or is that too early? Anything.'

I took a deep breath, hesitant about saying what I really wanted her to do, but knowing that it was the only possible course of action. 'There is one thing that would be really useful...'

Before I could get the words out, the doorbell rang again.

I sighed. 'That didn't take long. You can get rid of them for me. Whoever it is. Tell them I'm asleep, on the phone to the coroner, funeral director, anything.'

Philippa marched down the hallway with purpose and it felt so good to delegate my responsibility for dealing with other people. I was confident that she was a match for the most insistent of visitors.

I heard the front door open and a familiar voice floated through to the kitchen. Scarlett. Wary and puzzled. 'Oh. Hello. Where's Mum? I forgot my handbag with my keys and phone.'

'Hello, love,' Philippa said, her voice soft and compassionate.

I shot out ready to step in. But Philippa said, 'I'm so so sorry to hear about your dad,' and immediately Scarlett moved into her arms and sobbed onto her shoulder at an awkward angle, cradling Rowan while being cuddled herself.

I walked up to them and lifted Rowan onto my hip, half wanting to stand guard to make sure this promising scene didn't suddenly take a turn for the worse, while recognising that what happened between them was out of my control. With great restraint, I went upstairs with Rowan to retrieve Scarlett's handbag.

When we came down again, Philippa and Scarlett were standing clutching each other's hands. Philippa was leaning in saying, 'You'll get through this. You're strong and you've got the little one to focus on.'

I held my breath, crossing my fingers that Scarlett's reply would be gracious.

'Thank you,' she said.

Rowan must have sensed the unsettled atmosphere and started whimpering. 'Mama, mama.'

Scarlett took him from me and I watched Philippa's face to see if her eyes had narrowed or her expression had hardened. Instead, a flash of pain crossed her features before she said, 'He's an absolute stunner, Scarlett. A proper sweetheart.'

Scarlett stroked his head. 'Thank you. That's very generous.' And my heart swelled with pride, with love. With hope.

I handed Scarlett her bag and gave her a hug. 'See you soon, darling. Ring me.'

We both stood at the door, caught in a surreal moment of waving at Philippa's ex-husband as he reversed out onto the street.

'Thank you, that cannot have been easy for you,' I said as we walked back through to the kitchen.

Philippa pressed her fingers into her eyes, but a few tears forced their way out. She shook her head. 'Life's so short. I don't want to waste another second of mine being bitter. This is the life I've got. I want to put all my attention on everything I have, not what I don't. I need to be a good role model to Abigail, to show her that there are many different ways to enjoy life, especially if she's never able to have the baby she's so desperate for. So, no time like the present...' She breathed out heavily, then said, 'Anyway, before Scarlett came, you were about to tell me the one thing I could do to help.'

'I was going to ask you to call a truce with Scarlett, because otherwise I don't think there is a way that we could rebuild our friendship.' I swallowed. 'I've missed you so much. But I didn't have to ask in the end. You handled that with real grace.'

Philippa smiled. 'Better late than never. She's really going to need you now. She mustn't ever be in any doubt about whose side you are on.'

A LETTER FROM KERRY

Dear Reader,

I want to say a huge thank you for choosing to read *Whose Side Are You On?*. If you did enjoy it, and want to keep up to date with all my latest releases, just sign up at the following link. Your email address will never be shared and you can unsubscribe at any time.

www.bookouture.com/kerry-fisher

I loved writing this book because it encompassed two of the things that are very close to my heart – motherhood and long female friendships. I love the trust that exists between women who've grown up together, that incredible luxury of starting at any point in a story and knowing that the other person can fill in the gaps without the need to keep stopping and providing the background. As I approach another big birthday – lucky me – I am appreciating all over again the privilege of having friends I've known for years. The women who joined in all the (sometimes reckless) adventures when I was young and invincible. The same ones who stayed the course while our lives extended to include partners and children. The fabulous people who are showing up for life's difficult moments now we're older and we know we're not invincible – but still bring the same joy to the time we spend together and continue to embrace our adventures.

Which led my warped and meandering writer's mind to considering what – if anything – could harm those seemingly unbreakable friendships. One of the major things to consider before writing any book is 'What's the conflict?' Disappointingly, reading about happy people doesn't seem to be as interesting as reading about people having to overcome obstacles. It seemed to me that the conflict between the primeval need to protect your own child, while trying to stay loyal to a lifelong friend would be a suitably difficult situation. And so another book was born.

I always find it thought-provoking when I can't find a word to sum up important feelings or events neatly, especially if they are ones that most of us have experienced at one time or another. Included in that list is that we have 'divorce' for marriages ending but no tidy word for the death of a friendship. I know some women who might pick their best friend over their husband if push came to shove, so I think that is a definite lack in the English language! If anyone is aware of a word in another language that sums this up – please do let me know.

I'd also be interested to know whose side you were actually on... whether you feel Jackie should have told Philippa the truth upfront or whether you understood why Jackie behaved the way she did. Please do share any of your own lifelong friendship stories with me; I am always thrilled to hear about friendships that have lasted for decades. Very special indeed.

The other theme I wanted to explore in this novel is how parents might react when their children make choices they don't approve of. Despite the oft-touted mantra of 'I just want them to be happy', my observations suggest that the mantra frequently has a silent 'within the parameters I find acceptable' tagged on. I haven't yet been put to the test with my own children, but I have at least given myself a fictional trial run should the need arise!

Finally, I wanted to acknowledge that, like Jackie, some

readers will have suffered from post-natal depression. My heart goes out to you.

One of the biggest privileges of my job is receiving messages from people who've enjoyed my books. Sometimes readers have shared their own personal stories when they identify with an element in my novels. I am absolutely humbled by the raw honesty of some of these messages and the trust you put in me. Thank you.

I hope you enjoyed *Whose Side Are You On?* and would be very grateful if you could write a review if you did. I am always interested to hear what you think, and it makes a real difference to helping new readers to discover one of my books for the first time.

I love hearing from my readers – the best way to contact me is through my Author Facebook page, X or via my website. Whenever I hear from readers, I am reminded of why I am so lucky to do this job – pure motivational gold!

Thank you so much for reading,

Kerry Fisher

www.kerryfisherauthor.com

facebook.com/kerryfisherauthor
x.com/KerryFSwayne

ACKNOWLEDGEMENTS

With every book, the list of people to thank seems to grow, which makes me a very lucky author. I'm going to start with where the magic happens and words get turned from the first inklings of an idea into something readers might want to read. My lovely publishers, Bookouture, have a fantastic production team working so hard to send our books out into the world in the best possible shape. There are so many things going on behind the scenes without the authors even realising. I also have to single out my brilliant editor, Jenny Geras, who never fails to spot where improvements could be made. Her clarity of vision is an absolute gift. Thanks also to Kim Nash and the publicity and marketing teams for the many hours they dedicate to helping our books find an audience.

A shout-out – as always – to my lovely agent, Clare Wallace, who's been championing my books, calming my nerves and sharing her wisdom with me for well over a decade. And also to the rights team at Darley Anderson for working so hard to promote my books to an international audience.

A special mention to the warm and welcoming Global Girls Online Book Club – Jackie Claridge-Wood is a total power-house of organisation and enthusiasm. Huge thanks to her and the many other bloggers and FB book groups who give up so much time to review and champion our books.

Thank you to everyone who has helped me with fact-checking – in particular, to Tracey Blair and Jessica Redland –

but also to the people who generously talked about their own firsthand experiences of unexpected death.

Finally – a round of applause for all the readers who buy, review and recommend my books – and especially anyone who takes the time to contact me personally. Those messages never fail to lift my day.

PUBLISHING TEAM

Turning a manuscript into a book requires the efforts of many people. The publishing team at Bookouture would like to acknowledge everyone who contributed to this publication.

Commercial
Lauren Morrissette
Hannah Richmond
Imogen Allport

Contracts
Peta Nightingale

Cover design
Jo Thomson

Data and analysis
Mark Alder
Mohamed Bussuri

Editorial
Jenny Geras
Lizzie Brien

Copyeditor
Jade Craddock

RAISING READERS

Books Build Bright Futures

Dear Reader,

We'd love your attention for one more page to tell you about the crisis in children's reading, and what we can all do.

Studies have shown that reading for fun is the **single biggest predictor of a child's future success** – more than family circumstance, parents' educational background or income. It improves academic results, mental health, wealth, communication skills, and ambition.

The number of children reading for fun is in rapid decline. Young people have a lot of competition for their time, and a worryingly high number do not have a single book at home.

Our business works extensively with schools, libraries and literacy charities, but here are some ways we can all raise more readers:

- Reading to children for just 10 minutes a day makes a difference
- Don't give up if children aren't regular readers – there will be books for them!

- Visit bookshops and libraries to get recommendations
- Encourage them to listen to audiobooks
- Support school libraries
- Give books as gifts

Thank you for reading: there's a lot more information about how to encourage children to read on our website.

www.JoinRaisingReaders.com